THE WELCOME WAGON

"God-*damn* your half-breed hide!" Clutching his right hand to his belly, the man glowered up at Yakima from beneath his furry gray brows. The whites of his eyes were etched with tiny red veins—he'd no doubt been celebrating the coming of winter to Dead River with a whore and a bottle. Must be a tradition here, Yakima vaguely ruminated.

"He already did that," Yakima growled, staring down at the grunting, groaning local lawman, "when he sent me here to this hellhole with the sheriff of your fine county sporting a bullet in his belly and saddlebags filled with stolen gold. All I want from you, Marshal, is a safe place to stow the loot until Kelly's back on his feet. Now, I'm a little tired and saddle sore, and the prospect of spending a night here, much less a whole damn winter, has me ready to throw up what little grub I have left in my gut down the nearest privy hole. So, if I hear any more half-breed comments out of you, I'll smash your head so flat it'll do you for a dinner plate."

continued . . .

Also Available by Frank Leslie

DEAD RIVER KILLER

Frank Leslie

A SIGNET BOOK

SIGNET
Published by New American Library, a division of
Penguin Group (USA) Inc., 375 Hudson Street,
New York, New York 10014, USA
Penguin Group (Canada), 90 Eglinton Avenue East, Suite 700, Toronto,
Ontario M4P 2Y3, Canada (a division of Pearson Penguin Canada Inc.)
Penguin Books Ltd., 80 Strand, London WC2R 0RL, England
Penguin Ireland, 25 St. Stephen's Green, Dublin 2,
Ireland (a division of Penguin Books Ltd.)
Penguin Group (Australia), 250 Camberwell Road, Camberwell, Victoria 3124,
Australia (a division of Pearson Australia Group Pty. Ltd.)
Penguin Books India Pvt. Ltd., 11 Community Centre, Panchsheel Park,
New Delhi - 110 017, India
Penguin Group (NZ), 67 Apollo Drive, Rosedale, Auckland 0632,
New Zealand (a division of Pearson New Zealand Ltd.)
Penguin Books (South Africa) (Pty.) Ltd., 24 Sturdee Avenue,
Rosebank, Johannesburg 2196, South Africa

Penguin Books Ltd., Registered Offices:
80 Strand, London WC2R 0RL, England

First published by Signet, an imprint of New American Library,
a division of Penguin Group (USA) Inc.

First Printing, September 2011
10 9 8 7 6 5 4 3 2 1

For my cousin Shane
and all the fun old times in the Turtle Mountains

Chapter 1

"You best stay with the horses, Kelly." Yakima Henry glanced at the young sheriff's glistening bullet wound. "You're losin' blood so fast you'll be drier'n a broiled boot, you keep movin' around."

"Not a chance." Jack Kelly grimaced as he swung his right leg over his saddle horn. "I'm goin' with you, Yakima. Those bastards killed two good people in Douglas, and I'm gonna see that . . ."

His voice trailed off as he sagged out of the saddle. He would have dropped like a rock if Yakima hadn't grabbed him. The half-breed eased the young lawman to the ground, propping his back against the bank of the dry wash they'd been following as they'd tracked the bank robbers.

With his gloved right hand, Kelly clutched the wound into which Yakima had stuffed the young lawman's neckerchief after they'd been ambushed by the fleeing brigands. Two posse men had been killed. Kelly had taken a bullet. The dustup had given the other three posse riders a bad case of homesickness.

Unwilling to risk their lives trying to retrieve the

thirty-six thousand dollars in gold coins the murdering thieves had stolen from the bank, and bring to justice the six men who'd killed the bank president and his son, the frightened townsmen had reined their horses around and galloped back across the high cedar-stippled desert toward Douglas.

That had been several hours ago. Sheriff Jack Kelly and Yakima had pressed on, following the six riders' fresh tracks west toward the Wind River Mountains, the snow-mantled peaks of Bow Mountain and Gannet Ridge looming in the northwest. Yakima had wanted the young sheriff to return to Douglas with the others. But Kelly wouldn't hear of it. It was his job to bring those killers to justice.

It wasn't his job to die foolishly, Yakima had thought then as he thought now, grabbing his canteen off his saddle horn. But Kelly was young. He'd come from a jackleg ranch on Cactus Creek. He was proud of the badge the citizens of Douglas had deemed him qualified to wear. He couldn't give up. Not even with that bullet in his belly.

Yakima popped the cork on the canteen, holding the flask out to Kelly. "Take a drink, Sheriff. You're dry as a stump."

The sheriff shook his head. His face was taut with pain. He was a big man, nearly as big as Yakima, but the beard he'd attempted to grow had remained thin and patchy. He had large ears and thick, straight jaws. His dimpled cheeks, easy smile, and friendly eyes had attracted the young ladies of Douglas. Yakima had spied two hanging around the sheriff's office in the short time that Yakima had spent in the high-desert town northwest of Laramie, trying to drum up work with a new stage line that was reluctant to hire a half-breed.

Especially a half-breed loner stranger.

He'd gotten to know the young sheriff after busting up a saloon as well as two drunk ranch hands who'd falsely accused him of cheating at yellow dog for little more reason than they'd grown tired of losing to the "green-eyed dog eater." Kelly had arrested him, but when the bank was robbed, the sheriff released Yakima with the stipulation that the half-breed join the posse he'd hastily thrown together.

Yakima had agreed. Not so much because it was better than remaining in the cramped jail cell but because over the past day and a half he'd grown to like the affable, big-eared boy-sheriff, and knew he needed seasoned tracking help. The other men composing his posse were shopkeepers, one a blacksmith, another a wheelwright. None were manhunters.

The sheriff's throat worked as Yakima helped him tip back the canteen. Most of the water seemed to run down from the corners of the young man's mouth, streaking the dust on his lightly bearded chin. As if the canteen was too heavy, Kelly dropped his hands. Yakima lowered the canteen.

The sheriff choked, wagged his head.

"What're you tryin' to do?" he chuckled raspily. "Drown me?"

Yakima corked the canteen and set it beside the young lawman. "It's right here if you need it."

"Four left, Yakima." Kelly grabbed the half-breed's forearm. "Go easy."

"I will, Kelly."

"I wish I could help."

"I know you do. But you're better off here."

Kelly nodded, cursing. Yakima walked over to his big, rangy black stallion, Wolf, and slid his Winchester Yellowboy repeater from his saddle boot. He levered a cartridge into the chamber, off-cocked the hammer, and set the rifle on his shoulder.

He looked at Kelly. The young lawman was staring back at him from under the dusty, salt-stained brim of his hat. His face was shaded, but he had yellow rings around his eyes. He didn't say anything. Yakima turned away from the sheriff and the two ground-reined horses, and began striding westward along the shallow wash between stands of cedar and aspen.

A hawk gave its ratcheting hunting cry. There was no wind. The angling sun was slithering long shadows across the broken desert all the way to the broad purple barranca of the Wind River looming on the western horizon, beyond a low, tawny jog of sand hills and higher, rockier, and greener foothills.

Yakima and Kelly suspected the outlaws were holed up in a cabin nearby; just a few minutes ago they'd heard a horse whinny and a baby cry. Yakima and Kelly had killed two of the six men during the ambush. Another had taken one of Yakima's bullets to either a shoulder or an arm. He might be looking to tend that wound.

As Yakima walked slowly along the wash, the wild currant shrubs on the right fell back, opening slightly. A mud shack appeared about fifty feet beyond the bank, shaded by a tall, sprawling ash tree. Split firewood was stacked against the hovel's back wall. There was a privy and a small garden of corn, potatoes, and squash plants likely watered from a well.

The baby was crying again, though more softly now. Through the open windows on the near side of the shack, Yakima could hear a woman cooing to the child, likely rocking it, for there was the faint squawk of a chair. Men's voices sounded amidst the child's soft, intermittent cries. The men seemed to be in another part of the shack from the woman and the child.

Hunkering low behind the bank of the wash, and screened by shrubs, Yakima looked around carefully. West of the shack, off to his left, lay a stable connected to a hay shed by a corral of peeled, sun-bleached cottonwood poles.

Six horses milled inside the corral. A man was forking hay into the crib from an opening in the hay shed— a tall man in a striped serape and wearing a high-crowned hat thonged under his knobby chin. Yakima recognized him as the one who'd shot Kelly. His short blond beard glowed in the late-afternoon light as he worked, a crooked panatela smoldering between his lips.

Yakima would take him out first. Silently, if possible. Then he'd work on the men in the shack. . . .

Keeping his head below the lip of the bank, he continued on down the wash. He was halfway between the cabin and the sheds and corral when an eerie rasp sounded from ahead somewhere.

A stone-colored sidewinder lay coiled on a flat rock, in the shade of a large, cracked boulder on the wash's left side. The rattler was wound tight as a freshly woven lariat, and thick as Yakima's wrist. Its rattle rose, quivering. Its forked tongue slithered in and out of its flat, diamond-shaped head, testing the air, its beadlike yellow eyes staring—if snakes stared—from beneath protruding, hornlike scales.

A sand rattler. Deadly to man and beast and almost impossible to see when they nearly buried themselves in sand or slithered along the cracks of a canyon wall.

The half-breed froze, the flesh between his shoulders crawling with primal fear. He drew a breath, adjusting his gloved grip on the Winchester, and continued forward once more, stepping wide of the snake but keeping an eye on it. It swung its head, keeping its own malign gaze on him, shaking its rattle intermittently, lifting that ominous rasp that sounded like gravel shaken in a hollow gourd.

Yakima shook his head, trying to work his mind away from the sound. But the snake was a witch's finger prodding his very soul, not easy to fling away.

The rattling was the first sound he'd heard as he'd awakened from brain-addled unconsciousness to find his wife, Faith, gone . . . kidnapped by her old pimp and roadhouse manager, Bill Thornton. That had been the last day he'd seen her vibrant and alive, eager to spend the rest of her life with him at their horse ranch on the cedar- and mesquite-cloaked foothills of Mount Bailey. The snake had had nothing to do with her death, but the rattle of one—the very sight of one—spurred his own demons back to life, reacquainting him with the aching sadness and loneliness he knew would be his to parry for the remainder of his years.

Faith . . .

The rattling dwindled to silence the farther he moved away from the horned sidewinder, but her name the way he'd screamed it the night she'd died in his arms, her blue eyes reflecting the leaping flames of the burning roadhouse in which Thornton had been consumed, he would never outdistance.

He was glad to hear the baby start to cry again, louder. And for a man in the cabin to shout, "Can't you shut that kid *up*?"

A nice distraction. It also told him that his presence had not yet been detected.

When he found himself directly south of the hay shed, he glanced at the shack once more, now off to his right, beyond a small, brush-roofed well, and stole up out of the wash. He could hear the man moving around in the shed. Finished forking hay, he seemed to be arranging gear. There were several squawking thuds of tack being flung onto frames. Yakima heard him breathing heavily—it was warm for this late in the year, the sun was bright, and the altitude here was almost seven thousand feet above sea level, the air thin.

Yakima moved slowly to the shed's double doors. The right door was propped open by a sawhorse. Yakima pressed his shoulder against the wall to the right of the door, glanced inside. Suddenly, there were no sounds. In the inner gloom, with sunlight angling through cracks between the vertical, whipsawed wallboards, he spied no movement. Slowly, he spun around into the opening.

A faint sound rose behind him—the light tread of a boot on the straw-flecked ground. He wheeled again, just in time to see a tall figure lunge toward him, grinning, the man's eyes wide with eagerness and cunning.

He grunted as the pitchfork in his hands swept past Yakima's hip, an outside tine clipping the half-breed's calico shirt, tearing it.

The tall man's momentum propelled him forward and almost into Yakima before the half-breed rammed the Yellowboy's barrel into his solar plexus. The man dropped the pitchfork. He gave a loud *"gnahhh!"* of expelled air as he leaned forward. At the same time, Yakima flipped the Winchester end for end and slammed the rear stock with its brass butt plate hard against the underside of the tall man's chin.

The man's teeth clacked as his jaws slammed shut.

He groaned and flew backward, hitting the ground just outside the door on his back. Yakima gritted his own teeth, not wanting the man to call out to the other three men in the cabin. As the man groaned and flopped around in terrific pain, blood oozing out from the corners of his mouth, which was spotted white with bits of shattered teeth, Yakima picked up the pitchfork.

He heaved it.

It slammed down hard through the middle of the man's chest with a raking crunch, pinning the man to the ground. He flailed with his arms, trying to grab the handle just above the rusty, three-pronged fork. Lifting his head, leaving his sombrero on the ground, he looked at the fork; around the buried tines, dark blood boiled up. He groaned, clawed at the handle as though to try to remove it from his chest.

Finally, as if resigning himself, he sighed, dropping

his hands. His head hit the ground. His lower jaw hanging, blood and teeth dribbling off his lower lip and into the blond stubble on his sunburned chin, he stared up at Yakima. The light left his eyes. His body fell slack. He turned his head to one side. His legs shook and fell still.

Yakima turned to his left. The cabin was silent. No one appeared in the front windows or the door, which was propped half-open with a rock.

Quickly, Yakima leaned his rifle against the doorframe, grabbed the dead man's ankles, and pulled him into the hay shed, dragging the man's sombrero still thonged to his chin and carving a ragged furrow in the ground behind him. His light blue eyes remained open, glassy in death.

Yakima grabbed the Yellowboy and, hefting it in his gloved hands, glanced outside the hay shed at the shack. The hovel was gilded by the west-angling sun. Birds milled above its brush roof. A magpie was perched on the *ollo* hanging from a nail in a front post supporting the brush roof angling over its narrow porch, the bird peering into the Spanish-style clay water vessel as though trying to figure out how it could get a drink.

Aside from the piping of the birds, no sounds came from the shack. He couldn't even hear the baby now.

Had someone seen him, and now the three men were waiting for him?

Only one way to find out.

Holding the Winchester up high across his chest, Yakima strode across the dusty yard toward the cabin.

Chapter 2

He ran, crouching, and hunkered down behind the well coping. He edged a look over the well at the house. Still, no movement. But he heard voices now—the woman's and a man's. Another man laughed. There was the sharp crack of a hand across a face.

The man laughed again.

"You two don't hurt her!" another man's angry voice shouted. He seemed to be in the front part of the cabin, near the half-open front door. "She's still gotta take a turn with me, and then she's got some cookin' to do, by God!"

Yakima bolted out from behind the well and, staying wide of the shack's front door, ran to the porch. He stopped, breaking the momentum of his sprint, then placed one hand on the ironwood rail at the edge of the gallery, stepped over it slowly, and quietly moved forward to press his right shoulder against the adobe brick front wall, between the door and a grease-paper window that glinted pink and yellow in the waning sunlight angling over the purple western mountains.

He could hear the woman struggling with two men

in the shack's bowels, while the clinks of a fork on a tin plate sounded from just inside the door.

Yakima stepped inside the cabin, then stopped. He leveled his Winchester on an older man with long, thin gray hair sitting at a crude wooden table about six feet away from him, flanked by a fireplace and a chimney. A pair of faded leather saddlebags, both pouches bulging, lay on a chair beside the man—the loot from the Douglas bank holdup. Jerking his head up at Yakima instantly, the gray-haired gent dropped the spoon from his right hand, with which he'd been shoving dried apple pie into his mouth.

Aiming his Winchester out from his right hip, Yakima squeezed the trigger. The rifle thundered in the close confines, making the whole front room leap.

The slug slammed through his target's chest, just above the tobacco sack he wore on a rawhide cord around his neck. He flew straight back in his chair, both him and the chair hitting the hard-packed earthen floor with a loud thud. Surprisingly, he sprang up from the floor and tried grabbing the long-barreled Colt from the holster thonged low on his right thigh.

He didn't get the gun half out before Yakima shot him again. The second slug drilled the man through the side of his head, just above his ear, bouncing him off the front of the whitewashed stone fireplace and throwing him forward against the table.

A dingy hall opened in the wall behind the table, left of the fireplace in which a small fire smoldered. As Yakima levered a fresh cartridge into the Winchester's breech, a man's head appeared in a doorway on the left side of the hall, about ten feet from the kitchen. The man's eyes snapped wide as, clad in threadbare white balbriggans, he bolted into the hall and brought a pistol to bear on Yakima.

Yakima triggered the Winchester twice quickly, both ejected cartridge casings arcing over his right shoulder to ping off the wood floor of the gallery behind him.

The man in the hall fired his Remington wildly, the slug plunking into the top of the kitchen table only inches from where the old man still lay slumped forward, jerking as he died. Then the man in the hall rolled down the cracked adobe wall of the hall before falling to the earthen floor in a quivering, bleeding heap.

The baby was crying in another room down the hall. In the same room from which the other shooter had bolted, an exasperated shout rose. The woman screamed. A man grunted. There was the mad creaking of rope bedsprings, and then the clack of a shutter being thrown back against a brick wall.

Yakima bolted forward, skirting the table and dashing down the hall before turning into the first opening on the left from which a faded flower door curtain was drawn back. He held the cocked Yellowboy out in front of him, raising the gun as a half-clad man dropped out the window.

"Hold it!"

A thud rose as the man, wearing a battered hat and holding his shirt in one hand, his shell belt and pistol slung over his other shoulder, hit the ground outside the window. He grunted with the impact, boots crunching gravel.

Yakima lowered the rifle and ran to the window.

The man ran straight out from the shack. Long red hair, glistening orange in the late-afternoon light, buffeted down his back. His gait was awkward, as if the heels of his boots were badly worn. He ran around tufts of sage, rabbit brush, and wild mahogany, pumping his arms and legs. Yakima heard his anxious, rasping breaths.

The half-breed dropped to a knee, raising the gun to his shoulder.

"You'll get it in the back!" he shouted out the window over which there was no grease paper, only open air.

The man continued running, tracing a zigzagging course. He was trying to reach a low rise a hundred yards north of the shack, in the shadow of a bald ridge.

Yakima triggered a shot, purposely throwing it wide, kicking up dust and gravel beside the runner's right boot.

The man kept running.

Yakima ejected the spent shell. It hit the floor behind him. He pressed the stock against his shoulder once more. The man was running up the rise, crouching and really digging his boots in now, flapping his arms, frantic with the effort of getting over the rise to safety.

Yakima planted a bead on the center of the man's back where his red hair jounced wildly.

"Fool," he muttered as he squeezed the trigger.

The rifle thundered, jerked.

The runner flew forward, screaming and dropping his gear. He hit the top of the rise and rolled down the other side, out of sight. A tendril of dust rose.

Yakima ejected the spent cartridge, levered a fresh one into the Yellowboy's smoking chamber, and pulled the gun back into the room. He turned to the bed.

In the corner of his eye, he'd seen a copper-skinned figure slumped amongst the rumpled quilts and sheets, atop a lumpy mattress. Now he saw the woman clearly. No, a girl. A Mexican girl with maybe some Indian blood.

She was naked, her long black hair hanging wild. She rested on one hip, her knees drawn to her soft, brown belly. She was pressing a shoulder against the carved, ironwood headboard of the bed, covering her brown breasts with one slender arm. Brown eyes peered out from the tangle of black hair at Yakima. She curled and uncurled her toes.

In another room, the baby cried frantically.

Yakima was about to open his mouth to speak when she crawled off the bed and, appearing not to care that she was as naked as the day she was born, dropped to her knees to pull a dress out from under the bed. Her brown breasts sloped and swayed, heavy with milk, the nipples distended from suckling, as she shook the plain sackcloth dress out in front of her.

Standing, she dropped the dress over her head, and it slithered down her fine, plump body to cover her nakedness. She threw her hair out from the dress's collar as she wheeled to the door and disappeared down the short hall and into the other room. Yakima could hear her cooing to the crying infant.

Yakima rose from his knees and walked into the hall. He glanced down at the dead man lying at the base of the adobe brick wall, on his side, blood leaking from the two wounds in his chest and belly. Flies and a few fall-lazy wasps buzzed around him. The half-breed continued into the kitchen, where the old man had now slid down off the table and half sat, half lay against the side of the fireplace.

He skirted the table, glancing down at the saddle-bags, then picked up his pace as he headed out the front door, across the gallery, and swung toward the rear of the shack and the dry wash south, where he'd left young Sheriff Kelly. He followed a narrow path into the wash.

Wolf nickered as Yakima approached the two horses and Kelly, who was slumped back against the rock. His head was canted slightly back and to one side. His eyes were closed.

As Yakima moved up on the young sheriff, Kelly's chest didn't appear to be moving. The half-breed's blood quickened. He didn't know why Kelly mattered to him. He was just a kid from the sagebrush in love with a badge. But anxiety that his next move might be to dig the kid's grave raked at him, made him a little sick to the gut.

The sheriff opened his eyes and lifted his head. "Heard the shootin'."

Yakima drew a breath. "Yeah, I got 'em."

"They have the money?"

"From what I seen."

Kelly sighed in relief, blinked slowly. "The folks it belongs to will be glad to hear that."

"Yeah, but it won't do Reynolds and his son much good." Fred Reynolds was the banker the gang had drilled just after they'd forced the man's son, Darcy, to open the vault. "Gonna get you into the shack. Gettin' damn cold out here."

Yakima looked to the west. The sun was touching

the purple, snow-tipped peaks of the Wind River Range. Javelins of bright safflower light speared out from the bottom of the large orb and through the gaps between the sawtooth ridges. A breeze had risen, ruffling the willows and cottonwoods. The chill in it was like sandpaper against Yakima's sweaty back. The horses' tails ruffled.

He draped one of Kelly's arms over his shoulders and helped the man mount his horse. A few minutes later, he rode up out of the wash, leading the dun behind his black stallion, who was sniffing the air, likely detecting the scent of strange horses as well as blood.

Wolf didn't like the smell of either. The former usually meant civilization, which neither he nor Yakima much cared for. The latter meant trouble, neither of which he or his master cared for but which they were always getting into, it seemed.

No matter how hard Yakima tried to steer clear of it. . . .

Glancing back at Kelly, riding slumped forward but with his head up, his young, whiskered face betraying the pain of the bullet that had lodged somewhere in his belly, Yakima wished like hell he'd headed straight down to Arizona for the winter. How in thunder had he found himself in Wyoming this late in the year?

The trouble was, he had too many hard memories down in Arizona, especially in the high country just east of Tucson. And he'd been down to only a few bits of hardtack and jerky, and just enough green tea for about two weak cups.

He'd spent last winter in Dakota Territory, with a good woman named Aubrey Coffin. Compared to that frigid north country—despite the woman, whose warm company he'd enjoyed until spring had arrived and it had been time to pull his picket pins—a Wyoming winter would feel like Sonora.

He pulled the horses up to the front of the cabin now bathed in a rich golden glow, the cottonwood flanking it sprinkling yellow leaves onto its brush roof. The door was closed and white smoke slithered out the square, mud chimney. When Yakima had swung down from Wolf's back, he went back and eased Kelly off the dun, then helped him onto the porch.

He tripped the steel and leather latch, nudging the door open with his boot toe.

The dead men remained where he'd left them, a grim testament to the recent shoot-out that had spilled blood in the crude and sparsely furnished but well-kept little shack—a home in which a woman, possibly a couple and their child, had sunk a taproot. As Yakima had once unsuccessfully tried to do on the slopes of Mount Bailey in Arizona with Faith.

The woman sat in a rocking chair to the left of the hearth in which long flames leaped. A charred tin coffeepot chugged and steamed on a flat stone amidst the flames. The woman held a small, deerskin-wrapped bundle in her arms. She herself still wore the flour sack dress, with a red-and-yellow-striped deerskin drawn over her shoulders against the penetrating chill.

As she rocked, she lifted the heels of her bare feet, pressing her stubby brown toes into the hemp rug on the stone-hard floor.

She gave Yakima and Kelly a distasteful look despite the badge on the sheriff's brown leather vest, then jerked her head toward the mouth of the hall on the other side of the hearth from her and the child, and drew her mouth corners down. Yakima figured she meant to put Kelly in her bed.

He led the slumped, rawboned younker around the table and the chair in which the saddlebags still sat, and into the room with the rumpled bed. He grabbed a towel off a wall peg and tossed it onto the bed to catch some of the blood, then eased the sheriff down.

He stepped back as Kelly rested his head against the wallboard in which mountain lions and birds had been carved by a deft hand. The sheriff grimaced and clutched his bloody side. He didn't appear to be bleeding as badly as before.

"Gonna have to dig that bullet out, Kelly."

"Huh?" Shivering, Kelly looked up at him. "Musta nodded off."

"Gonna have to dig that bullet out. You won't stop bleeding till it's out."

"Where's the loot?"

"In the kitchen."

"Fetch it in here, will you?" A wry smile etched itself on the young man's face, his eyes gazing up at the half-breed. "Come a long way for it. . . ."

Yakima retrieved the heavy saddlebags and set them on the floor near Kelly. The young man raked thick fingertips across one of the pouches, and gave a relieved sigh. "Obliged, Yakima." He winced, crossed his arms on his chest, and shivered. "Damn, I'm cold!"

Yakima reached for a quilt, feeling overwhelmed suddenly, knowing he had to try to get the bullet out of Kelly as fast as he could. He was no doctor. The sheriff would likely die while Yakima dug around in the kid's guts for the lead, but it had to be done.

He covered the sheriff with a skin, then turned to leave the room. The woman stood in the open doorway, gently rocking the child in her arms.

"Split some wood," she ordered coolly, canting her head toward the shack's front door while continuing to rock the child. "Boil some water. I will see to the lawman."

Yakima looked at her, a little skeptical. He looked at Kelly, who lay back with his eyes closed, groaning and sweating.

Yakima turned back to the expressionless, round-faced young Mexican woman. She was young, probably not much over twenty, but the lines in her face, the maturity in her dark brown eyes, and her sober expression after the obvious torment she'd endured here at the hands of the three bank robbers, were a testament to the hard life she'd led.

She probably knew at least as much about tending a wound as Yakima did.

He sidled around her and headed outside.

Chapter 3

Yakima hauled water from the well and set it to boil, then got busy splitting wood. When he had enough wood to keep the fire built up that night, he hauled the three dead men out of the shack and the barn, dragging them out to where the fourth man lay on the other side of the low rise.

They were a ragged lot of killers. He did not take much time in giving them a proper burial. When he'd stripped the men of their guns and valuables, placing the booty in a croaker sack he'd found in the woman's stable, he dumped them into a ravine not from the rise. As dust rose from the ravine, he flung the croaker sack over his shoulder and started back toward the cabin. He saw something to his left, and stopped. There was a clear patch of ground in the middle of which was a neatly mounded grave fronted by a crude wooden cross. Over the cross was draped a wreath of dried-up wildflowers. On the grave itself was a relatively fresh spray of Indian paintbrush and goldenrod.

Yakima stared at the mound for a time, a pensive cast to his green-eyed gaze, the cool breeze blowing his Indian black hair back from his broad, scarred face.

After a time, he hauled the croaker sack into the cabin and dropped it on the floor. It would be his payment to the woman for tending the sheriff, a task she was apparently still involved in. She was nowhere in sight, and the faded flower curtain had been drawn over the bedroom door beyond which Yakima had deposited Kelly. She had the baby in there—he could occasionally hear the child fussing and the woman cooing soothingly as she worked.

He considered checking on her progress, but then decided to tend to his and the sheriff's horses instead. It was almost dusk when, having watered, fed, and rubbed down the animals before turning them into the stable with the four he knew to be the outlaws' mounts and two other mustangs, he returned to the shack.

The baby was in a cradle on the table. The cradle was carved with the same birds Yakima had seen in the headboard of the bed. The woman was working in the kitchen. A fire leaped in the hearth. She turned a dark-eyed glance at him over her shoulder.

"He is still alive," she said, "but I can't say for how long. I probably did more damage getting the bullet out."

He looked at the bloody basin of water on the table near the baby. Beside the basin lay the bullet. Yakima picked it up and inspected it—it was cracked and flattened, as though it had bounced off the sheriff's ribs.

She turned back to the rabbit she was chopping with a meat cleaver. Around the cutting board she had a few root vegetables and an onion. She was tossing the rabbit into a cast-iron skillet. "He needs a doctor."

Yakima closed the door and doffed his hat. The baby was awake but appeared content, sucking on one finger while pointing at something in the low rafters with another. His breaths rattled in and out of his chest and flicked spittle from his wet lips. Absently, fleetingly, Yakima wondered if the child was sick.

He considered what the woman had said. Douglas was ninety miles away over a treacherous series of mesas. Too far for a wounded man to travel. "How far's the nearest sawbones?"

"Dead River, to the west. On the other side of the pass. Half the distance to Douglas, maybe, but over a steep pass."

Yakima hadn't heard of it, but this was a big country. He'd head that way first thing in the morning. If Kelly was still alive, that is.

He went over and slid the curtain away from the bedroom doorway with his hand. Kelly was sleeping peacefully under a large buffalo blanket. His clothes were piled up on the floor, near the lumpy saddlebags. There was a bottle of what appeared homemade whiskey and a stone mug on the wooden nightstand beside the bed, and the smell of cooked licorice root in the room. She must have put a poultice over the sheriff's bullet wound.

The curly cinnamon buffalo hide rose and fell slowly as Kelly slept, his head turned slightly toward Yakima, the sheriff's young forehead deep-creased with lines that made him look ten years older than his twenty-four.

Yakima dropped the curtain back into place and returned to the kitchen. He saw that the woman had moved the coffeepot to the far side of the hearth, where it no longer chugged and sputtered. Steam curled out of the spout, adding the enticing aroma of the Arbuckles' to the smell of raw rabbit meat and roots as well as the slightly acidic but homey smell of the child.

Yakima turned to the woman, who was grinding dried sage in her small, brown hands and sprinkling the herb into the stewpot with the meat and vegetables.

"Coffee?" she said. "Help yourself."

She glanced at a shelf on which several tin cups and stone mugs were arranged with wooden bowls and plates and a handful of bent, rusty, wooden-handled eating utensils. He sidled up to the woman—her head came up to only his shoulder—and took a mug down from the shelf.

He could smell the smoky, slightly gamey smell of her. She also had the distinctive, enticing smell of woman, and that and the other smells of the shack were vaguely comforting. They also made him feel a twinge of lonesomeness. He grabbed a leather swatch from the hearth and filled a cup with the steaming black brew.

He remembered suddenly how he'd found her naked on the bed, and felt a little chagrined for not inquiring sooner.

"You all right?"

From another shelf, she grabbed a tin tray with a cake of lye soap on it and a scrap of cotton cloth off a nail near her worktable, and swung around, setting both abruptly onto the table. She jerked her chin at the front door. "Outside—go wash."

She swung back around, grabbed the stewpot by its wire handle, and hauled it over to the fire.

Yakima's ears warmed with chagrin once more. In light of her understandably sour mood, he supposed he'd best not ask where her man was—if she had a man—or risk having that cleaver thrown at him. He had a cold feeling the man was in the grave near the draw. Sniffing under his arms, he could smell only the woman and the child and the herbs of the shack, maybe a little gunpowder from his rifle. But he supposed she could sense his gamey trail smells, his sweat, that of his horse, and of course the blood smells of the dead men.

Feeling a little indignant, he set his cup down, grabbed the soap and the towel, and headed outside. There was a rickety stand on the gallery bearing a tin washbasin, and a water bucket on the floor beside the stand. The light was almost gone. It was cool now, and a breeze was blowing. He could smell the sage-tang of coming rain. Dead leaves dribbled off the roof and scuttled across the yard.

Yakima removed the necklace of grizzly claws he'd fashioned himself, from a bruin that had nearly done him in a few years ago and the meat of which had kept his larder stocked for several weeks, in the Arizona mountains. He looped the ornament over a rusty nail protruding from a roof support post. He couldn't tell if such totems warded off trouble, or if they'd improved his luck with bears, but he'd been raised by a Cheyenne woman who had believed such things, and many of her superstitions had stuck without his being fully aware.

Next he removed the leather sheath containing a five-inch blade from behind his neck, secured there with a braided rawhide thong. The Arkansas toothpick was constructed of five inches of hammered Damascus steel, and he kept its double edges honed sharp enough to shave with. The savage little weapon, built for throwing, had saved his hide more times than Yakima wanted to count.

Shucking out of his sweat-damp, grime-crusted calico shirt, and sliding the top of his long-handles down to his waist, he shivered at the raw chill against his skin. He ran fingernails across his broad chest with its pectoral muscles ridged like stone slabs, over his yoke-like shoulders rounded and defined by the hard, itinerant labor that sustained him. He scratched his sides, the back of his neck, and his head, ruffling his thick tangle of long black hair, then threw his arms up, his shoulders, back, stretching, twisting himself at the waist, working out the saddle kinks. His neck and spine popped and cracked as they loosened.

He groaned luxuriously, sucked a deep breath of the bracing air, threw his hair back behind his large red ears, both of which owned the ragged white scars of bullet creases, and grabbed the bucket.

He'd just lifted the bucket over the basin when the cabin door opened. The woman stepped out with a small, steaming pot. She stepped past him, brushing her shoulder against his naked side, and splashed the hot water into the basin, half filling it. Backing away, she glanced up at him, dropped her eyes briefly to his naked torso, then pivoted back into the shack and closed the door with a loud click.

"Obliged," he muttered.

He added cold water to the hot, then dipped his face in the basin, waggling his head around to fill his ears and soak his hair. He applied soap to his broad callused hands and worked it into his face and chest and the back of his neck with his fingernails, scrubbing hard.

He did the same to his belly and underarms, then splashed the water up, gooselike, to rinse himself off. Removing his cartridge belt, he dropped his pants and threadbare balgriggan undershorts and gave his privates a good soaping and rinsing, ridding himself of several days of trail filth. He had spare long-handles in his saddlebags. They were in a little worse shape than the ones he had on, but he'd put them on later.

When he'd finished washing he dried himself with the towel and tossed the dirty water into the yard. Barechested, feeling chilled but refreshed, he stood at the top of the gallery steps and stared out at the twilight. The horses were vague silhouettes in the stable. Stars were trying to emerge through the faint light remaining behind the indigo western ridges, the snowcapped peaks now showing only pale blotches. Several stars were kindling to life above the yard though a thin layer of scalloped, wind-churned clouds obscured them.

In the far distance, a coyote yammered—a faint, eerie sound beneath the keening of the wind and the scratching of the blowing leaves.

He donned his shirt and wide leather cartridge belt and holster filled with his horn-gripped Colt .44, then returned to the cabin. The stew was bubbling in the pot suspended from an iron rod in the hearth.

He could smell the spiced rabbit, the sage. He hesitated when he saw the woman in the rocking chair. She was suckling the child, making no effort to cover her bare breast. Yakima wondered if he should go back outside and give her some privacy, but by the disinterested way she rested her eyes on him, he knew it wasn't necessary. Victorian formalities were not observed out here.

He hung his gun belt over the chair he'd been sitting in earlier and reached for his coffee mug. He stopped when he saw it was empty. The woman gave a grunt and tossed her head at the pot in the fire. She'd returned the coffee to the pot to keep it from getting cold.

"You didn't need to go to all that," Yakima said.

She did not respond but only looked down at the baby, brushing a brown hand across the top of the child's head as it fussed and sputtered against her nipple.

Yakima refilled the cup from the pot, then sagged back down in his chair.

"Indio?" the woman asked as the child began making content sucking noises, almond-shaped eyes squeezed shut, his lips tugging at the nipple. His breathing sounded hollow, phlegmy.

"Half," Yakima said, blowing on the coffee. "You?"

"Mestizo." She wrinkled the skin above the bridge of her nose. "Half Mexican, half Pima. You a lawman, too?"

"Nah," Yakima said, "just a posse rider." He sipped from his cup. Feeling that her inquiries had given the nod to his own, he said, "Your husband . . . ?"

"Dead." She'd said it matter-of-factly, staring at the window flanking Yakima as the child continued to suckle and the stew bubbled, the gravy dribbling down the sides of the pot to sizzle occasionally in the fire's glowing bed of coals.

She offered nothing more, and Yakima no longer felt brave enough to inquire further about her life—a lonely one it must be, this far off the beaten path. Just her and the child. He remembered the grave. Faith's dead eyes drifted into the field of his inner eye's vision, and he sipped the coffee and brushed the thoughts from his mind like a fly buzzing around his face.

The stew padded his belly nicely, rejuvenating and warming him. He washed it down with more coffee, which she laced from the bottle she'd had in Kelly's room, though taking none of the firewater for herself.

After supper, while she cleaned the kitchen and scrubbed the pans, he went out, split more wood, and checked on the horses. It had gotten cold. A mist fell from a gauzy black sky. Likely, it would freeze, and there would be ice or snow on the ground by morning.

He hauled his saddlebags and bedroll from the stable to the cabin and spread the roll on the floor. He checked on Kelly, whose sleep, albeit a restive one, was likely due to the whiskey and herbs the woman had given him. She was trying to bring his temperature down by swabbing the young sheriff's chest with cold water.

Yakima went outside once more to evacuate his bladder. Returning to the cabin, he shucked out of his clothes and climbed into his blankets. The woman returned from Kelly's room with her own skins and blankets and spread them on the floor in front of the fire. She already had the baby in its cradle, positioned near her and the fire's warmth. She'd set a small pan of water in the fire, and it steamed near the child, whose breath once more rattled in his chest.

She heated a larger pot of water on the fire, shucked out of her clothes, and, sitting in a kitchen chair before the flames, the baby's cradle on the floor at her feet, gave herself a sponge bath. Yakima turned away, but something told him it wasn't required.

Later, she tossed the water outside. He watched her

walk naked, her damp, copper skin burnished by the light of the dancing flames, her full, brown-tipped breasts jostling, to her own pallet. She pulled on a flour sack gown, let it drop down over her breasts, the hem touching her naked thighs, and curled up in her blankets, singing under her breath to the child.

Yakima felt a primal stirring in his loins.

He turned over and willed himself asleep.

Chapter 4

Yakima woke before dawn and dressed quietly so he wouldn't wake the woman and the baby. When he'd built up the fire, he strode softly into Sheriff Kelly's room. He couldn't see him from the doorway, but he could hear the young man's raspy breathing.

Kelly had made it through the night. Which meant Yakima was headed for Dead River.

He stole quietly out of the shack and stopped on the porch. Having felt the chill in the floor and seeping through the walls earlier, he knew it was cold. He'd donned the green plaid mackinaw he always carried wrapped and tied around his bedroll and a pair of fleece-lined leather gloves. His breath puffed in the pale blue air. A light snow had fallen, glowing on the dark ground, but the stars shimmered.

He broke the ice on the horse trough in the corral and pitched hay to the horses. While they ate and drank, he wondered what he should do about the outlaws' mounts. If the woman didn't want them—they'd be expensive to tend through the winter—she could turn them loose or sell them. One of the other jackleg ranchers in the area would surely take them in. They were good mounts, obviously chosen for both speed and stamina.

He saddled Wolf and the sheriff's dun and led them across the yard to the shack. Thick smoke rose straight up from the chimney, which meant the woman was up and had added wood to the fire. He would split more wood for her, building her a good supply before she called him to breakfast. But he'd split only a couple of logs before the door clicked open. There was only a lilac smudge of light above the eastern horizon, so the woman's head was an indistinct silhouette against the weathered gray door.

"No need for that," she said, keeping her voice low. "I am leaving."

Yakima sniffed, brushed a gloved hand across his nose, and lowered the splitting maul. "Where . . . ?"

"With you. Me and my son will spend the winter in Dead River."

"You sure the child should travel?"

"There is a doctor in Dead River."

Yakima stared at her.

She started to turn back into the cabin. She stopped, turning back to him, her face customarily stony. "My decision has nothing to do with you. I do not need a man, just a job and a doctor for my baby."

She held his gaze for a moment, as though making sure he understood, then went in and closed the door. Yakima looked around, feeling chagrined. She had a way of doing that, slick as a hot knife through butter. He snorted a laugh and hammered the splitting maul into his chopping block.

He walked back to the corral and saddled the remaining horses. With two cedar posts he found behind the stable, and some rope that he cut with his Arkansas toothpick, he rigged a travois for the sheriff. He'd rigged enough travois that it took only a few minutes, wrapping the rope around each pole and forming a web of sorts between them and then securing two heavy saddle blankets over the ropes, padding the contraption as best he could. He rigged the travois with flat rawhide strips to his saddle.

That job complete, Yakima tied the spare mounts tail to tail for trailing to Dead River, where he'd sell them and give the money to the woman—she needed all the help she could get, being alone with a little one—and led them back to the cabin, where he could smell the previous night's rabbit stew lacing the pine smoke rippling from the chimney.

Propped up in bed but looking haggard and pale, Jack Kelly managed to eat one of the woman's *huevos revueltos*—tacos spiced with bits of sweet green pepper and the rabbit stew from last night. As the sun rose over the eastern buttes, the woman cleaned up the kitchen and secured the cabin for the winter. Yakima climbed onto the roof and laid a heavy plank over the chimney to keep birds and rodents out. Then he led Kelly outside and helped the sheriff onto the travois.

Kelly hadn't said much in the time he'd been awake, and he seemed wobbly on his feet. Now, he said, "Travelin' in style, eh?"

"Couldn't find a decent hack out here."

"Takin' me back to Douglas? We need to get that gold back to the bank."

"There's a doc closer, over in Dead River."

The sheriff poked his hat brim off his forehead and squinted against the morning sun, his breath puffing in the chill air. "Yeah, I reckon that's a good idea. I need to get back to Douglas, though, damn it."

"You need rest and a doctor," said the woman, who came out of the cabin in a heavy wool coat and wool cap and with the deerskin bundle of the baby secured in a sling strapped to her shoulder and secured across her chest. "You're tore up inside. You have a fever."

"All right, all right."

Yakima threw a blanket over the sheriff, clad only in a ratty coat, and drew it up to the man's chin. He squatted beside the young lawman. "Liable to putrefy, Kelly. Listen to her. She knows what she's talkin' about. Hell, the gold ain't gonna lose none of its value before you get it back to Douglas."

Before the man could protest further, Yakima straightened and turned to the woman. "Ready?"

She nodded. Yakima helped her onto the horse she'd chosen to ride, a mouse brown mustang gelding with a speckled white hindquarters. All that she'd packed from the cabin were a pair of saddlebags and a carpetbag. The child seemed content, flinging its little mittened hands around beneath the woman's chin.

Yakima tossed the saddlebags stuffed with the stolen gold over the back of one of the outlaws' horses, then swung up onto Wolf's back. He glanced over his shoulder, but he couldn't see much of the sheriff from that angle.

"Let me know if you need to stop and rest, Kelly. We're in no big hurry."

"Just make sure we don't lose that loot, you half-breed devil. That's all I'm worried about."

Yakima chuckled as he swung Wolf away from the cabin and clucked the black westward across the yard. Kelly was just trying to get his goat in the best way he knew how, remembering that one of the men whose jaw Yakima had knocked sideways had instigated the dustup by calling him a "half-breed devil."

Mostly, Yakima didn't mind being called a half-breed. Alone, it described him, after all. It was the words that usually accompanied it he took umbrage with—especially when he drank hard liquor, which wasn't often. Imbibing in firewater had caused him to wake up with what felt like an Apache war hatchet cleaving his brain, in the cell of some strange calaboose way too many times in his thirty long years.

He led Kelly's travois and the horses out of the yard, toward the saddleback ridge looming about ten miles west. The woman handled her horse like an experienced rider, despite the bundle strapped to her chest. She and the baby bounced in the saddle as she pulled the mustang up beside Yakima and rode a few feet off his right stirrup.

"You know," Yakima said when they'd ridden nearly a mile and the woman's shack had been consumed by the snow-damp pleats and folds of the hills behind him, "I don't reckon we swapped handles."

She glanced at him, lines of befuddlement scoring her copper forehead. It had gotten warmer now, snakes of steam rising from the ground, and her thick black hair hung loose about her shoulders. He wondered if she was just being coy or if she really was averse to excess conversation.

"I'm Yakima."

He waited.

She turned her head forward, eyes dark, round face expressionless. "I am Alta Banos."

"The boy?"

"Christian Banos, after his father."

"Pleased to make your acquaintance," he said, pinching his hat brim.

She said nothing, just kept her eyes straight ahead as though he'd said nothing at all. The baby gurgled and pressed a mittened hand to the underside of her chin.

"Well, anyway," Yakima said, turning his own eyes to the trail. "We got that settled. Now I reckon we can stop with all the chatter. Some coyotes are still prob'ly trying to get their beauty sleep."

In the corner of his eye he thought he saw her glance at him and quirk her lips in a grin. But when he turned his head toward her, she was staring straight up the trail once more, that oblique expression in place.

As they rode westward, they climbed gradually into rolling hills and rimrock toward the pass whose name, Alta informed him, was Crow Ridge. The trail they followed swerved toward a creek lined with cottonwoods and aspen, and the incline grew steeper as they rose higher up the mountain.

After an hour, Yakima reined Wolf to a stop. He glanced at the woman who'd been riding silently beside him, the jouncing of the walking horse having lulled little Christian to sleep in his deerskins. Clouds had gathered, veiling the autumn dun-and-red land in a steely grayness. A breeze had picked up, blowing cool against their backs.

Yakima swung down and walked back to the travois. Kelly's eyes were open. The jostling apparently hadn't lulled him to sleep as it had the child. He looked paler, his cheeks shrunken behind their thin veil of sandy whiskers. His eyes were ringed with jaundice-like yellow.

He narrowed one as he looked up at Yakima from beneath his hat brim.

"I was just checkin' to see if you were still kickin'."

He meant it as a joke, but the sheriff didn't laugh or even smile. He looked grim.

"If I kicked off, would you take the money back to Douglas for me?"

Yakima pulled the blanket down and lifted the right flap of the sheriff's coat. "You think I'd hightail it to Mexico?"

"I'm just askin'. I reckon I'm the worryin' sort."

The wound didn't appear to have opened; no blood shone over the poultice Alta had packed it with. He dropped the coat back down over the sheriff's belly. "Why's this job mean so much to you, Kelly? What's your stake in that town?"

Kelly looked straight down their back trail as though considering something. His eyes were dark, lines of consternation spoking them. As Yakima pulled the blanket back up to the young lawman's chin, Kelly said, "Will you keep this under your hat?"

"I only talk to Wolf, and he's not the gum-flapping sort."

"A few years ago, when I was still on my old man's ranch out by Cactus Creek, I . . ." He glanced up at the woman, then turned back to Yakima and lowered his voice. "I fell in with the wrong two ranch hands, and we . . . we robbed the Rawlins stage. Got eight thousand dollars and a diamond stickpin off a drummer's wife and a big, loud Ingersoll pocket watch with a ten-dollar bill folded up inside."

Yakima straightened. "They throw you in the cala-boose?"

Kelly shook his head. "We was never caught. But that whole thing has haunted me ever since. I couldn't even spend my share of the money." His voice hardened with self-recrimination. "But I was too goddamn yellow-livered to send it back to the stage company. I buried it. Never seen it again. Every time I went into Douglas to buy supplies or to get a drink with the boys, I felt like the folks knew what I'd done. Got so's I couldn't sleep at night. When I did, I dreamed I was waitin' in line to be tossed into a big lake of burnin' kerosene."

"Hell."

"That's right. All that taught me what hell was like. And it made me appreciate bein' respected and looked up to. Bein' trusted. I couldn't stand it if folks thought I lit out with that money myself, Yakima."

He stared up at the half-breed beseechingly.

"Your secret's safe with me, Kelly. And if you kick off, so's the gold."

He turned away, hesitated, and then continued moving toward his saddle. He'd glimpsed something on his left, on the rocky slope rising on the other side of the creek that gurgled in its shallow, treelined bank.

Two figures. Two man-shaped figures scurrying down the slope, weaving around the rocks. He hadn't wanted to take a close gander, and let them know he'd spied them, but he thought he'd seen rifles in their hands.

Casually, as though he'd been intending to stop all along, he said to Alta, "The sheriff needs a rest. Let's take a break and make some coffee."

Behind him, he heard a rock tumble into the creek.

Chapter 5

Slowly Yakima led the horses into a hollow in the rocks on the right side of the wagon trail they'd been following. He made no sudden moves, and resisted the urge to look at the creek beyond which the two men he'd seen were scrambling around. Alta gigged her own horse up beside Yakima and gave him a faintly incredulous look as he helped her and the baby down from the mustang.

"A couple men followin' us," he said, keeping his voice low.

"I know."

Keeping her horse between him and her and the creek, he slid his horn-gripped Colt from its holster, extended it butt-first. "Can you handle one of these?"

Instead of reaching for his weapon, she lifted the flap of her blanket coat to reveal a pistol holstered on her right hip. It wasn't one of those he'd taken off the dead outlaws, but a Colt .41-caliber New Line revolver. Octagonal-barreled, silver-plated, and factory-engraved, the old popper was a little rusty, but it was well oiled, and it sported a sound walnut handle. Alta carried it in a soft brown holster attached to a leather cartridge belt whose loops were filled with glistening brass.

"Figures," Yakima muttered, dropping his own pistol into its holster and looping the keeper thong over the hammer. "Gather a little wood for a fire. I'm gonna head on across the stream, see what they want."

She nodded and turned to loosen the mustang's cinch. Yakima walked back to the travois behind Wolf. The sheriff's eyes were closed, his chest rising and falling slowly.

The half-breed looked around, kicked at a couple of insignificant branches, trying to get the interlopers to believe he was on a firewood quest. He strolled off the south side of the trail, heading down a hill littered with dead leaves toward the creek.

He was about fifty yards west of where he'd seen the men in the rocks on the creek's opposite side. Pushing through a thick stand of cedars, chokecherry, and hawthorn shrubs, he crossed the creek by tight-roping a beaver dam. The cool-looking dark water slid over the dam, a few inches deep, soaking his boots, but a liberal coating of bear grease kept his feet dry.

On the creek's other side, he slanted downstream through cedars and boulders. Something moved above him and to the right. A man hotfooted down a steep slope, shoving a spyglass into the pocket of his thigh-length bear coat and holding a Winchester in his other hand. The Winchester hung from a leather lanyard around the man's neck. He was bearded, with heavy jaws; he wore a weather-stained, broad-brimmed tan hat.

Yakima ducked under a rock ledge sheathed in

rabbit brush, and dropped to one knee. A narrow gap in the boulder-strewn knolls passed nearby, and he could hear other men moving toward him, boots crunching rocks and gravel, branches raking across pant legs. The smell of smoke told the half-breed the men had an encampment farther back in the rocks that sloped up toward the chalky southern ridge.

A man appeared, moving at a crouch along the trail. Yakima dropped to both knees and pressed his back up tight against the stone ledge, squeezing the Winchester in his hands. He could see the man through a thin screen of gnarled juniper. He was short, wiry, and bearded, wearing a cloth cap and a torn blue wool coat. His eyes were deep-sunk and flat, his lips thin and grim.

Three more men came along behind him—two other short men and then the tall man whom Yakima had seen mincing his way down the steep bluff from where he'd apparently been keeping an eye on the half-breed and the woman and Kelly. All four wore fur or wool coats against the penetrating chill at this altitude. On the outsides of their coats, they wore bandoliers bearing cartridges of different calibers.

When the last man had tramped past his hiding place, Yakima stepped out onto the trail. The men were filing off toward the creek, all four holding their rifles up high across their chests. None spoke. They moved furtively, staring up the rise on the other side of the creek, in the direction in which Yakima and Alta had pulled their horses into a hollow in the rocks.

One of the men stepped into the creek. The water gurgled over the top of his calf-high moccasins. The others followed and were about to step into the stream also, when Yakima loudly racked a shell into his Yellowboy's breech.

"Private party, boys!"

To a man, they stopped, shoulders tensing.

The man in the creek jerked around suddenly, leveling his Henry repeater. Yakima fired the Yellowboy from his shoulder. The man in the creek hit the water with a scream and a splash, throwing his rifle over his head.

The other three whipped around then, too, and Yakima drilled the two nearest him before the third one, nearest the creek, fired his rifle from his hip, then dove behind a boulder. He jerked his head out from the right side of the rock, a pistol in his hand.

Yakima's Yellowboy's leaped and roared twice, blowing rock dust and chips from the side of the boulder. The man behind the rock screamed and jerked his head back behind his cover. Yakima heard him thrashing around. The half-breed ran, leaping a deadfall log. He ran past the boulder and aimed his smoking Yellowboy behind it, where the tall man lay belly-down near the creek.

He clutched the wound in the side of his neck with his right hand. His pistol lay in the grass at the edge of the dark water. His rifle leaned against the back of the boulder. The man snapped his head around to glare up at Yakima. He had gray eyes and a long, bony face. His nose was short and upturned. He'd lost his hat; his hair was thin, lying flat against his scalp.

He hardened his jaws. His gray eyes shone with a wolflike fury. The hand clutching his bloody neck quivered. He said nothing.

Yakima aimed his cocked rifle at the man's head.

"What were you after?" Yakima said with quiet menace, his own eyes set beneath heavy black brows like twin chips of jade. "The woman? The horses? The saddlebags? Maybe all three . . . ?"

The man only glared and kept his hand clutched to his neck from which thick, dark red blood pumped with each beat of his heart. It dribbled across his hand and into the yellow aspen leaves and wiry brown grass and gravel at the edge of the stream.

"All right," Yakima said. "Time to visit your friends."

The man stared up at him in mute defiance until the Yellowboy roared and blew a quarter-sized hole through his forehead, painting the gravel behind him with his brains and the back of his head. Yakima ejected the spent cartridge and seated a fresh one as he looked at the other dead men.

The one in the creek was on his back, the current scraping him across the rocks and gradually nudging him downstream. His hat had gotten caught up between two half-submerged rocks. It bobbed there, gently turning a slow circle. Suddenly, the current tore it free and sent it bobbing off down the stream past its owner.

Yakima quickly thumbed fresh shells from his cartridge belt, sliding them through his rifle's loading gate. He looked around carefully, making sure he wasn't being stalked by more would-be bushwhackers. Following the smell of the fire, as well as the thin strands of blue smoke webbing toward him from the direction of the southern ridge, he tramped cautiously back along the crease in the low buttes.

There might be more men where the four he'd taken down had come from.

He followed the trail up a low rise and into a box canyon in which a dying cook fire cracked and sputtered. What appeared to be a haunch from a small deer was cooking on a wire rack over the fire. Off to the left were four unsaddled horses, saddles and other tack piled against the ridge wall. From the trash strewn about this small alcove in the ridge, the men must have camped here the night before and hadn't yet set out today. They'd probably been nursing hangovers; several empty busthead bottles lay amongst a few airtight tins. One of them, however, must have been keeping an eye on the trail for someone to rob, and summoned the others.

Yakima walked over to where the men's gear was piled against the base of the ridge. The horses nickered and sidestepped away from the stranger. There was nothing unusual about their gear . . . except for a blood-stained burlap sack. The top of the sack was tied with a strip of rawhide.

The rotten-meat stench around the sack was so strong that it made Yakima's eyes water. He breathed through his mouth as he jerked the rawhide knot open and spread the mouth of the bag wide to have a look inside.

What he saw wasn't much of a surprise despite the grisliness of his discovery—three human heads, dead eyes staring out from beneath drooping lids. One, capped with shaggy, lice-flecked cinnamon hair, had a ragged round hole in its forehead, just above its right eye. Its lips were stretched back from long, crooked yellow teeth.

Yakima released the bag and straightened.

His stalkers had been bounty hunters. The heads had bounties on them. They'd likely belonged to killers of one stripe or another. Yakima himself had no paper on him—at least, none that he knew about—but the bounty men might have heard about the robbery in Douglas and thought him, Alta, and Kelly had belonged to the gang of bank robbers. They'd probably seen the overstuffed saddlebags thrown over one of the horses.

Maybe they'd just wanted the money themselves. The money and the woman. Yakima had rarely met a bounty hunter who'd been any more scrupulous than the men he hunted. Often, they were less so. Bounty hunting was relatively easy, if you didn't mind stealing into remote camps under cover of darkness and shooting your prey as they slept.

He turned the horses loose, then removed the meat from the rack over the fire. He wrapped the haunch, only a little charred, in a deerskin that was draped over a rock for drying, then shouldered the bounty as well as his rifle and made his way back down the grade to the creek. He forded the creek again at the beaver damn and strode across the trail and into the camp, where Alta sat on a rock by the fire she'd built, bunching her lips and narrowing one eye as she aimed her cocked New Line at him.

With her tangled blue-black hair and wild eyes, she had a feral look. Not unlike some Apache women he'd known in Arizona.

He stopped in his tracks and looked at her.

She must have enjoyed having a man in her gun

sights. She was probably recalling the indignity she'd endured at the hands of the thieves and would-be rapists who'd invaded her shack. She didn't depress the Colt's hammer and lower the weapon for several seconds. When she did, she gave an almost dejected grunt and returned the piece to the cross-draw holster under her coat.

"Who were they?" she asked.

"Two-legged coyotes." Yakima tossed the deerskin and meat onto the ground beside the fire she'd built. "They brought lunch."

As the woman unwrapped the meat and slipped a knife from another sheath hidden beneath her coat, Yakima checked on Kelly. The man's hat had blown off. He opened his eyes as Yakima set his hat back on his head.

"Heard the shootin'. Wanted to help but . . . thought I'd better stay here with the girl. She's probably pretty skittish after that affair in the cabin yesterday."

Yakima glanced at Alta slicing up the roasted venison, muttering to herself as she worked. He remembered last night, when she hadn't seemed skittish at all. "Right."

After they'd eaten and downed some coffee, and after Alta had suckled the fussy Christian, they continued their journey. An hour later they topped the breezy saddleback ridge and saw Dead River—a mess of false-fronted buildings and timber shacks and stock pens spread like smoking wreckage across a broad, northern horseshoe in the ridge-surrounded Dead River Valley.

Chapter 6

Several faces appeared in windows on both sides of Dead River's broad main street as Yakima led his oddly composed procession down the middle of it.

Smoke from chimneys hung in blue tatters beneath downdrafts in the chill gray air, while several men were out in front of their establishments, splitting more wood to feed their stoves. Already, stacks of split wood were prominently fronting or siding the mostly peeled log structures, or filling the trash-littered alleys between them.

On the low ridge to the north of the town, trees and shrubs shone with the duns and reds of a mountain fall. Sumac shrubs along the creek curving along the base of the slope to the south of the village were cloaked in vivid scarlet. The stream was steel blue, stitched with the occasional white ruffles of small rapids.

On Yakima's left was a barracklike general store, a pine railing running along the sides of its broad loading dock. Two big wagons were parked out front, both teeming with children and middle-aged women. There were three dogs in the wagons, as well, one barking at

a big brown-and-white collie that was running frantically around the loading dock as several bearded men
in fur coats backed-and-bellied grain sacks out of the
warehouse side of the store, handing them down to
others inside the wagon boxes.

The men looked purposeful, several with pipes
clamped in their teeth. The children looked dour. The
women sat stiffly in the wagons' drivers' boots, clad in
heavy cloaks, plain wool skirts, and wool caps that
were tied beneath their chins. These folks' demeanors
told Yakima this might be their last trip to town for the
year for all of them. They'd likely spend the next four
months snowbound on their ranches or hay farms,
huddled before roaring fires and dreaming of the first
green shoots of spring.

"There," Alta said, pointing toward the street's right
side as she rode off Yakima's right stirrup, her infant
gurgling in its harness beneath her chin.

Yakima saw a building—one of the few bare-plank
structures he'd seen so far—that appeared to have
been a livery barn at one time. A badly faded sign over
the large double-hung doors announced FEDERATED
LIVERY, though below it, a smaller signboard jutting
into the street and supported by a cottonwood post
announced ABERNATHY'S FURNITURE, while yet another,
jutting out from the base of a stairs that climbed the
outside of the building, on its east side, read WINTHROP
HOWE, MD.

A secondary sign beneath the main one advertised
TOOTH EXTRACTIONS, PATENTED ELIXIRS, and SLEEP
TONICS. One more, very small, was mounted over a

bottom story window. It read AFFORDABLE HELP FOR FEMALE COMPLAINTS.

Yakima had seen enough such signs to know that the "help" offered was usually for those females who found themselves in the family way without wanting a family.

"This fella sounds like a snake oil salesman," Yakima growled as he drew Wolf to a stop before the hitchrack at the bottom of the outside stairs.

He swung out of his saddle. A woman caught his eye on the other side of the street, and he couldn't help taking a moment to look her over. The sign on the two-story building identified it as MISS VENORA'S WILD COYOTE SALOON & DANCE HALL, but the girl standing on the second-story balcony, leaning forward against the rail and smoking a slender cheroot, was no ordinary saloon girl.

She was dressed in an alluring dress of black taffeta, with fishnet stockings and high-heeled black, gold-buckled shoes. She wore a blanket around her shoulders to ward off the chill, but between the blanket's ends, he saw that a gaudy red corset pushed up a pair of full, creamy breasts.

The girl's rich chestnut hair dropped in thick swirls to her shoulders. Her face was heart-shaped. There was a mole on her cheek, a smaller one on her chin. He was too far away to tell for sure, but he thought her eyes a deep, inviting brown. Their intoxicating almond shape was complemented by the dark paint that shadowed their lids.

Yakima's pulse quickened. A beguiling little gal, for

sure. What in the hell was a whore like her doing in a town this far out in the high and rocky?

Meeting Yakima's brash gaze with a brash one of her own, she spread her lips suddenly, showing a full set of small white teeth.

A stone thumped off Yakima's right shoulder. He turned to see Alta glaring at him, then jerking her chin at the doctor's office.

"Cold here," she grunted. "I have to get the little one inside."

"All right, all right."

He walked over to where Kelly lay back against the travois, his hat tipped over his head. His head was turned to one side. Yakima couldn't tell for sure under the blanket and his heavy coat, but he didn't seem to be breathing.

His pulse quickening, he placed a hand on the young sheriff's chest. Kelly lifted his head with a jerk, knuckling his hat brim off his forehead. He looked around. "Jesus, you gave me a start." He blinked as if to clear his bleary, bloodshot eyes. "We to Dead River already?"

"You gave *me* a start, you jasper. For a second there I thought I made the trip for nothin' . . . when I could've been hightailin' it for Mexico with them saddlebags."

Kelly shivered and crossed his arms under the blanket. "Some colder up here, ain't it? Liable to get stuck here if we don't get out in a week or so. Passes on either side are so high the prospectors around here say they see angels dancin' around on 'em on a Friday night."

Yakima squatted and draped the sheriff's left arm over his shoulder. "Ain't this in your jurisdiction?"

Kelly nodded as Yakima helped him to his feet. "So

far from Douglas, I only get over here once or twice a year. A good lawman here—Dusty Burkholder. He'll hold the gold for me."

"What—you still don't trust me?"

"Why should I trust you?" Kelly grunted as Yakima guided him over to the boardwalk at the bottom of the doctor's outside staircase. "You beat up two cowboys in my town, damn near destroyed a saloon, and now you're talkin' about Mex—ah, *shit!*"

He missed the boardwalk and nearly dropped to his right knee, on Yakima's off side. Alta was there, grabbing Kelly around the waist and draping his arm across her shoulders, helping Yakima guide the young sheriff up onto the boardwalk.

"Jus' so . . . damn weak," Kelly muttered as Yakima and Alta fairly carried him up the stairs, one slow step at a time. If the travois ride hadn't already done it, Yakima didn't want to open up the young lawman's wound here at the end of their journey.

At the top, steadying Kelly between him and Alta, Yakima rapped on the outside door. No response. He heard only the voices of the men loading the wagon and the ring of a blacksmith's hammer, the distant barking of a dog.

"Wait here," he said.

He opened the outside door, pushed open the rough-timbered inside door, and stepped into a small office outfitted with a horsehair sofa and a rolltop desk. A potbelly stove ticked to Yakima's left, opposite the desk. There were two doors, one on the office's far side, another to Yakima's right. On the other side of the one to his right, he heard movement.

"Doc?"

A man cursed. A woman laughed. There was a thud of a foot on the floor, and then a louder thud—as though of a large body dropping to a knee—that shook the office and made the cheap panes rattle in the window frames. The woman gave a startled gasp, then laughed again as the man cursed and grunted.

"Everything all right?" Yakima called.

The knob on the door on the room's right side twisted. A second later, the door opened, ramming against a man's shoulder before the man stepped aside and jerked the door open far enough for him to slide his bulk through. He was a man of average height but immense girth, clad in a rumpled three-piece suit. One white shirttail stuck out beneath his brocade vest, and a large, soft hand fumbled at the last button of his fly.

"Good Christ," he said, breathing hard and sweeping a thick lock of silver hair back from his flushed forehead with his other, beringed hand and regarding Yakima with both chagrin and annoyance. "What in God's name can I do for you, young man? I was . . . I was just having lunch."

He jerked the door closed. Behind it, there was the muffled sound of the woman's laugh again. Just before the door had closed, Yakima had caught a glimpse of a ruffled bed and a naked woman with long red hair sitting on the edge of the bed and pulling a stocking up one of her long, porcelain-pale legs.

"Sorry to interrupt your lunch, Doc," Yakima said, "but I got a wounded man out here. Can I bring him in?"

"Ah, hell," the doctor sighed, plucking a pair of wire-rimmed spectacles off his desk and mounting them over his nose, twisting the bows behind his ears. "I thought things would be settling down. Winter's on the way, for chrissakes."

He looked at Yakima through his spectacles, running his eyes up and down the half-breed's long, broad frame ensconced in buckskins and mackinaw, with long black hair hanging down from his flat-brimmed hat.

"Who on earth are you?"

"Name's Henry."

"You're a stranger. We don't get many strangers this time of year. Hell, people *leave* Dead River this time of year. They don't *arrive*." The sawbones sounded truly miffed.

"I'll remember that for next year. Can I bring Sheriff Kelly in now, before he bleeds to death on your stairs?"

"Kelly? What the hell's *he* doing here? Why, Douglas is way over on the other side of Crow . . ."

He let his voice trail off as he began tramping as though through deep snow toward the door on the room's far end. Yakima moved back out onto the stairs, where Alta was supporting Kelly, little Christian sound asleep against her chest. They guided the sheriff into the doctor's office. The portly sawbones came out of the back room, rolling up his shirtsleeves.

His incredulous gaze grew even more incredulous as it slipped from the pain-racked sheriff to Alta standing on the other side of the lawman from Yakima.

"Why, Alta Banos!" the pill roller exclaimed. "What on earth . . . ?"

"My man," she said in her matter-of-fact way as she and Yakima guided Kelly on past the doctor and into the examining room, "is dead. Three months."

"Why?" the doctor inquired, shocked. "How?"

"Horse threw him. A snake bit his chest."

As Yakima eased Kelly onto the pedestal-table in the middle of the small room, Alta turned to the doctor and peeled the deerskins away from little Christian's head. "Before he died, he give me this. Little Christian. He look just like his *padre*."

The doctor's scowl opened to an admiring smile. As he walked over to Alta and the child, placing his hands on the boy's little head, Alta said, "He is not well. His breathing."

"I'll check him over when I'm through with Kelly."

"Reverend Ekdahl still here, Doc?"

"Why . . . yes, of course."

"He have anyone for the winter—to clean, cook?"

The doctor looked a little befuddled. He hiked a shoulder. "Not that I know of . . ."

"Adios," Alta said without further ado, and headed on out of the examining room and then out the front door. Yakima heard her light tread on the outside stairs.

As the doctor turned his attention to Kelly, the sheriff grabbed Yakima's forearm. "The gold still on the street?"

"Don't worry," the half-breed said. "I'm headed back out there. You rest easy, Kelly. I'll be around if you need anything."

"Gonna be snowed in if you don't leave soon," the doctor warned, unbuttoning the young lawman's coat but shifting his watery glance to Yakima. "The old Indian who chops wood for me—Blue Thunder—says a storm's on the way to the high country. The passes to either side of Dead River will be covered by midnight. Blue Thunder himself done headed on over the western pass several hours ago. Has a white woman waiting for him in an old prospector's shack," he added with a wry smile.

"Hell, it's only October," Yakima said.

"Snow comes early to this leg of the Wind Rivers. Those who intend to and haven't already are hightailing it over the passes to the low country."

"Any way outta here to the north or south?"

"Wind Rivers to the north, the Mexican Range to the south." The doctor shook his head as he inspected the sheriff's wound. "No way over either range once the snow hits. 'Less you're a bird." He grimaced. "What happened here, Sheriff? When were you shot?"

As the doctor continued to examine Kelly, Yakima moved on out of the little room in time to see the redhead slip out of the other door and pad on the balls of her feet across the main office and outside. She obviously didn't want to be seen, so Yakima stopped just outside the examining room.

He saw only that she was a well-built girl, full-hipped and big-breasted, with rich red hair spilling down her shoulders almost to her rear. She wore a gaudy dress under a long, striped wool coat and high-button canvas shoes. A little beaded purse swung from her right hand.

The half-breed waited until she'd slipped her shoes on—he could see her out the window beside the door—and then headed on down the stairs. He himself went out and dropped down the stairs behind her. As she angled across the street toward the Wild Coyote, glancing skeptically at the ragtag string of horses, where Alta was adjusting the cinch of her own mustang, a man came out of the building she was heading toward.

He pinched his hat brim at the redhead, then hitched his pants on the saloon's front gallery, staring suspiciously toward Yakima and the woman.

"I take it you have somewhere to go," Yakima said as Alta glanced toward the tall man on the other side of the street.

She nodded as she walked over to the mustang's left side, the reins in her hand. "You?"

"I'll manage."

Yakima lifted his hat, ran his hands through his hair as he looked around at the town around him, the log shacks and false-fronted business establishments looking grim in the gray light. The breeze had gotten colder, and he thought he'd spied a few stray snow granules. He had no fondness for the mountains in winter. From what he'd heard, Dead River would probably get as cold as Dakota Territory, and the snow would likely pile up deeper and for just as long.

"You can come with me. The reverend has extra rooms."

"Reverend, eh?" Yakima shook his head. "I don't put much stock in sky pilots, and most of them I've run into have returned the favor."

"Help."

She canted her head toward the saddle, and lifted her left, moccasin-clad foot, as though to toe a stirrup. Yakima crouched and formed a step with his hands, hefted her and the child into the leather, then stepped back and watched her ride on up the street toward the opposite side of Dead River.

The chill breeze blew chimney smoke this way and that around her. Tumbleweeds danced. Two ranch hands clad in heavy blanket coats cantered their horses from the direction of a saloon farther up the street, and rode on past Yakima, urging their mounts into trots, crouching low and tipping their hat brims against the wind.

Yakima watched them gallop toward the east end of town, hooves thudding, dust broiling. As they passed the two freight wagons that had been parked in front of the mercantile but that were now being driven out of town in the same direction, one of the men shouted something, likely concerning the weather. The driver of the first wagon shouted a return that Yakima couldn't make out above the breeze and a yellowed newspaper rustling nearby.

The street around Yakima was vacant now, excepting the tall man in the long buffalo coat staring at him from the whorehouse gallery, fists on his hips, ragged hat tipped low on his forehead. Yakima had just turned his attention toward the tall man when the man started walking toward him.

As though expecting trouble, the man flicked the keeper thong free of his holstered Colt's hammer, and spread his coat just wide enough that Yakima glimpsed the town marshal's badge pinned to his shirt.

"You know what you look like?" the man said in a slow, menacing Texas drawl.

"Sight for sore eyes?"

"History—if'n you don't fork that big stallion and trail these cayuses the hell out of my town. See, I don't plan on winterin' up with no half-breeds!"

Chapter 7

Before Yakima realized it, he'd buried his right fist in the potbelly of the marshal of Dead River, and the man had dropped to his knees with a loud groan of expelled air.

The marshal clawed at the Colt on his right hip, beneath the buffalo coat, but he hadn't lifted the six-shooter half out of the leather before Yakima kicked out with his right boot and sent the gun turning end over end in the air behind the sheriff.

It thudded to the dusty, shit-littered street.

"God-*damn* your half-breed hide!" Clutching his right hand to his belly, the man glowered up at Yakima from beneath his furry gray brows. The whites of his eyes were etched with tiny red veins—he'd no doubt been celebrating the coming of winter to Dead River with a whore and a bottle. Must be a tradition here, Yakima vaguely ruminated.

"He already did that," Yakima growled, staring down at the grunting, groaning local lawman, "when he sent me here to this hellhole with the sheriff of your fine county sporting a bullet in his belly and saddlebags filled with stolen gold. All I want from you, Marshal, is a safe place to stow the loot until Kelly's back on his feet. Now, I'm a little tired and saddle sore, and the prospect of spending a night here, much less a whole damn winter, has me ready to throw up what little grub I have left in my gut down the nearest privy hole. So, if I hear any more half-breed comments out of you, I'll smash your head so flat it'll do you for a dinner plate."

Apparently, the only thing the marshal heard from the entire rant was the sheriff's name. "Kelly?" It sounded like a choke, as he was still trying to regain his wind.

"He's up at the doc's gettin' tended. He'll appreciate how well you've treated his sole remaining posse rider."

Looking chagrined as well as out of breath, the marshal lifted a foot and pushed off his thigh with a grunt. He only straightened his legs, remaining half-crouched over his belly. Again in a pinched voice, he said, "Why the hell didn't you say so? I heard the bank over to Douglas was robbed." He pointed to the bulging saddlebags on the coyote dun, and straightened a little more. "Boy, you pack a punch—don't ya?" He winced, swallowed, and jerked his dimpled chin. "That the loot?"

"Yep. And me an' Kelly both would feel a whole lot better if we had it under lock an' key."

The lawman ran the back of his bare hand across his soup-strainer mustache and peered up at the doctor's office over the furniture store. The cool breeze smelling of balsam from the surrounding ridges nipped at his hat brim. "Kelly gonna make it?"

"I sure as hell hope so."

Yakima wondered if he—or Kelly himself—could

trust the marshal of Dead River to return the stolen gold to Douglas. He himself would like to get the hell out of here as soon as possible, before it wouldn't be possible again for several months.

He nixed the idea as soon as it had swept across his mind. He couldn't leave the young lawman. He'd stay here until Kelly was either dead or back on his feet, and help him get the money back to where it had come from.

"How 'bout it, Marshal . . . ?"

"Hold on, damn it. I'm still tryin' to get a lungful. You bruised me up some. I ain't as young as I used to be—pushin' fifty, for chrissakes."

He snorted, drew a breath, wincing, but managed to straighten his back. "All right—that's better. I reckon I had it comin', and I do apologize. I reckon I've never felt right about Injuns—even white men with only a few drops in their veins—since I rode with Colonel Chivington against Black Kettle and Little Crow at Sand Creek. I know it ain't right, but it's somethin' I'm workin' on."

"It's comin' kinda slow, ain't it? Besides, in case you haven't heard, Sand Creek was a massacre, not a fight. Those Indians were unarmed."

"This is always clearer when viewed through the lens of the past. Besides, them Injuns had been kidnapping white girls and long-looping settlers' stock for years."

He removed his right glove. "Burkholder's the name." Apologetically as well as by way of introduction, the marshal extended his big, gnarled paw toward Yakima. "Call me Dusty. Most folks around here do."

Yakima shook the man's hand, his jade eyes still skeptical. "Yakima Henry."

"Yakima? That's a different name. Well, come on,

Yakima. Can I call you Yakima? Follow me. We'll stow that loot in one of my jail cells. I got three, and only one's occupied."

Yakima grabbed Wolf's reins off the hitchrack and, leading the black as well as the string of outlaw mounts, followed the stiff, bandy-legged lawman into the mouth of a southern side street that intersected the main one two buildings west of the Wild Coyote.

The marshal's office, identified by a shingle under the gallery roof, sat alone on a sage-stippled lot a block away from the main street. It was a low-slung, shake-shingled log building with smoke curling and tearing from the dented tin chimney pipe that poked out the side of the building and then jutted straight up above the roof. A perpetually grieved mountain jay cawed from a branch of the jack pine standing snug against and towering over the building's west wall, as though helping to hold it up.

Yakima tied Wolf to the hitchrack, grunted under the weight of the gold-filled saddlebags that he draped over a shoulder, and followed the aging marshal up the porch steps. Burkholder stopped at the door, glanced at Yakima, and pressed two fingers to his lips, grinning.

He pushed the door open suddenly, and the young man sitting behind the marshal's cluttered desk quickly dropped his boots off the desk with a surprised grunt and a squawk of his swivel chair's dry hinge. His crossed boots had nudged a short stack of wanted circulars off the desk edge, and they fluttered and danced now in the air beside it.

"Shade, what'd I tell you about kickin' your damn feet up on my desk!"

"Shit!" said the broad-faced young man, a cap of yellow curls sitting down tight against the crown of his large, square skull. He was red-faced, as though from a recent sunburn, but something about his little dark blue eyes beneath orange brows told Yakima that brick red was his natural color—due more to a colicky temperament than the high-altitude sunlight. The deputy scowled, hardening his heavy, freckled jaws. "You're gonna give me a heart stroke one o' these days—bustin' in here like that!"

Burkholder said, "You're here to remain alert and watch the prisoner and listen for gunfire or other sounds of trouble. I didn't pin that deputy star on your vest so you can have a place to sleep while kicked back, lookin' important."

The deputy rose from the chair, then crouched to begin retrieving the wanted dodgers. He looked more annoyed than sheepish as he glanced over the marshal's shoulder at Yakima. "Who the hell's the Injun?"

"This here's Yakima Henry. He come in with Sheriff Kelly."

"Kelly?" The deputy plucked the last dodger off the floor. "What the hell's he doin' here? The old rock worshipper, Blue Thunder, said it's gonna snow hard startin' tonight. Might last all week. Hell, Kelly's gonna be stranded here till June!"

The yellow-haired deputy didn't seem pleased by the prospect of having the county's highest-ranking lawman kicking around Dead River all winter.

"Doesn't have much choice. Yakima says he got a bullet in him."

The deputy looked at Yakima again, suspiciously. "Oh, yeah?"

Burkholder ignored the deputy and walked over to one of the three cells at the back of the room, flanking the cluttered desk. "How's our prisoner who was stompin' with his tail up half the night?"

"Tryin' to sleep, if it's all right with you, Burkholder," came the low, muffled, angry voice of the man inside the cage.

"No, it ain't all right." Burkholder grabbed a key ring off a nail in a broad ceiling support post, stuck one of the keys in the lock of the cell in which a man dozed belly-down on the single cot, and opened the door. "Come on out of there, Potter. I'm turnin' you loose. It's about to storm, anyways, so you'd best high-tail it back out to the Circle Six. Don't care to feed you another meal, anyway."

The cot creaked as the prisoner—short and husky and full-bearded—rose onto his right arm and scowled at the sheriff, who moved over to the next cell. "I thought you was gonna keep me till tomorrow."

"I changed my mind. My prerogative. Now hustle yourself on out of there, Eldon." Burkholder threw the cell door open and gave the short, beefy prisoner a commanding glare. "And don't let me catch you in town again—and especially not in the Wild Coyote again—till after Christmas!"

Eldon Potter grunted and groaned and blinked his large red-rimmed brown eyes as he stumbled on out of the cell. He stopped in front of Yakima, his head coming up only to the half-breed's breastbone, and scowled, making his unkempt vomit-flecked mustache droop down the sides of his thick-lipped mouth. "Who's the dog eater?"

The deputy, a hip hiked on the side of the sheriff's desk, laughed.

Yakima's eyes blazed in his best imitation of a kill-crazy warrior. "Vamoose, Shorty, or my squaw'll be swampin' out my tipi tonight with what's left of your *hair*!"

Potter stumbled back with a start, glaring at Yakima. He wore a hickory shirt under a denim jacket and cheap checked trousers. Long, greasy, stringy auburn hair hung from the sides of his head to his shoulders. The top of his bulb-shaped head was as bald as a pumpkin. He gave a snort, brushed a hand across his mustache as he took Yakima's imposing measure once more, grabbed his gun belt with its holstered Schofield and a funnel-brimmed tan hat off pegs by the door, and left with a curse.

The sheriff was opening and closing the door he'd just unlocked, the door of the cell nearest his desk, scowling at it. "This damn thing don't seem to be latching right," he muttered wonderingly, continuing to open and close the door.

"What's in the saddlebags?" the deputy wanted to know.

The sheriff told him.

"No shit?" the young firebrand said, letting his heavy lower jaw hang as he slid down off the desk and walked over to Yakima. "Let me have a look."

"Get away, boy," Yakima said, growing impatient with Dead River's local badge toters and more than a little anxious about the safety of the stolen gold. "Why don't we try Potter's cell, Burkholder?"

"That's *Marshal* Burkholder to you, breed," the deputy corrected Yakima.

"Easy, there, Shade." Moving over to the cell that Potter had vacated, the sheriff glanced at Yakima. "Don't mind the kid. His ma runs the Wild Coyote, and he gets a little full of himself sometimes. Shade Darling, meet Yakima Henry." He chuckled as he drew the cell door wide. "Whatever you do, don't call him a 'breed.'"

He chuckled again as Yakima hauled the gold into the cell and dropped the heavy pouches onto the cot. He swung around. The kid stood in the doorway. The freckle-faced Darling was nearly as tall as Yakima, but not as broad. His dark blue eyes were glassy with jeering. Little red pimples were sprayed across his spade-shaped chin.

"What the hell's a goddamn breed doin' cartin' that loot around. Don't tell me Kelly was fool enough to make him a *deputy*!"

"Ah, Christ, Shade," the sheriff complained.

Yakima stared at Shade Darling, who grinned at him insolently, as though daring the half-breed to throw a punch. Yakima kept his face implacable—hard as chiseled granite, green eyes lightless. Miraculously, he'd checked his impulse to give the deputy the same treatment he'd given the marshal. He didn't doubt he'd get away with it—even working together, these hoople-heads weren't capable of hog-tying him—but if he was going to be stranded here in Dead River awhile, it might be wise to make as few enemies as possible.

"Out of the way, Darling," Yakima said with subtle

mockery, holding the kid's laughing gaze. "I'm gonna mosey over to the Wild Coyote, give your ma some business so she can afford to keep havin' your diapers laundered."

Yakima placed his left hand on the kid's chest—instinctively keeping his right hand free for his six-shooter, in case he needed it—and pushed the deputy out of his way. He strode to the door, swinging his head around to make sure the firebrand wasn't fool enough to reach for the hogleg holstered on his left thigh.

"You stay away from Fabienne, ya hear?"

"Fabienne," Yakima muttered, raking a pensive hand across his jaw. "Now, that ain't a name you hear every day. She sounds purty." He sliced a warning look at the deputy scowling at him. "You just make sure that gold is here when me and Kelly come for it." He added with a sly grin, "Fabienne'll be in very good hands."

As Darling lurched for him, he swung around and went out.

It was colder now. The breeze had picked up. Yakima lifted his coat collar to his jaws, and plucked his reins from the hitchrack. He'd seen a livery barn just down the street from the marshal's office. Now it was obscured by swirling snow.

He'd stable his horses, then head back to the main part of town. He was hungry and thirsty. He remembered the exotic-looking girl smoking on the saloon's second-story balcony.

Fabienne . . . ?

Chapter 8

The man who owned Wind River Livery and Feed—
G. W. McMasters—was cranky at having his supper
interrupted by an unexpected visitor, with a storm on
the way. He had little use for five horses here at the
start of winter, but when Yakima asked if he knew of
anyone else in town who might be interested, the man
offered him twenty dollars apiece for the horses as
well as their tack and the possibles in their saddlebags.

Alta hadn't wanted any of the thieves' guns, prefer-
ring the one she already had, so Yakima threw the burlap sack of hoglegs into the deal. He managed to dicker
McMasters out of twenty more dollars for all four of the
rifles he'd taken off the dead bank robbers, and paid the
man in advance for two days' stabling, feeding, and
grooming of Wolf, pocketing the rest.

It was a tidy sum. Even after splitting the booty with
Alta, he had enough to get him through a few days'
stay here in Dead River—possibly the entire winter, if
it came to that—and back to Douglas or onto the trail to
somewhere in the sunny Southwest, where he'd secure
work for the winter.

Hungry and seeing no need to heed Shade Darling's warning—if you let a man push you too far, you were only doing an injustice to yourself and the pusher, after all—he headed back to the main part of town. It was dusk, and the wind was blowing the snow sideways. He could catch brief glimpses of the spruce-and-jack-pine-stippled ridges surrounding the settlement.

So far, the danderlike flakes were forming only small piles against the sides of buildings and on the lee side of shrubs, trash heaps, and woodpiles, clinging damply, for the ground was still relatively warm. The sky was low and the color of dirty laundry. Yakima paused at the side of the main street, which was called Pine Street, and stared westward.

At the far end of town stood the crisp, white-frame, steepled church toward which Alta and Christian had headed. Flanking the church was a sprawling timber and stone lodge set back in the Douglas firs and birches that was probably the church's parsonage, though Yakima had never seen a preacher's digs that large. Weren't sky pilots men of paucity? Whoever he was, Alta knew the man. Yakima hoped the young widow had found a place to light there for herself and the little one.

Yakima gave the sky a last, skeptical glance and, bearing the weight of his Winchester and saddlebags, pushed into the Wild Coyote Saloon and Dance Hall. The moaning of the wind was replaced by the patter of the piano being played at the room's far end by a dapper, middle-aged man in green pants, green jacket, red suspenders, red socks, and a red-feathered green hat—a costume that made him look like a large leprechaun.

In the middle of the room, a potbelly stove ticked and

chugged. Just now the redheaded whore whom Yakima had seen earlier in the doctor's office, dressed now in a frilly orange-and-black ballroom gown obscured by the colorful quilt she clutched about her bare shoulders, was chunking a birch knot through the stove's open door.

When she'd closed the door and turned the squeaking latching lever, she brushed a hand across the quilt and turned her head toward Yakima. Her eyes widened as she appraised the big, dark-skinned, green-eyed, long-haired creature standing before the saloon's closed winter door staring back at her from beneath the flat brim of his black, low-crowned hat.

"Look what the bobcat dragged in." She glanced at the bar that ran along the long room's right wall. Three townsmen stood sideways to the bar, one with a whore, all looking toward the newcomer. "You want a drink or a girl?" The redhead arched her brow enticingly. "Or . . . maybe you have enough pocket jingle for both . . . ?"

"Got any grub?"

The redhead looked at the corpulent, bald, bearded man standing behind the bar. "Tully?"

"Stew's ready," said Tully, his voice pitched with disapproval as he eyed the half-breed bitterly.

The redhead kept her auburn eyes on Yakima. He figured her to be in her late thirties, early forties—still a well-setup woman though there were lines cut into the skin around her eyes and long red mouth. She'd probably been here for as long as the place had been in existence. "Stew suit your fancy?"

"Bring it out."

Yakima dropped down the three steps to the saloon

floor, which was carpeted in several large, mismatched Oriental rugs, from the front of the room to the stairs at the back. The rug was deep but burned, worn, and torn in places, and flecked with wood ash, some tobacco ash. Game trophies and old, hand-forged ox shoes decorated the red-and-gold-papered walls. The air of the place was a not uninviting potpourri of liquor, beer, tobacco and wood smoke, roasting meet, and various perfumes.

The half-breed kicked a chair out from the first table he came to. Glancing at three girls lined up at the bar, all three staring at him with various expressions, he dropped his gear on the chair. The whores at the bar were two blondes and the brunette he had seen on the second-floor balcony. She stood with the others but she was not of them. There was something wild and beguiling about her singular, dark-eyed beauty—something that bit a man hard deep in his loins and held there, chewing, like a hungry mountain lion.

No wonder Shade Darling didn't want to share her with the likes of a half-breed drifter. He'd share her with other citizens, because he had to. But not with a stranger.

Fabienne . . .

The girl's eyes smoldered back at him. The corners of her rich mouth quirked knowingly, as though she were reading the hunger in his primal gaze, but she did not smile. Yakima looked away from the girl as he set his rifle on the table before him. The redhead had followed him over to the table, and now she said, "Something to wet your whistle?"

Yakima's gaze flicked to the girl, whose knowing, ancient eyes were still glued to him. He could almost feel them caressing him like very soft, feminine fingers. He wanted whiskey. But not with the girl here. With the girl and whiskey, things could get out of hand faster than a summer cyclone. And he had to keep his mind clear for Kelly and the stolen loot that was supposedly under lock and key at the town marshal's office.

"Beer."

The big leprechaun was still tapping the piano keys, swinging his head from one side to the other and humming, having a grand old time by himself over there though no one else seemed to be enjoying the raucous melody. The redhead walked around behind the bar and filled a dimpled beer schooner from a wooden tap. Yakima sagged into a chair at his table, doffed his hat, threw it over the brass receiver of his Yellowboy, and ran thick fingers through his long, tangled hair.

The redhead returned with the beer, setting it on the table before him. The big, bearded barman, Tully, came out through a curtained doorway behind the bar and set a steaming plate of stew and wheat bread on the table before Yakima. Curling a bearded lip at the stranger, revealing a gold eyetooth, Tully went away, but the redhead remained. The stew was darkly rich, with large, near-black chunks of venison and little squares of well-cooked potatoes, carrots, turnips, and translucent bits of wild onion.

The redhead slipped into a chair across from Yakima. He glanced at her skeptically as he took up his fork and knife and began shoveling grub without ceremony.

"I'm Miss Venora," said the redhead in a raspy voice that sounded to Yakima's practiced ears as affected. "Venora Darling, that is. I run this place."

"Congratulations."

"I want you to know that I don't normally allow Indians in here, but—"

"Not an Indian," Yakima said, hunkered down over his plate. "Black Irish."

She looked at him as though considering this and then, realizing he was joshing, she continued with her previous sentence. "But I make an exception for you because you look somewhat civilized. Looks like you've been around whites some, and . . ."

She let her voice trail off as Yakima looked up at her, still chewing, enjoying the taste of the stew and the ale and the company of the girls at the bar though he hadn't spoken to them yet. He didn't like Miss Venora—had she said her last name was *Darling*?—and he felt warm tar dribbling into his veins as he said, canting his head toward the bar, "How much for Miss Fabienne?"

"Oh," the redhead said, wagging her head slowly, frowning. "No, no. She's only . . ."

"For town folks?"

The piano was getting on his nerves.

"For those town folks who can afford her and are in good standing here at my humble establishment, Mr. . . ."

"How much?"

"Fabienne is five dollars an hour. Twice what I ask for the other girls. She's French, you understand. Only came here last year . . ."

Yakima set his fork down, ran a sleeve across his mouth, and reached into his shirt pocket for the roll of greenbacks he'd acquired at the livery barn. He peeled off two silver certificates and set them on the table in front of his plate. "Here's for the girl and a hot bath."

The woman's amber eyes were riveted on the roll of bills in Yakima's thick, callused hands. Her lips were parted, as though she had intended to continue with her objections; then, reconsidering, she reached out with her right hand and plucked the two notes off the table. She held each up to the hurricane lantern hanging over the table, then folded them three times and shoved them down into her corset, between the tops of her two pillowy breasts that were bulging up against her long, pale neck.

As Yakima resumed work on his plate, eating hungrily, Miss Venora glanced toward the bar. In the corner of his right eye, he saw the auburn-haired girl push away from the bar and walk past him on her way to the back of the room. Beneath the raucous notes of the off-key piano, he heard the girl's tread on the stairs, heard the faint squawk of the loose railing.

In the corner of his left eye, he saw Miss Fabienne, clad alluringly in lacy black and red silks and taffeta, move along the balcony above the saloon, then turn away down a hall and out of sight.

He felt a slight but persistent hammering in his chest. He kept his head down, eating, hearing the piano and the wind howling outside and the muffled conversation of the men and girls at the bar. He felt Miss Venora's eyes on him. He looked up at her, and she looked as though she were watching an animal in a cage—one that both frightened and amused her.

When he finished his plate, he swabbed it clean with the last of his bread and downed the last half of his ale, swallowing hard, enjoying the malty, hoppy taste of the beer on top of the well-seasoned venison. He lowered the glass, belched, and set it on the table.

"Can I get you another? I'm having a bath hauled to your room."

"Why not?"

He wasn't in any hurry. It was going to be a long stay here in Dead River until Kelly was able to ride again. Then, of course, there was always the possibility—a good one, judging by the noise of the building storm above the tooth-gnashing clatter of the leprechaun's piano—that he'd be here till the crocuses bloomed.

He sipped the second beer. Customers came and went. The girls looked bored with the clientele, as though dreading having to settle for the next several months with the slim pickings in Dead River. A few shopkeepers started a poker game. One, a gent in his fifties with shaggy salt-and-pepper muttonchops, cajoled one of the girls, a little blonde with too much lipstick, into hooking her rump over his knee "for luck."

The piano-playing leprechaun took a break and ordered an ale from the bald barman, Jim Tully, which he sipped while straddling a chair backward and observing the game.

Outside, the wind moaned.

A cat appeared from somewhere, and Tully set a pan of milk for it near the woodstove.

Figuring that both the girl and the bath were ready for him, Yakima finished his beer, grabbed his gear, and climbed the stairs at the back of the room. His heart thumped in anticipation of the girl. He wasn't sure why. He'd known beautiful whores before. Hell, he'd married one. Maybe because he'd been warned away from her. Whatever it was, he figured on enjoying the next hour or so, then heading off to find somewhere to hole up for the rest of the night and forget about her.

Madame Venora had whispered her room number. He stopped at a door with a small plaque bearing the brass number 5, rapped the back of his knuckles against it. Her voice sounded sweet and sonorous, girlish, as she said, *"Entrez!"*

He turned the knob and went in under the weight of his gear, and stood there awkwardly in the open doorway, his lungs instantly filling with the smell of incense and burning piñon. There was a fire in the small hearth to the right. A canopied four-posted bed to the left.

The girl sat with her back to him, facing a mirrored cherry vanity. Yakima's breath purred as it caught slightly in his throat. At first glance, she appeared naked, but then he realized she wore an extremely sheer black shift that fell to the floor beneath her brocade-upholstered bench.

The shift served only to veil her slender, curving back. She sat at enough of an angle that he could see the rounded side of her left breast beneath her upraised arm. She was brushing her hair with an ivory-handled brush, tilting her auburn head slightly to one side. The face in the mirror was intoxicating. It became even more disarming as she smiled into it, her eyes on his own reflection.

"What took you so long?" she said in her sexy French accent, the voice itself tinkling like a slender spring runoff over polished rocks.

Yakima nudged the door closed with a boot and dropped his gear on the floor. "Saw no reason to rush things."

Why was it he felt he knew her? Instantly, he felt comfortable in this room though he'd slept in such a well-appointed room maybe twice in his life, with other high-priced parlor girls he'd managed to scrape up the eagles for.

He walked over to the corner of the bed and shrugged out of his coat. To his left, between him and the snapping hearth, was a steaming, high-backed copper tub. The tub glowed golden in the firelight. The water shone like liquid fire.

She set the brush down on the table, rose slowly, turning as gracefully as a forest sprite, and strode toward him. The shift hung straight down from her neck, to which it clung loosely. As Yakima dug his fingers into the knot of his neckerchief, trying to loosen it, the hitch in his throat grew almost painful.

Beneath the shift, the girl was naked. Her pale, full breasts jostled from side to side as she strode toward him, looking up at him coyly from beneath her dark brown brows. Her eyes were like brown velvet. The firelight shone in them, the flames resembling small gold bayonets.

She smelled rich and intoxicating. Slighty musky.

She reached up and brushed his hands away from his neck, and then both her own, small, slender hands worked at the knot. Her lips were full and very faintly etched with vertical lines. They parted slightly, and he could see the white ends of her teeth. She pressed the point of her tongue against the underside of her front teeth, and the corners of her mouth rose slowly, showing a glistening wetness.

Her breath puffed gently against his chest. It smelled

faintly of licorice. Her breasts brushed lightly against his shirt. He raised his hands to them, brushed the tips of his fingers against their curving sides.

As she untied the knot of his neckerchief loose and pulled the ends away, she rose on her toes and pressed her lips against the side of his jaw. Her mouth felt like silk. Her lips left a moistness that ignited another fire through his jaw and into his left ear, making it ring.

Beneath his kindling anticipation of her, he hadn't expected her to be all that much. The only one who'd turned out to be better than he'd expected was Faith. But there was a sexy, charming innocence about this girl that, coupled with those ancient eyes, made him feel stuck like some butterfly to a wall with a stickpin.

Her breasts pushed against him, jostling and warm and pliant, and he felt the heat of her spread down his throat and chest and into his groin.

He unbuttoned his shirt, shrugged out of it, let it drop to the floor. Next off was his cartridge belt. He let that, too, drop to the floor. As he continued shucking out of trail-grimed clothes, she sat back on the edge of the bed and crossed her all-but-naked legs, watching him, sticking a fingernail between her lips and taking turns biting at it and sucking it.

Her eyes danced across him, her expression by turns wistful and skeptical and hard to decipher. When he was naked, her eyes dropped to his crotch, and she threw her head back on her shoulders, shaking her hair back from her eyes and giving the bare leg hanging over the opposite knee an eager little wag.

He felt a little embarrassed by the obvious heatedness of his need, as well as by the scars that covered nearly every dark, bulging muscle on him and that were like a government survey map of a life lived violently. He swung over to the tub and dropped down into the hot water, kneeling and shoving his head under.

He lifted his face, blowing water from his lips and running his hands through his hair, squeezing excess water from it. When he opened his eyes again, she was on her knees beside the tub, raking a cake of sweet-smelling soap against a wooden-handled brush bristling with horsehair.

"We get you scrubbed up," she said, gritting her teeth as she continued raking the soap hard against the brush.

When she had the brush well lathered, she said, "Close your eyes." And she very gently and slowly scrubbed his face, working up a lather. When he'd rinsed his face, she lathered the brush again and went to work on his neck and his back, scrubbing hard now, grunting with the effort, her hair dancing about her slender shoulders. Her breasts slid this way and that against the side of the tub.

The hardness between his legs grew until he fairly throbbed with need.

She scrubbed his broad chest and belly, hard and taut as a bullet-dimpled adobe wall. She ordered him to stand, and, ignoring his jutting member, went to work very businesslike scrubbing his legs and haunches, gently cleaning between his legs and his fully extended member, caressing him with the tips of her soapy fingers.

Yakima sank back on his heels and groaned.

Rinsing the brush out in the tub around his shins, she smiled up at him devilishly from beneath his throbbing need, and rasped, "I like that you're ready for me."

He dropped down into the tub, submerging his entire body including his head, and came up blowing water from his lips. She stepped back as he came out of the tub, dripping, and tossed him a towel from her vanity bench. She watched him dry himself, standing before him, her dark eyes shimmering in the firelight, her full breasts rising and falling as she breathed. Her soft belly, slightly bulging out from her waist, expanded and contracted.

His body now dry, his damp hair brushing his shoulders, he strode forward, pressed his hands against her back, and closed his mouth over hers. Then he stepped back, lifted the black wrap up over her head, and cupped her breasts in his hands, rolling the nipples between his thumbs and index fingers.

They were hard as small stones.

She leaned against him, placed her hands on his bulging pectorals, and pressed her lips to each of his shoulders. Very slowly, she ran her mouth across his chest before bending slowly at the knees and wrapping her arms around him; flattening her warm, soft hands against his buttocks, she kissed her way down his belly until she knelt on the floor between his legs.

As she closed her warm mouth over him, he buried his hands in her hair and squeezed his eyes closed. "Oh, *Jesus*," he heard himself groan.

Chapter 9

Yakima left the forbidden French whore dozing a couple of hours later.

Laden with saddlebags and rifle, he walked toward the balcony at the end of the hall. He stopped several feet before he got to the rail and stared straight out across the top of the saloon hall, where a thick cloud of tobacco smoke shimmered in the light from the gas lamps below. A din rose with the smoke. The piano was being played wildly now, though it would stop for several minutes between hammerings, as though the leprechaun playing it were royally inebriated.

Bottles clinked, men and women laughed. The roulette wheel clicked as it spun, and dice thudded across green baize as the craps players threw. Boots clomped, chairs scraped raucously on the floor. There were intermittent shufflings of cards.

Yakima stood still in the hall, bracket lamps flickering, lengthening his bulky, hatted shadow out before him. He could hear the sounds of coupling behind closed doors—men and women groaning together, leather bedsprings straining. Somewhere, a headboard was hammering a wall.

Even above the whorehouse din, he could hear the wind blowing outside, making the timbers creak. Drafts from all corners made the lamps flicker.

Yakima considered going downstairs and joining the party. Something held him back. He nearly always felt a restraining inner hand that kept him from mixing naturally with others. If he went down there, he'd likely just be sitting alone, drinking alone, fending off the advances of another, lesser whore. Feeling alone, with no friends here or anywhere, and nowhere to go.

Growing owly from too much drink, he'd likely be fighting within the hour. . . .

His belly surged with a near-crippling lonesomeness that had trailed him like hungry wolves since he'd been a boy raised by a lonely, ostracized Indian woman. Faith had given him sanctuary for a time. They'd been friends as well as lovers—no man ever got two shots at that in one life.

Faith was gone. The wolves were back, slathering at his heels. He could hear their footfalls in the imagined brush of the wilderness closing on him from the hallway's papered walls.

He strode off in the opposite direction. There had to be a back way out of this place. Anyway, he'd spent himself on Fabienne. That was all he could hope for these days—a few blissful moments of wild coupling.

Whores were best because they asked no questions. Demanded nothing but monetary fulfillment. There was no point in wearing out his welcome with the

French girl. She'd seemed to enjoy his company as well as the fervent hammering he'd given her—it would have been damn hard to manufacture the love cries she'd loosed as she'd ground her heels into his backside when their final release had come.

But he had to remember that whores were the best actresses anywhere in the world. He did not delude himself into believing he'd been anything more than just another paying customer. But how would he know? He knew nothing about her. He wanted to know nothing about her.

After a short search, he found a back staircase that dropped into a dark storeroom. He stumbled amidst the barrels and hanging sides of salted meat, and finally pushed out into an alley beside the saloon. Wind-driven snow blasted him, nearly throwing him back against the door. It sucked the breath from his lungs and ripped his hat off his head, blowing his hair in a wild tangle about his face and ears.

He stumbled through the darkness and snow—there was only an inch or two on the ground so far though most of it the wind had probably piled in drifts—until he'd run his hat down. He didn't try to wear it but held it in the same hand in which he held the Yellowboy as he hoofed it out into Pine Street and tried to get his bearings.

He'd seen another hotel in town, one called the Canon House. He saw it now to his right and on the other side of the street—a narrow, two-story, slate-roofed place with a few windows lit on the first floor, none on the second. The flophouse likely had plenty of vacant rooms, as it appeared that most people who were going to leave Dead River for the winter had already left.

But Yakima saw no reason to pay good money for a room when all he needed now was to sleep. He'd pay for a town bath and a woman—but why pay to sleep when livery stables were often just as comfortable as any overpriced hotel room? As long as you were paying to stable your horse, you yourself could usually bed down in the same stall for free.

He headed for McMaster's place down the side street from the marshal's office. As he passed the jailhouse, he saw the buttery glow of lamplight in the two front windows. Likely, Shade Darling was there, guarding the stolen loot. Yakima was glad. He'd been just as glad not to run into the man in the Wild Coyote or elsewhere, because he wasn't in the mood to rearrange the man's face. He wouldn't take any shit off him, but he didn't feel like expending himself. Besides, he'd had enough trouble over in Douglas.

And that trouble had led him into this trouble that could very likely last him the whole winter. . . .

He put his head down against the western wind, sucked a breath out of the wind that was blowing snow and hay and tumbleweeds as well as several fistfuls of shit and grit from the street, and tramped on to the dark bulk of the livery stable. He ducked through the paddock on the town side of the stable and continued to the small side door he was relieved to find unlocked.

Inside, he closed the door on the wind and was met with the familiar smells of horses, ammonia, oats, and hay. The barn was as dark as the inside of a glove, so he lit a match and made his way down the central alley, looking for Wolf. He had to fire several matches as he passed horses hanging their incredulous heads over the stall partitions on his left and two parked rental buggies and a small spring wagon on his right.

Wolf snorted and nickered as Yakima approached. The horse bobbed its head in greeting. Yakima quickly snuffed the match out between his fingers and grabbed the horse's sleek snout, closing a hand over its leathery nostrils to keep it from lifting a whinny that would likely wake McMasters, who lived in the back shed connected to the barn by a small red door nearly hidden by tack and rope hanging from pegs over and around it.

The wind ripped at every timber in the walls and ceiling, but beneath the cacophony, Yakima thought he could hear the surly old gent snoring back there. He probably had a fully stoked stove near his cot, and a belly awash in tanglefoot.

It was cold in the barn. Breath jetted from his own and the horses' nostrils. As Yakima slipped into Wolf's stall, the horse watching him, black eyes glistening in the darkness a little above and to either side of the white, Florida-shaped streak on his face, he envied McMasters the stove.

The half-breed mounded up some hay in the stall's back corner, dropped his saddlebags, and leaned his rifle against the side stall partition, within easy reach. His tack straddled the front partition. From his saddle he removed his oilcloth-covered blanket roll that consisted of two heavy wool blankets and a rain slicker. He hung his hat on his saddle horn. Plopping down in the fluffed-up hay mound, he rolled onto his side and drew the blanket roll over him.

He sighed, relaxing. He lay there awaiting sleep and listening to the wind.

At length, Wolf gave a blow beside him, and then he heard the big beast drop to its haunches and roll onto its side in the hay. Yakima could feel the cold wind of the horse's scissoring hooves before the beast lay still on its side only a few feet away. Then the stallion's warmth settled against him, as welcome as an extra blanket.

Wolf snorted. The horse's breathing grew deep and regular. A comforting, familiar sound. Yakima drew his knees up and crossed his arms on his chest. He shivered against the chill that even Wolf's heat couldn't hold at bay. Soon, his own breathing grew slow, and gradually the wind's howling and the barn's creaking faded under a soothing wave of sleep.

He woke the next morning when McMasters's door scraped and rasped. When Yakima opened his eyes in the first wash of gray dawn light, he saw the liveryman staring over the partition at him. McMasters's bony, angular face was a gray oval beneath his black, leather-billed watch cap. The man's gray soup-strainer mustache shone nearly white in the gray light angling through a window over Yakima's head.

The man nibbled his mustache thoughtfully, blinked his washed-out blue eyes, and ran a gloved hand down his face. He strode away heavily, hacking up phlegm and spitting.

Yakima turned his head in the hay. Wolf was a hulking black lump beside him, a few feet away. The horse's side rose and fell as he breathed, still asleep. Steam snaked off his sleek black hide.

Yakima glanced at the window. The sky shone like worn burlap. A good morning to sleep in. . . .

He closed his eyes and let sleep wash over him once more. When he opened his eyes again, he blinked in surprise to see washed-out, brassy sunlight forming a trapezoid on the mussed hay and straw beside him. Wolf stood, hanging his head and regarding Yakima expectantly. The horse switched its tail, glad its master was at last awake. Apparently McMasters hadn't fed the horse though Yakima had heard him feeding and watering the others as he'd dozed.

Feeding his own horse would be Yakima's payment for using the livery barn for a hotel.

Yakima gave a snort and climbed to his feet. The cold grabbed him. He shuddered as he let the blankets fall away from him. Christ, it was going to be a long, cold winter. . . .

As he forked fresh hay into Wolf's stall and hauled water from the well behind the barn, he was vaguely aware of hushed voices and footfalls out in front of the place. Finally, he grabbed his rifle, donned his hat, and slid open one of the front, double-hung doors.

He looked up in time to see a club angling down fast toward his head. He pivoted to his left, raising his rifle, and the board slammed into his elbow and shoulder, cushioning the blow to his head.

His smashed hat tumbled off his shoulder. Reacting instinctively, Yakima gave an enraged snarl as he swung around and rammed his Yellowboy's butt into Shade Darling's midsection.

The deputy grunted and stumbled back, dropping the long two-by-four he'd used to nearly clean Yakima's clock. Two other men flanked the deputy, who wore his five-pointed badge on his wool coat and whose breath shone in the chill air lit by wan sunlight angling through low, thin clouds. One of the others was Darling's former prisoner, Eldon Potts, whose thick beard was rimed with frost. The other man was Darling's size and clad in an elk-hide coat.

Yakima sidestepped, crouching, gritting his teeth.

"Drop the rifle, Injun," said the unknown man flanking Darling's right shoulder, stepping around to track Yakima with the Winchester he was aiming straight out from his right hip.

Before Yakima could do anything, Shade Darling raked out a sharp curse and bolted toward Yakima, dropping his head and bulling into Yakima's belly before the half-breed could set his feet. Darling was nearly as big and heavy as Yakima, and the half-breed was lifted a good foot from the ground. The hard-packed earth fronting the livery barn came up to whack him hard about the back of his head and his shoulders, hammering the wind from his lungs.

For a moment, his vision blurred and birds chirped in his ears. Darling's broad red face shone before him beneath its tight cap of yellow curls, and the young firebrand was sporting four eyes and two noses. The eyes and noses shifted until there were only two of the former and one of the latter. Darling was starting to bring his right fist back toward his shoulder when Yakima head-butted him.

The deputy grunted as his head snapped back and he sagged to one side. Yakima kicked the firebrand off him and leaped to his feet, crouching as the other two moved toward him. They both had rifles, and the taller man on the left was bringing his Winchester to his shoulder and narrowing an eye, drawing a bead on Yakima's chest.

"No!" Shade Darling, blood dribbling from the cut in his forehead, wobbled to his feet, shaking his head to clear it, and gritting his teeth. "No guns! We're gonna beat the holy hell out of this son of a bitch! And then we're gonna tar and feather him, and string him up!"

Eldon Potts laughed beneath the brim of his bullet-crowned leather hat.

Vaguely, Yakima thought that tarring and feathering was severe punishment for sleeping with a whore he'd paid good money for. He didn't have time to dwell on it. As the three set the rifles down and then formed an arc around him, raising their fists, he backed into the street to give himself more room to work. Darling was trying to move around him, the tall deputy working his fists in front of his face, like a pugilist, his face flushed scarlet, pimples standing out on his chin, cobalt blue eyes shiny with rage.

The man in the middle, Eldon Potts, was shorter than the other two, but broad-shouldered and with a hard potbelly. The other man was tall and hawk-faced, with a long neck, stringy brown hair, and two silver front teeth he showed as he grinned cunningly, moving toward Yakima with the others, clenching his rifle in his hands.

Darling lunged toward the half-breed, swinging his right fist. Yakima ducked the swing, leaped off his left foot, wheeled in the air, and slammed his boot deep in the deputy's gut.

It was one of the several Eastern fighting techniques

he'd learned from a Shaolin monk he'd laid railroad track with several years ago in western Kansas and the Rockies. The moves had proved damn effective. They did again now as, continuing to leap and bound off each foot in turn, he had the other two men down in dusty heaps, groaning, cursing, howling, dribbling blood down their lips, and holding their injured parts.

The man with the silver teeth bolted off his heels and made an enraged dash for Yakima, swinging both his fists. Yakima parried the attempted blows with his wrists, then rammed his right fist into the side of the man's face, knocking his jaw sideways with a wicked cracking sound.

Deputy Darling just then threw his own right fist against Yakima's forehead. Yakima ducked to avoid the deputy's carelessly flung left, then crashed his own left fist into the man's nose, feeling the wetness of the instant blood burst and seeing the man's nose turn sideways against his face as his eyes crossed.

The short, bald, stocky Potts leaped toward Yakima. Yakima ducked, grabbed the man's arm, and almost effortlessly flipped him over his back. The short man's body slammed against the front of the livery barn with a thunderlike crash before dropping straight down to the ground on his head. Potts got up, blubbering and making another dive at the half-breed, who leaped high, spun, and hammered his left heel into the back of the short man's head.

Potts flew back, hitting the ground in a flurry of broiling dust and feathery snowflakes.

Behind Yakima, a shadow moved. He dropped his head just as a gun butt skidded off the crown of his head, and buried his fist into Marshal Burkholder's mackinaw-clad belly a little harder than he'd buried it the first time. Even with the coat's padding, the older gent groaned and dropped to both knees at once. His pistol dropped to the ground near Yakima's left boot.

"Christ!" the marshal grunted, losing his hat, his thin gray hair whipping around in the morning's cold wind.

Yakima stepped back, his own long black hair blowing like a tumbleweed. The low clouds blew around the sky. Shadows scudded around the street. Yakima's original three attackers were down and writhing. Yakima looked down at the marshal, who had his forehead lowered in front of his knees, his shoulders quivering.

A block toward the main street, several townsmen in shabby suits and winter coats stood, staring warily toward him. A mongrel dog was running around them, wagging its tail. One of the men, wearing a long, wool coat, absently puffed a pipe. Vaguely, Yakima saw that one of his observers was a woman.

Yakima clenched his fists at his sides and looked down at Burkholder. "Is it now against the law for a dog eater to frolic with the whores in this town?"

Burkholder coughed and choked, grinding his forehead into the shit-littered street. Stray snowflakes blew around him. He lifted his head and angled his long, pain-racked face up toward Yakima.

"Ain't against the law to frolic . . ." He coughed, groaned, clamped his arms against his battered belly. "Dog eater or not, it *is* against the law to *kill* 'em!"

Chapter 10

Yakima felt as though he'd been struck across the back with an ax handle. He stared down at the marshal, who continued to spasm as he sucked small drafts of air into his lungs. Yakima lifted his gaze to the people—four men and a woman in a green knit hat, earmuffs, and a spruce green cape—staring at him from fifty yards away.

In the corner of his left eye, he saw another man—the liveryman, McMasters—sitting on the top corral slat in a heavy wool coat and his billed watch cap, slowly chewing a tobacco quid and looking around in mute interest at the men groaning on the ground before him.

The question must have been easy to read in Yakima's eyes. McMasters spat a wad of chew onto a snow-dusted pile of frozen brown horse apples, rubbed his jaw with a gloved hand, and narrowed an accusing eye. "She's dead, all right. That whore. Deputy's mama said you was the last one to see her." He gave an evil grin. "That puts you in a bind, now, don't it?"

Yakima turned and scooped his Yellowboy out of the dust. He brushed the dust from the gun, then stepped past Burkholder, who was now staring at him incredulously from his knees, and started up the street. As he moved toward the main street, he swung around a couple of times, aiming his Winchester out from his hip, in case the marshal or his deputy or Potts or the silver-toothed man tried to drill him from behind.

The men near the intersection parted for him. The dog stepped aside, as well, lowering its tail and its ears and groaning deep in its chest. The woman held her ground—a frosty-eyed woman with brown hair and wearing a long wool dress and black, lace-up boots against the cold. An attractive but severe and stone-faced woman. Her cape fluttered in the breeze. Yakima walked past her and turned the corner to head east along the all but deserted main street.

There were no saddle horses tied to the hitchracks fronting the Wild Coyote. Yakima mounted the board-walk, opened the closed winter door, and walked into the main saloon hall, pulling the door closed on the cold morning and turning to the dingy room that, in stark contrast to the previous night, was as silent as a crypt.

There was only the burly barman Tully, and the madame, Miss Venora Darling. Tully, wearing a black wool cap and a red apron, stood motionlessly behind the bar, staring darkly at Yakima. Miss Venora stood on the other side of the bar from the apron, facing Tully and sipping from a steaming stone mug. Following Tully's riveted gaze to the half-breed, she gasped. Black coffee sloshed down the sides of her mug.

"You!"

Yakima dropped down the steps and walked past

the woman, keeping the barman in the corner of his left eye. "Just came to check on my handiwork."

"How dare you! My son was supposed to *arrest* you!"

"He tried."

Yakima climbed the stairs. Turning his head to one side, he glimpsed Tully moving quickly behind the bar. Yakima whipped around, levering a round into the Winchester's chamber, and saw Tully lifting a sawed-off, double-barreled Greener from beneath the bar. Yakima's rifle leaped twice in his hands, stabbing smoke and flames and blowing out a good-sized segment of the back-bar mirror behind Tully.

Glass clattered onto the shelves below the mirror and from there to the floor.

Miss Venora screamed and crouched and covered her ears with her hands, dropping the coffee mug. The barman threw himself down behind the bar, and Yakima didn't see him again before he'd gained the second story and was moving along the balcony, holding his smoking repeater on his right shoulder. As he began to turn down the hall toward the whore's room, Tully lifted the top of his head from above the bar, his eyes dark and fearful, lips stretched back to reveal his snaggly teeth and the single gold eyetooth.

Fabienne's door was partway open.

Yakima pushed it wide. Two whores he'd seen last night downstairs, now dressed in cotton wraps, both gasped at the same time when they saw him—the big half-breed in the open doorway, holding a rifle on his shoulder. They'd heard the gunshots and shattering glass, and thought they were about to die. They backed away from him, standing side by side and desperately clenching each other's hands.

Yakima moved slowly into the room and looked at the bed. There were a washbasin and two sponges on the bed beside Fabienne, who reclined on her back, totally nude. There was a bullet hole in the middle of her chest, about two inches above the cleavage separating her breasts that were deathly pale now, like candle wax mixed with a pinch of lilac. Goose feathers lay everywhere—some sticky with dried blood. The pillows they'd come from was on the bed's far side. It, too, was sticky with blood.

The lovely whore's head was turned to one side, facing Yakima, her heavy-lidded eyes half-open and staring somewhere off over the edge of the bed.

Her eyes became Faith's eyes, her dead eyes staring and reflecting the dancing light of the burning roadhouse in which her killer had been consumed beyond the reach of Yakima's vengeance. And then the death-glazed eyes switched back to Fabienne's.

Again, Yakima felt as though someone had laid an ax handle across his back, cracking his shoulder blades. His vision blurred. His pulse pounded in his ears. Heart swelling, he lowered his rifle, took it in his left hand, and turned to the bed. He lifted his right hand and stretched it out slowly, feeling it shake, and gently wrapped it around the dead girl's upper arm. She was as cold as an unlit candle.

Her image blurred. He blinked, cleared his throat, and turned to the two whores—the short blonde and the brunette. Both were watching him more curiously now than fearfully, likely wondering why they weren't dead.

"Did you see anyone?" His voice sounded strange to his own ears. He took a deep breath and cleared his throat again. "Anyone up here around her room? Besides me . . ."

The brunette said nothing. The blonde hardened her eyes slightly, angrily. "Never saw *you* leave."

"You hear the gunshot?"

She shook her head. "It got right loud last night around here."

The brunette's eyes watered up as she frowned uncomprehendingly at the half-breed. She dropped her lower jaw, muttering, "Why? *Why?*"

Yakima looked at the bloody pillow and the blood-splattered goose feathers. The girl's killer had used the pillow to muffle his shot.

Yakima looked at the two whores again. He knew there was no point in telling them he hadn't killed her. He was the last one who'd visited her, as far as they knew. He was a stranger and a half-breed, to boot. That was enough to convict him in their eyes. In the eyes of the entire town.

He turned and walked out of the room. At the end of the hall, he looked over the balcony. Tully stood below him, out away from the bar, holding his double-barreled Greener across his broad chest and fat belly that pushed his apron out. Miss Venora stood pressing her back against the bar, arms stretched out along the edge of the counter to each side.

Both people were looking up at Yakima, anxious. There was one more person in the saloon—the woman Yakima had seen outside.

The severe-looking, gray-eyed, brown-haired woman

now stood at the bar near the saloon's front door. In her silk-gloved left hand, she was slowly, thoughtfully turning a half-empty shot glass. A bottle of whiskey stood on the bar in front of her.

The men he'd seen outside, and a few more, now stood outside the saloon's front windows, looking grimly in through the beveled glass. A few pressed their faces up close to the glass, shading their eyes with their gloved or mittened hands. Yakima looked at Tully. "Lower that cannon or I'll blow you to hell."

Tully's fleshy face flushed. He glanced at his boss, Miss Venora, and then turned his head still farther toward the woman at the bar. He looked perplexed, not wanting to appear the coward. He also didn't want to die. It was the woman at the bar who went easy on him.

"Do it, Jim." She'd said it quietly, evenly.

Yakima had no idea who the woman was, but she appeared to pull some weight with the Wild Coyote's bartender. Tully lowered the Greener, held it down low by his side in his right hand. He kept his eyes on Yakima as the half-breed walked along the balcony, then dropped slowly down the stairs, holding his own Winchester on his right shoulder.

Yakima walked to a table near the bottom of the stairs, set his rifle on the table, kicked out a chair, and sagged into it.

"I'll take a shot of whiskey," he told Tully.

A whiskey couldn't make the situation any worse than it was. Everyone thought him a killer, and when he'd blown out the back-bar mirror he'd reinforced their judgment of him as a ruthless savage. Under normal circumstances, he could just ride away and hope to stay one step ahead of the wanted circulars. But the weather wasn't cooperating, and he had Kelly to think about—if the sheriff was still alive—as well as the stolen loot he'd promised the young lawman he'd see to.

Tully scowled at him distastefully, then strode around behind the bar. Angrily, he slammed a glass onto the bar top, splashed whiskey into it, and then carried it over to Yakima. He stared down at the half-breed, one brow arched, the gold eyetooth peeking out from under his furred upper lip.

"Might as well start me a tab," Yakima said, lifting the whiskey to his lips. "I reckon I'll be here awhile."

"Mister," the barman said, "you got some awful gall!"

"If I killed that girl, I would have gall. You got that right, Tully." Holding the shot glass to his lips, Yakima stared up at the broad, fat man from beneath his own black brows.

Tully glanced at Miss Venora, who hiked a shoulder, then pushed away from the bar and headed toward the stairs. Tully stomped off then, too, and reached through a small, curtained doorway and pulled out a broom. As he began sweeping up the glass behind the bar, the other woman grabbed her bottle and shot glass off the bar top and strode around the tables toward Yakima.

She'd removed her knit hat and her earmuffs. Her hair, he saw now, was piled loosely atop her head. It was slightly gray-streaked. There were crow's-feet around her eyes that no longer looked completely gray but tinged with lime green. He guessed her to be in her late twenties, early thirties, though in this rugged, dry country, she could be much younger.

Her eyes were ever so slightly bloodshot. He looked at the bottle as she set it on the table in front of him.

She stood across from him, holding her shot glass in front of her, staring grimly, skeptically down at him. "You're right, mister."

"How's that?"

"If you killed that girl, it would take gall to come back to the scene of your crime. Or . . ." She arched a brow and threw back the last half of her shot, then wiped her mouth with the back of her hand and sat down in a chair across from Yakima. "Or maybe you don't remember shooting that poor girl through her heart."

Yakima studied her. She suddenly didn't seem as prim and severe as she'd first appeared. She appeared harder now, at close range. Her clothes had been nice in a conservative fashion at one time, but the cape and the sleeves of her wool day dress looked old and wash-worn, the lace cuffs unraveling. "Who the hell are you?"

"Ramsay Kane. I'm the mayor of Dead River . . . when I'm not teaching school. So, I guess you could say I'm the executive law enforcement officer."

"A woman mayor."

"You don't like it?"

"What's for me to like? I've been a lot of places, seen a lot of things. A woman mayor is the least of my surprises." Yakima threw his shot back. He spread his lips as the cheap snake venom burned down his throat. He liked the warmth it put in his belly. "And about the chief law enforcing thing . . ." He shook his head. "Please don't try to arrest me. You seen those others."

"Saw."

"Forgive me. I can spell my name and read it on

wanted circulars when I see it, but that's about it."
Yakima couldn't help taunting her a little.

"What *is* your name?"

"Yakima Henry."

"An Indian . . . with green eyes . . ."

"Takes all kinds, don't it?"

"I have some Indian blood."

"I see you enjoy the busthead. Only schoolteachers
with Injun blood would enjoy a swig now an' then."

"I don't drink and go crazy."

"Is that what you think happened?"

She tucked her bottom lip under her upper teeth,
and wrinkled the skin above the bridge of her nose. "I
don't know. You're a stranger. I've never known a half-
breed that wasn't half crazy, including several of my
own cousins and uncles. What are you doing here in
Dead River, Mr. Henry, so late in the year?"

Yakima told her.

When he'd finished, she reached forward and splashed
whiskey from her bottle into his glass, then sank back in
her chair.

"So, what are you thinking?" he asked her, when he
saw the pensive way she appeared to be studying his
hand wrapped around his shot glass.

"I'm thinking we have a killer on the loose in Dead
River."

"He . . . or she . . . might have lit out of town."

"Not last night. Maybe this morning. If so, he . . . or
she . . . will likely be back. Both passes are snowed in."

"Anywhere to hole up between town and the mountains?"

"A few. There's some prospector shacks out there in

the scrub and rocks. A person would be less conspicuous in town, though."

Yakima looked beyond her toward the front of the saloon. No one was staring in the windows, but the small crowd was still out there. He could hear the men talking amongst themselves. Upstairs, a woman sobbed. He kept his face expressionless, but a hard fury burned through him.

Fabienne . . .

"Who would want to kill her?" he asked Ramsay Kane.

"If not you, you mean?"

"Yeah."

"Certainly none of the men in town. The reason they're all wanting to string you up is that she gave so much pleasure to them all. Of course, Shade Darling wanted to marry her, but his mother wouldn't hear of it." The woman laughed caustically. "And lose her best moneymaker?" She sobered again. "But he's the one you'll have to watch out for. He bit his fist every night when his mother had Fabienne entertaining her clients, but he was able to resign himself. But not to you—a breed. No, you'd best watch out for him until you can pull your picket pin and ride on out of our fair town."

"But I'm a killer."

Miss Kane—Yakima assumed she wasn't married, as few schoolteachers were—set her glass down hard on the table, grabbed her bottle around its neck, and gained her feet. "Most likely. But I doubt it's provable in a court of law. Good day, Mr. Henry." She glanced at the front windows, beyond which men could be seen milling about, their voices raised in confusion and anger, their breath frosting the glass.

Clutching the bottle against her chest, like a small child, she glanced wistfully back at the half-breed. "Best watch your back, and I'm not just talking about Shade Darling now, either."

She grabbed her hat and earmuffs off the bar and headed into the street.

Chapter 11

A few minutes after the teacher had left, Yakima polished off his own whiskey, then grabbed his Yellowboy and headed outside.

The sun that had been angling up through the low clouds was now obscured by the same clouds, and a fine snow stitched the air. Not much had fallen the night before, and most of what had had been blown clear of the street. It was bunched up against the buildings and boardwalks, thin as wind-tossed desert sand.

Yakima stepped out into Pine Street, holding his rifle butt under his arm and lifting his coat collar against the knifelike breeze. Several men who'd been loitering around the saloon, probably trying to work up enough pluck to take the law into their own hands and either gun him down or arrest him since the marshal hadn't been able to do it, scrambled off in several directions. They disappeared into their shops and drew the shades over their front doors.

Yakima looked at the ridges encircling the town, all obscured by the cottony clouds from which the insubstantial snow continued to fall. It looked as if it could snow all day. If the passes weren't already socked in, they likely would be by tonight. He wondered about two unrelated things: Sheriff Kelly and Fabienne's killer.

Was Kelly still alive, and was the killer still in town?

He glanced at the doctor's office on the other side of the street and south about forty yards. The portly doctor, in brown wool vest and shirtsleeves, was just now helping Shade Darling up his steep staircase, the deputy's head drooping toward his chest, his arms crossed on his belly. The other two men were close behind Darling. Potts was followed by Marshal Burkholder, who was staring menacingly over his left shoulder at Yakima.

The doctor obviously had his hands full. Yakima would check on Kelly's condition later. Meanwhile, since he had nothing else to do, he decided he'd ride around and see if he could cut any sign of anyone leaving town in the last few hours. He'd have loved nothing better than to find out who'd killed the whore. Whoever he was, he was a vicious dog that needed to be put down fast and thrown to the wildcats.

He stared up at the doctor's office. Shade Darling was holding up the line of men filing up the stairs behind him. The deputy had stopped at the top and was staring across the street toward Yakima. He was too far away for the half-breed to make out the man's expression.

A creeping sensation crawled up Yakima's spine though the notion he was entertaining had occurred to him several minutes ago. Had the deputy killed the girl in a fit of jealous rage, knowing Yakima would likely be blamed for it? The possibility was as jarring as having a sack of rocks slammed against his head. If so, it meant Yakima was at least partly responsible for Fabienne's death.

The image of her face as he'd first seen her, leaning against the Wild Coyote's second-story balcony rail, blossomed behind his eyelids. Then he saw her lying dead upstairs, her death-glazed features looking too much as Faith's had looked. He'd been responsible for Faith's death. He hadn't gotten to her in time to keep Thornton from killing her. He hoped to God he wasn't responsible for this girl's death, too—all for one night of careless frolic.

His mind pitched as he moved west along the street, keeping an eye out for men lurking in the breaks between buildings with rifles, preparing to back-shoot him. He still couldn't wrap his mind around what had happened. The pretty whore . . . dead . . . very possibly because of his wild-assed, defiant, half-breed nature.

He wished like hell he'd just gone on down the trail to Arizona, bad memories or no. After all, he thought bitterly as he tramped over the cold, hard side street past the marshal's office, life was a back trail littered with bitter memories.

He went back to the livery barn and saddled Wolf. A minute later, he led the mount out the barn's open double doors and into the street.

"You coming back?" asked McMasters, standing outside the doors behind him. He looked cautious, skeptical under the leather brim of his watch cap.

"I ain't runnin', if that's what you think," Yakima said. "Just gonna take a ride, work the green heaves out of my black and get the lay of the land."

"I was figurin' on a peaceable winter." McMasters

scowled and puffed the stogie that poked out the side of his mustached mouth.

"Me, too."

Grainy snowflakes collecting on his hat brim, Yakima gigged Wolf on down the side street, into the town's ragged outskirts and beyond.

A crow cawed from the limb of a short, gnarled pine. It watched Yakima in black-eyed annoyance as, hunkered on his haunches beside his horse, the half-breed reached out with his right hand and traced the outline of the shoe print in the hard sand between two stones.

Yakima lifted his hand, entwined it with the other one as he rested his elbows on his knees and looked around the rocky bench. He looked over his left shoulder at Dead River nestled in the steep-walled hollow behind him—grim and dark against the grayness of the day. Smoke rose from several chimneys and formed a blue haze that was almost indistinguishable from the clouds. Yakima could hear the dull thuds of someone chopping wood.

The trail rose out of the town and twisted over the rocky, cedar-stippled hogbacks. It disappeared in the hollows between the hills before it finally appeared again a hundred yards down from Yakima's position here on the bench. He was on the trail, and the shoe print he'd just come upon was the first one he'd seen since he'd left Dead River, heading toward the eastern, saddleback ridge.

He looked at it again. The way it was angled meant the rider had likely ridden onto the trail here, from the south.

Yakima rose and, leaving Wolf ground-tied, strode slowly off the trail, his head down, his red neckerchief whipping in the breeze above the collar of his mackinaw. He scoured the ground with his eyes, then squatted again when he found what he'd been looking for.

Another print. He looked around, found another south of the first, and then he found a full set in the soft sand of a dry wash that snaked along the bottom of the bench. A light dusting of snow partly covered the indentations. The shoe with the crack belonged to the horse's right rear hoof.

Judging by the poor condition of most of the tracks except for these in the relative shelter of the wash, and the snow that obscured even these, they'd been made late last night. Someone had swung wide of the town and headed for the trail up here a couple of hundred yards beyond it, as though they hadn't wanted to be seen leaving.

Yakima looked upslope to the east, where rock outcrops, firs, pines, tamaracks, spruces, and clouds concealed the pass. He wondered if the man had left early enough to make it. Or was the pass still open?

Deciding to try to find out the answer to both questions, Yakima walked back to the trail, grabbed Wolf's reins, and stepped into the saddle. He tapped his heels against the horse's flanks, and the stallion cantered on up the trail that curved around granite scarps and deep ravines, the incline gradually growing steeper.

The higher Yakima climbed, the more snow he saw lying in the forest on either side of the trail. Fremont squirrels and chipmunks quarreled. Deer dashed through the trees, their short, black-tipped tails flapping.

Below, the ground wasn't covered but only dusted, and in open stretches the wind had swept most of the ground clear.

Here, the ground was covered first by an inch or two, then, a little farther on, three or four inches. Yakima followed a bend in the trail, rounding a natural stone tower and climbing ever higher. Here, the snow made for treacherous going—he could feel Wolf's hooves slipping on the granite floor of the trail beneath the snow. The slight rain that had preceded the snow had laid down a thin coating of treacherous black ice.

He reined the horse to a stop and stared up through the corridor that the trail carved through the pines, toward the pass that was only about a half mile away but completely lost in the clouds and the snow that fell here much harder than below. The large, icy flakes were mantling Yakima's shoulders and crusting in Wolf's mane.

Something screeched to Yakima's left. There was a heavy thud to his right. In the periphery of his vision, he saw bark chip fly from a pine trunk. A half second later, just as he grabbed his Winchester from his scabbard and leaped off the right side of Wolf's back, the rifle's report flatted out over the silent woods.

Yakima hit the ground on his shoulder, and rolled, coming up off his heels, ramming the butt of his Yellowboy against Wolf's hip, and yelling, "Git, boy!"

The horse wheeled a little uncertainly on the slippery slope, then, trailing its bridle reins, galloped back down the trail in the direction of Dead River. Another bullet screeched through the air over Yakima's head, and *spang*ed loudly off a rock behind him. He threw himself backward and rolled off the side of the trail, then scampered on all fours behind the pine that the first bullet had plowed into.

He levered a round into the Yellowboy's breech. He doffed his hat, set it on his thigh, then, clutching the rifle with both gloved hands, edged a cautious look around the tree's right side. There were few branches on the lower halves of the columnar lodge poles, so he could see a good ways up the snowy, needle- and slash-carpeted slope on the other side of the trail.

There was a stony dyke about a hundred yards away, and he could see a figure with a rifle rise from a notch in the top of the bench, step cautiously along the bench's snowy crest, past a thumb of jutting rock, then drop down the thumb's opposite side and out of sight.

Yakima bolted out from behind the pine and ran up the snowy slope. He wished he'd thought to don his fur-lined moccasins before making the ride—they'd be more effective on the snowy terrain. As it was, his stockmen's boots slipped and slid and twisted his ankles as he angled up the slope and then made a dash across the trail into the forest on the other side.

He steered east of the stone bench from which the bushwhacker had fired on him, on the uphill side, moving as quietly through the trees as he could, looking around cautiously and holding his repeater in both hands across his chest.

After fifteen minutes that seemed like an hour, he saw the man downslope from him. The shooter stood beside an Engelmann spruce, as still as the tree itself, his back to Yakima. He wore a black, bullet-crowned, narrow-brimmed hat and a brown plaid mackinaw to which the damp snow clung like wool. He also wore high-topped boots with the cuffs of his blue denims tucked inside.

He was waiting, watching, listening for his quarry.

A breeze had come up, jostling the snow around. The rustling of the breeze in the branches and the occasional thuds of falling pinecones covered Yakima's quiet footsteps as he stole slowly down the slope, weaving from tree to tree. He kept his eyes on the back of the man who stood below him. The bushwhacker occasionally turned his head from side to side as he scanned the downslope.

For some reason, he didn't seem worried that Yakima might have worked around him.

When Yakima was ten feet away from the man, he raised the Yellowboy to his shoulder and aimed at the coarse brown ducktails of hair thinly streaked with gray dropping down from beneath the man's felt hat to feather over the collar of his mackinaw.

Clicking the Yellowboy's hammer back, Yakima said, "Give me one good reason why I shouldn't blow a hole through your fool head."

The man's back tensed. He started to turn his head to the right, so that Yakima could see the long, broad, dark nose jutting like an ax handle from his weathered face.

"No, don't turn around, you son of a bitch."

The man jerked his head back forward.

Just then Yakima realized his own mistake.

A slender twig crunched under a furtive boot behind

him. He could hear the low whistle of a heavy object arcing through the air above him, felt the tooth-gnashing agony of it slamming against the top of his head with a solid thud that was the last thing he heard before the snowy forest blinked out.

Chapter 12

Yakima felt something cold and rubbery against the back of his neck.

He jerked with a start and shivered. He lifted his head that felt as large as a wagon wheel, and just as heavy on his shoulders, and turned. Wolf's head was only a few inches from his own, the horse's breath warm and smelling of the grass he'd apparently been grazing, against Yakima's face. His large, almond-shaped eyes regarded his rider curiously from either side of the long white blaze. His whiskers brushed against Yakima's jaws and lips. He was a loyal cuss—Yakima would give him that.

Yakima looked around, blinking against the snow peppering his eyes like sand. It was coming down harder. He had a good covering of the white stuff himself, and he shivered again as he rose and an icy handful slithered down his collar to drop between his shoulders.

His hat lay beside him. Nearly an inch of feathery snow covered it. Judging by the rate it was currently falling, he figured he'd been out a half hour. Maybe closer to an hour. He lifted a hand to his tender head.

The tenderness increased as he touched the painful knob welling from the crown of his skull. His snow-caked hair was sticky with fresh blood.

Whoever had come up behind him had brained him with a hard branch or a pistol butt. Vaguely, through the fog swathing his brain, he wondered why his bushwhackers—there must have been at least two—hadn't finished the job they'd set out to do.

He looked around. He had to force his eyes to focus. The current braining on the heels of the one he'd received earlier that morning wasn't helping him think through the myriad problems he'd been confronted with here in Dead River.

When he stood, he had to fight to keep from throwing up what little food he had in his stomach—only some jerky and stray bits of hardtack he'd fished out of his saddlebags on the way up here. His knees were spongy. He decided that he had better build a fire and make a little tea and try to get some strength as well as his wits back before heading back down the pass to the town.

As he led Wolf down the grade toward a hollow sheathed in shrubs and rocks, he looked around for tracks but wasn't surprised to find none. The snow had covered the gunmen's tracks. He had no idea what they were doing up here, or why'd they'd bushwhacked him, but it certainly gave him something to chew on.

Were they responsible for Fabienne's murder?

Maybe they'd left him alive so he could continue to take the blame.

Where had they gone? Up over the pass? Not likely. Probably back to the town—unless they had a shack or something out here in the high and rocky where they intended to hole up until the passes opened again, or they felt enough time had passed that they could reenter Dead River without suspicion. . . .

Such thoughts were sharp barbs yanking at the half-breed's throbbing brain. Grunting and groaning and muttering curses at his current brush with his old pal Misfortune, he gathered deadfall wood from the sheltered places beneath trees and in the lee sides of rocks and managed to coax a small fire to life with some paper and dry pine needles and cones. He heated a tin cup of water for tea, and when steam finally curled from the water's ash-flecked surface, he added a few sprigs of green tea from a small burlap pouch.

"Tea better than coffee," his old friend the Shaolin monk had once told him. "Tea keep your mind clear and your feet light!"

He'd laughed then in his raucous way. Ralph, he'd called himself, because no one in this hemisphere would have been able to pronounce his real handle. He'd been a good friend to Yakima, and he'd taught him not only Eastern fighting techniques but also a foxy game of stud poker.

Ralph had won the Winchester Yellowboy at a backwater saloon's sole gambling table in Dakota Territory, and he'd given the weapon to Yakima because he didn't believe in firearms. But poker had gotten Ralph killed in the end—he'd won too much money off the wrong men. And, possibly, they'd taken his customarily gay laughter for mockery.

They rode to his camp one night when Ralph was alone. They shot him, hanged him from a tree, and burned his body almost beyond recognition.

Yakima sipped his tea while holding a snowball to the back of his head with his gloved hand. Behind him, Wolf foraged through the snow for grass and stretched his neck to nibble wet aspen leaves. Yakima had loosened the black's latigo straps so he could breathe freely, and he'd slipped his bit from his mouth so he could graze.

The rocky, forested slope of the pass was so quiet that Yakima could hear the furry flakes slithering down through the dense pine boughs to land atop each other, one after another, piling up fast. Occasionally, a crow cawed. A pinecone skipped off several branches before hitting the ground near Yakima's hollow with a soft thud.

He stared off into the falling snow, the trees standing black against it. Part of him wished he could stay here in this hollow by himself—just him and Wolf. He'd always hated towns. They were only good for women and supplies. Whenever he'd stayed in a town longer than a few hours, trouble grabbed him as surely as a bobcat would come leaping out of the waist-high brush to snare a cottontail with its saberlike fangs and razor-edged claws.

But he also felt compelled to return to Dead River. He had unfinished business there, not the least of which was finding out who'd killed Fabienne so savagely while she'd slept in the bed still warm from her and Yakima's coupling.

He sipped the tea that tasted the way fresh-cut alfalfa smelled. It warmed and soothed him, dulling the ache in his head. The snow helped bring the swelling down. When he finished the tea, he kicked snow and dirt and pine needles on the fire, then stowed the cup in his saddlebags.

He tightened the latigo straps, slipped the bit into Wolf's mouth, mounted up, and reined the horse out of the hollow and back to the trail. He figured it was a little after midday, but the leaden sky and the snow made it look like dusk. When he gained the bottom of the valley in which Dead River lay, the town sat huddled against the snowfall that all but obliterated it from view until he entered the outskirts, and the corrals and stock pens passed behind him.

There was more wind down here, but slightly less snow was falling than up on the pass. Still, it was hard to see anything but the outlines of the false-fronted buildings. He could smell gusting wood smoke, see the occasional lamp in a store window, but he saw no one on the street.

The blow to his head had made him dull, but he had more work to do before he holed up out of the weather. He wanted to check on Kelly, but first he rode over to the livery barn, dismounted, and slid one of the front doors open. McMasters was inside, trimming a rangy roan's hooves by the light of an old bull's-eye lantern.

Snow sifted in over Yakima's shoulders. He held Wolf's reins in his hand.

"You see anyone new to town today, McMasters?"

The old liveryman scowled at him. "You're the newest I seen. Expecting friends, are ye?"

"If two men come around here, one wearing a brown plaid coat and a nose nearly as long as that roan's, you let me know. I'll be uptown."

The liveryman had the roan's hoof clamped between his knees. Now he dropped the hoof and gave Yakima a devil-eyed glare, his rugged, patch-bearded face flushed with fury. "I ain't beholden to you!"

"I didn't say you were."

Yakima gave the man a hard stare, cowing him. He closed the door, swung back into the leather, and gigged Wolf into a canter back toward the main part of town, keeping an eye out for a brown plaid coat and an anvil-sized nose. Those two men—if there were only two—had to be around here somewhere unless they had a place in the country between the passes.

He reined up in front of the doctor's place. Instead of swinging down from the saddle, he stared up at Howe's windows that shone dark behind the slanting snow that was piling up on the boardwalks and forming drifts against the stock troughs.

Before him, the furniture shop's front door opened, and a dark-haired man stood there in a leather apron, sucking on a stove match. He just stood there in his half-open doorway, regarding Yakima obliquely. He had thick, dark brown hair that hung in a wave over one dark eye. Sawdust clung to his apron. Somewhere between thirty and forty, he was pale and unshaven.

"He ain't up there," he grunted. He jerked his head westward along the street. "Took Kelly over to Preacher Ekdahl's. Ekdahl has plenty o' empty rooms over there at his school, and Howe likes to spend his free time over to the Wild Coyote." The man looked faintly disapproving of the doctor's hobby.

Yakima pinched his hat brim at the man, whom he

assumed was Abernathy of the signboard above his head. "I appreciate the help," he said, faintly skeptical, wondering why the man had volunteered the information when everyone else in town treated him as though he carried the plague.

The man just stared at him, blinking away the snow dusting his lashes.

Yakima swung Wolf back into the street. Suddenly, a commotion rose behind him, and he turned his head back to see a woman in a long black dress with a white collar pushing past the carpenter to run out onto the boardwalk. Her gray eyes were fairly red with fire as she stomped her stout black shoes to the edge of the boardwalk, raising a long, crooked finger and jerking it accusingly at Yakima.

"You brought trouble here, heathen!" she screeched, her voice cracking and trembling with emotion. "What you see so far—the dead temptress from across the street—ain't nothin' compared to the trouble you got stackin' up for *your*-self here in Dead River! *Leave* here, you red-skinned *Satan-spawn*!"

"Mama," said the carpenter, grabbing the woman's arm. "Get in here, Mama. Leave him be!"

The woman fought away from her son and raised her witch's finger at Yakima, throwing her arm toward him as if she were hurling a war lance. Even louder, she screeched, *"Leave here on your black horse and don't come back or you'll have the whole town payin' for your wicked ways!"*

The woman sounded so shrill and demonic that Wolf buck-kicked, and Yakima had to check the frightened beast under a tight rein as he stared back at the woman in shock. Her son said, "Mama, stop this nonsense. Get back inside. Come on!"

When he'd wrestled the wiry, stoop-shouldered old crone back through the door and held her there with one hand, he looked back at Yakima, his own face now flushed with anger. "Get on outta here, breed! Don't come around here no more. Can't you see ya done upset my ma?"

He cursed, bolted inside, and closed the door behind him.

Yakima felt as though he'd been ambushed again. His head throbbed. Bells tolled in his ears.

He stared back at Abernathy's furniture shop as though expecting another diatribe fired across his bow, the old woman's crazy eyes staying with him like a bad smell or a haunting dream. Finally, he gave Wolf some slack and the horse cantered on up the street.

He hadn't ridden a block before another door opened—this one in a little, shabby store which a crude sign identified as F. T. SULLIVAN'S SEWING SHOP. Dead River's mayor stepped out of the store, wearing the same hat, earmuffs, and cape as before though now she was wearing high-topped fur boots, as well. Holding a small parcel in her hand, from the top of which a scrap of red bolt cloth flapped, Miss Ramsay Kane looked at Yakima uncertainly, turning her head to peer eastward along the street, as though she'd heard the old woman's tirade.

She looked again at Yakima as she closed the door of the small store behind her. Yakima didn't slow his pace but turned away from her and kept riding, trying to blink the pale, haunted visage of the carpenter's mother from his retinas.

What the hell was wrong with this town?

Whatever it was, he was trapped here.

With an early-winter storm settling down, heavy as an African elephant.

Chapter 13

Yakima reined Wolf to a halt at a large sign forming a portal, like a ranch portal, over the trail out from town but only about fifty yards from its edge and not far beyond the white-frame church.

THE REVEREND GUSTAV EKDAHL'S HOME FOR WAYWARD CHILDREN.

Beyond the portal lay the sprawling shake-shingled structure of rock and hand-adzed logs he'd marveled at before. The place almost looked Victorian, with several turrets and a broad stone chimney running up the front center of the dwelling, just beyond a wide front gallery, and an octagonal room on the right front corner. There were three peaks and several dormer windows, all shuttered against the storm.

Despite its grandiose structure, the place had a dark, run-down look. Yakima would have thought it abandoned if not for the man sweeping off the broad porch steps—a tall, middle-aged gent with long, thick, silver hair blowing in the wind. He had a silver mustache, and he wore a long, ragged-looking buffalo coat over worn broadcloth trousers and high-topped boots. He wore no hat or gloves.

As Yakima put Wolf under the portal sign and on into the yard, where snow-dusted rabbit brush, cedars, and a few willows grew, the man stopped sweeping and, standing on the third step down from the porch, turned his lean body toward Yakima. The half-breed reined Wolf to a stop in front of the house, looked it over again, puzzled by the size of the place in a town as small and remote as Dead River, then turned to the tall man on the steps.

The man stood blinking his long Nordic eyes that were set wide atop broad, tapering cheeks. His brushy mustache ruffled in the wind.

Yakima pinched his hat brim at the man. "Reverend Ekdahl?"

The man said nothing. He only blinked as he gave Yakima an oblique, stony stare.

"I'm looking for Sheriff Kelly. Jack Kelly. I was told the doctor had hauled him over here."

The man dipped his chin slightly. "He's here." He canted his head slightly to one side and opened and closed his hands on the broom handle. "You're the one who killed the girl. . . ."

Yakima saw that he wasn't going to be invited, so he swung down from the saddle and tossed Wolf's reins over the wrought-iron rail to the right of the porch steps and fronting a stone stock trough. Yakima mounted the porch steps that were quickly accumulating a fresh layer of fuzzy snow despite the preacher's recent sweeping. He returned the man's stare, his own dark gaze as implacable as the sky pilot's.

"Don't judge lest ye be judged."

The preacher quirked the left side of his mouth. "Stand against the devil and the devil will run from you."

"I ain't running, Preacher. Where's Kelly?"

The man drew a lungful of cold air as he rolled his gaze across Yakima once more, then tossed his head at the house's two heavy-timbered doors. "Alta told me about you. She's inside. She'll show you to Kelly."

Yakima brushed past the man, topped the porch, and drew one of the doors open by its large wooden handle carved in the shape of a winged angel. He stomped the snow off his boots, swiped as much of it as he could from his coat and pants with his hat, pounded his hat free of the snow against the wall, then went inside. The warmth that pushed against him was soothing. He moved down a short foyer to see a broad parlor-like room to his right. A fire snapped and popped in the broad hearth. Two overstuffed sofas and a deep bullhorn chair faced it. Facing out from the far wall was a grand piano across which stretched a frayed elk hide.

Books spilled from shelves lining the walls—heavy, dusty tomes whose spines were cracked from use. The shelves bowed beneath their weight, and cobwebs hung from them and from the corners of the herringbone-patterned ceiling. More were stacked here and there on the floor and on reading tables.

On the walls were crucifixes, paintings of Christ and scenes from the Bible—Yakima recognized them from his own days at a similar boarding school. There were also posters of crudely painted bucolic or symbolic scenes complemented by Bible verses. They were old and yellow, their corners curled. They'd likely been done by the "wayward children" that the preacher obviously schooled here—or had schooled here, at one time. So far, Yakima hadn't seen a single child in the town.

There was a broad open doorway to his left and through which emanated the smells of fresh dough and roasting meat. He could hear someone moving around in there.

He went through the doorway and around a long, scarred table of halved pine logs at which sat twenty or so chairs, ten on each side, all very neatly lined up side by side. Yakima remembered similar long dining tables in the Catholic boarding school he'd been sent to after his mother had died when he was twelve, and his belly recoiled at the fleeting but poignant memory of the horrific experience—over a dozen children treated like unwanted cattle and told they'd burn in hell if they did not adopt the white man's ways.

This area of the room was L-shaped, and in the long part of the L he found the vast kitchen as well as Alta, who was kneading bread dough on a table half as long as the one Yakima had just passed.

Little Christian sat in a high chair, bits of jerky on the tray before him. He was shaking a homemade rattle and gurgling raspily but contentedly. He smiled when he saw Yakima, and squealed, and then Alta looked up from the bread dough, her hair hanging wildly in her eyes. She blew several strands, then swept some more aside with her hand, leaving a streak of flour on her dark cheek. Her eyes widened, and her lips parted slightly.

Yakima went over and ran his hand across the top of little Christian's head, and the boy squealed louder, showing his wet gums in delight as he continued to shake the rattle, pounding it on his tray.

"Christian," Alta admonished, walking over to the chair and placing her hand on the rattle. Dressed in a brown plaid, lace-edged muslin day dress that contrasted the girl's thick mop of wild blue-black hair and dark eyes, she looked at Yakima, said a little coyly, "You are still here. . . ."

"Hard to light out with the snow comin' down." Yakima looked at Christian. "How's the boy?"

"See for yourself. The doctor gave him a tonic."

Christian swiped a wet hand at Yakima and shrieked. He wore a quilted brown bodysuit trimmed in tiny crosses. Alta smiled.

Yakima ran his hand across the top of the child's head once more, then gave the infant his finger to squeeze. To Alta, he said, as he looked around at the vast well-appointed kitchen—a kitchen obviously meant to cook regular large meals—"Everything workin' out with the preacher?"

A shadow seemed to pass across her large chocolate eyes, and for a moment her mind seemed elsewhere. Then she dropped her gaze back down to the child and said in her customarily uninflected fashion, "There is work here, a place to stay for me and the little one. That's all I ask."

"A lot of kids to cook for?"

"No." She shook her head and looked back behind him at the long table. "There have been no children to cook for in a long time."

Again, he saw—or thought he saw—that fleeting, haunted cast to her gaze.

"The reverend," she added somberly, "isn't so young anymore, so he closed the school. There is just him here now. And the sheriff."

"Can I see him?"

She wiped her hands on a towel, brushed her lips across Christian's temple, then strode off down the kitchen, past a large black range over which pots and pans hung from iron hooks. On the range, a cast-iron pot bubbled, sending up the rich, gamey smells of elk stew with its steam, making Yakima's mouth water. He'd had nothing but jerky and hardtack crumbs all day, and it was getting on toward early evening.

He followed Alta down a couple of halls and then up narrow, switchbacking stairs, the old boards creaking under his feet. They came to a narrow hall paneled in rough pine, with more pictures of Christ and Bible scenes hanging from nails. Again, his chest tightened at his own bitter memories of a place very similar to this. To the right was a set of narrow double doors. A wooden sign over the doors read DAUGHTERS OF OUR LORD JESUS CHRIST. To each side of the doors were steel brackets as though to hold a locking bar though there was no bar there now.

Directly across the hall was another set of double doors, identical to the ones on the left. Over them, a sign read SONS OF OUR LORD JESUS CHRIST. Alta rapped her knuckle on one of these doors, turned the latch, and poked her head inside before pushing the door wider, stepping aside, glancing at Yakima, and canting her head toward the open door.

Yakima moved on into the room. The portly doctor was there, stuffing his stethoscope into his leather medical kit that sat on a cot—one of many in the long, narrow, low-ceilinged room—directly across from the one that Sheriff Jack Kelly occupied.

He glanced behind as Alta stepped away from the door; then he could hear her moccasined feet moving off down the hall.

"Well, look who the cat dragged in," the doctor said, closing and fastening the straps of his medical bag, regarding the half-breed with much the same expression as everyone else in the town.

Bald disdain.

"You bring me any more business?" the medico wryly queried.

"Not this time."

Kelly half sat on the bed, his back and head propped against several pillows. He looked gaunt, but his eyes shone clearly in the light from the lantern hanging from a ceiling post in the aisle between him and the sawbones.

"I take it he filled you in," Yakima said to the sheriff.

Kelly nodded. He studied Yakima with barely concealed suspicion. He, too, was wondering if Yakima had really killed the girl. The half-breed couldn't blame him. Kelly had likely been raised with all the same prejudices of anyone else on the frontier. And he really didn't know Yakima much at all. In fact, he'd thrown him in his own jail over in Douglas for being drunk and disorderly.

The doctor picked his fur hat and his bag off the bed, and, brushing past Yakima with his ankle-length bear coat hanging open, he said, "I'll be running along. Might just go over to the Wild Coyote and pick me out one of the few remaining *doves du pave*." Half out of the room, he poked his head around the door and held his hat against the side of his mouth and smirked as he whispered, "Don't tell the reverend."

He pulled his head out and shut the door.

Yakima looked at Kelly. "Well, you're still kickin'."

"I'll make it. Doc says I have a fever, and he has trouble keepin' the wound closed, but I'm a tough nut." Kelly pointed his chin at the cot on the other side of the aisle from his own. "Have a seat. Nice digs, eh? Tell me about the girl. Who you think killed her?"

Yakima tossed his hat on the cot, ran his fingers through his wet hair to which bits of ice still clung. "My guess is Burkholder's deputy shot her. But I hope not."

"Why not?"

"Because then I might as well have done it myself." Yakima sagged down on the end of the cot, leaning forward and resting his elbows on his knees. "He warned me off her. Warnin' me off somethin' puts a hump in my neck. Always has."

"It's just your nature to cause trouble, I reckon."

"Cause it when I don't stumble into it." Yakima lowered his head and ran his fingers more brusquely through his hair, avoiding the still-throbbing goose egg at the crown of his skull. Chagrin like tar washed through him. He really had to try harder to stay away from towns, stay away from the wrong women and trouble in general.

He lifted his head again, gave Kelly a serious look. "I didn't kill her. But I'll find out who did."

"How you gonna do that?"

"Hell, I don't know. I just came down from the

eastern pass. A couple fellas laid me out after they damn near drilled me with a third eye."

Kelly looked pained. "Say again?"

"They left me there. Maybe to take the blame. I don't know. But I'm gonna keep lookin' for 'em. One of 'em I got a pretty good look at before the other kissed the top of my head with a pistol butt."

"Kiss . . . *what*?" The sheriff stitched his brows and dropped his lower jaw.

"Don't worry." Yakima set his hat on his head and heaved himself to his feet. "You just rest, Kelly. I'll get her figured out. Not to worry."

"Not to worry. Christ . . ." That made the young lawman worry about something else. "Hey, what about the money? You got it over at the jailhouse?"

"Should be safe . . . as long as Burkholder and his deputy can be trusted. Don't think about it. Rest. I'll go over and check on the loot right now. Best get ole Wolf stabled."

He looked out one of the only two small, sashed windows in the room that must have been fifty feet long, twenty feet wide, and with ten cots abutting each wall. The snow was coming down the same as before— medium-fast out of a sky the color of rifle bluing. "Looks like it's gonna snow all night." He shivered and looked around. "Cold up here. No woodstove?"

"Nah, just a grate in the floor. I reckon the only heat's what comes up from below. The preacher don't cotton to visitors, so he's got me tucked away up here. The old bastard."

Yakima looked at the cots under the low, peaked ceiling and felt a pang of loneliness, remembering his own bitter days. "Them kids must have got right chilly up here of a winter."

He could feel the cold pressing through the pine walls and the ceiling slanting close above his head.

Kelly looked around then, too, quietly pensive. Finally, he hacked phlegm from his throat and spat into a chamber pot beside his bed. "I hope we can get outta here soon."

Yakima shook his head. "Don't count on it. My ma always said you can predict how much snow a place's gonna get by how high the seed pods start on a skunk cabbage. The pods on the cabbage around here are nearly as high as my cartridge belt."

Kelly sighed and ran his hands through his hair, dropping a little lower on his cot. "It's still fall, though. The sun'll melt this off in a few days. Maybe a week." He watched Yakima tramp wearily toward the door. "Keep me privy to what's goin', will ya, Yakima? And try to stay out of trouble. Maybe I oughta deputize ya. Would that help?"

At the door, Yakima grinned. "I doubt it."

He moved out the door and headed down the hall and down the several short stretches of meandering stairs.

Chapter 14

When he finally made his way back to the sprawling old house's first story, he stopped in the doorway to the kitchen. He'd intended to say good-bye to Alta, but he saw Preacher Ekdahl standing on the other end of the dining room in his buffalo coat, holding a steaming stone mug in his hand. He had his back to Yakima, and he was looking out one of the several long windows in front of him.

Beyond him, a short, dark figure was tramping off through the cedars amidst the falling snow and failing light. Yakima recognized Alta's black hair and her blanket coat. She wasn't wearing a hat, and snow clung to her hair as it fell down her back. Her figure was dwindling quickly into the gauzy distance, but she appeared to be carrying something in her right hand.

"Cold out there for a walk," Yakima said.

The preacher turned his head toward him. He didn't say anything, just stared at Yakima, his gray-blue eyes reflecting the window light.

Yakima turned away, strode on down the foyer to the double doors, and went out and crunched across the porch on which a half inch of snow had fallen since the preacher had swept it. Wolf, standing at the hitchrack, head hanging, looked like a blue roan or a steeldust. Yakima stepped into the black's saddle, swung the horse away from the house, and cantered off in the direction in which he'd seen Alta walking. He saw her tracks angling out from the rear of the house, and followed them through the piñons and cedars and all-but-buried clumps of sage and rabbit brush.

A hundred yards northwest of the house, where the slope began climbing toward the steep northern ridge, Yakima checked Wolf down beneath a pine bough. Alta stood about fifty yards beyond him, under the skeleton-like remains of a cottonwood, all the tree's bark having rotted off, and most of its branches missing, as well.

The girl stooped beneath a low-hanging branch and brushed snow away from a low rock mound that was fronted by a crude wooden cross like the cross that was fronting her husband's grave on the other side of the eastern pass.

Another grave. This one as remote as the elder Christian's. No one not looking specifically for the grave would find it out here. Yakima couldn't help wondering why it wasn't in the town's cemetery or at least in the cemetery he'd seen flanking the church, only a couple of hundred yards away.

Alta leaned forward and draped the small wreath of woven pine boughs trimmed with red velvet ribbons over an arm of the cross. As she did, Yakima backed Wolf away. He'd meant to give her a ride back to the house, as the snow was piling up fast, but now he saw that she was having a private moment with the lonely grave. He could stay and give her a ride when she finished, but the somber air about the girl compelled him to leave her alone with her thoughts.

He knew the need himself. Besides, maybe she didn't want anyone to know the grave was here, marked by the dead cottonwood.

Yakima swung the horse around and retraced his ruffled trail through the brush, around to the front of the house, past the church and cemetery, and back to the main part of Dead River. The air was blue, as the sun was going out quickly, and the cold was blowing its frosty breath down Yakima's mackinaw. No one else was out—not even any recent tracks in the foot of snow that had covered the street and that blew now in ghostly swirls as the wind picked up. Lamplight shone in the windows. The big leprechaun was back playing the piano in the Wild Coyote. As he passed the place from which he could hear the tinny notes beneath the groaning breeze and the brush of the blown snow, he wondered about Fabienne. A cold, lonely place to die so young . . .

Yakima gave an involuntary shudder. That led to the unwanted image of Faith lying cold and dead in her own grave. How much of her was left after these two long years? Did she look anything like she had—blond-haired and blue-eyed—or was her beauty only dust now?

A handful of dust . . .

He remembered the way she'd smiled, one corner of her mouth rising slightly higher than the other, showing the ends of her teeth, and how she'd rise from their bed mornings and toss her hair behind her head so that it gathered back behind one shoulder. . . .

As though clearing a cluttered table with his arm, he swept the reverie out of his mind.

Feeling Wolf shiver beneath him, he headed straight for the livery barn, where he found McMasters kicked back in a chair in his back room by a hot fire, with a bottle and a dime novel. The old man was owly as usual, so Yakima put Wolf away himself, tended the prized stallion, then headed back out into the cold twilight, closing the barn's small side door and trudging through the snow that had drifted in cake-frosting swirls inside the corral.

His Yellowboy rode his right shoulder, in case he needed it. If he ran into the men who'd bushwhacked him, he'd need it.

The town marshal hadn't shoveled his steps. Yakima tramped up through the calf-deep snow to the front door, hammered it twice with his fist, and pushed it open.

"Don't worry. This ain't a social visit," he told Burkholder, who sat crouched over paperwork at his cluttered desk, a guttering lamp and a plate of food before him. "I'm just checkin' on the sheriff's loot."

"It's still here."

Yakima nodded and began to pull the door closed. Burkholder waved to him.

"Get in here, damn it."

"Jails make me fidgety."

"I said get in here! Don't worry. I ain't gonna try to arrest you again."

"That's a load off."

Yakima kicked his boots clean against the sill, then stepped inside. Like the liveryman, the town marshal had a good fire going in his stove. Burkholder slid his chair out from his desk, entwining his hands behind his head as he indicated the slat-backed visitor's chair beside the desk.

"Come on in and have a seat."

Yakima looked around skeptically. Only Burkholder was here. The half-breed doubted that his deputy was in any condition to do his job this evening, even though all it would likely entail during the storm was keeping an eye on Kelly's loot locked up in the center cell. Still, the place gave him a claustrophobic feeling. Slowly, cautiously, he moved into the room, doffing his hat and slapping it against his thigh.

"You mind leaning that long gun down against my desk?" Burkholder asked.

Yakima did the marshal's bidding, knowing he could grab it quickly if he needed to. Then he sank down in the chair, glancing at the plate of food on the lawman's desk—a thin steak, mashed potatoes and gravy, and green beans. Only a few bites had been taken from the pile of gravy-drenched potatoes. The gravy had congealed into a cold mass.

"Wanted to talk to you about the French girl," Burkholder said, opening a desk drawer and hauling out a bottle. "Somethin' to cut the cold?"

"Why not?"

Burkholder filled two tin cups. Yakima glanced at the food again. He found himself salivating, felt his belly heave.

"You gonna eat that?" he asked as the marshal slid a cup toward him.

"No." Burkholder set the bottle down hard and grabbed his belly. "Guts don't feel quite up to it yet . . . after this mornin'."

"In that case, as things go," Yakima said, dragging the plate toward him, "your misfortune is my gain."

He removed his gloves, picked up the steak in his fingers, and began hungrily chewing bites off.

"Good Lord, man—when's the last time you ate?" the marshal asked, leaning back in his chair while hooking a finger through his cup's handle.

"Except for a few bits of jerky, last night. At the Wild Coyote." Yakima chewed, swallowed, and tore off another piece of the cold, overcooked, and only mildly flavorful beef sirloin. "That Tully ain't a half-bad cook. I almost feel bad for breaking his mirror."

"That's got Miss Venora pretty riled up, you know. Mirrors don't grow on trees, and the Wild Coyote ain't quite as wild—present circumstances not withstanding—as it used to be. Not as many folks around Dead River these days. Town's dyin'. Ranchers over both passes leavin' on account o' the bad winters and low stock prices. Venora don't make nary a dime all winter, when there's only about twenty people here in Dead River, and half o' them can't pay till spring. Only newcomer we've had in years is big Jim Tully over to Miss Venora's."

"Like Preacher Ekdahl," Yakima said, sucking grease from his fingers. "And that old mother of the furniture maker's. Bet she don't pay at all."

He smiled at his feeble joke.

The marshal frowned as he swallowed a sip of his hooch. "Huh? Miss Annabelle? How'd you meet her?"

"We had a real nice chat. Who's her long-suffering son?"

"That's Saul Abernathy. Him and his mother are about the only two people in Dead River who attend old Ekdahl's church services through the winter. Most folks give it up, figure it ain't worth fightin' the cold and the snow to go get yelled at." Burkholder snorted. "Me included." He took another sip of his whiskey. "Now, about that mirror . . ."

Yakima dropped the bone and a chunk of gristle on the marshal's supper plate and nudged the plate away from him. "Tell her she's lucky it's only her mirror I blew to pieces and not her bartender." Yakima sucked another finger, then cleaned his hands off on a wanted dodger atop the marshal's desk. "You think your deputy, Darling, might have killed Fabienne?"

Burkholder looked incredulous. "Not a chance!"

"He warned me not to see her."

"And you shouldn't have. Put both the girl and Miss Venora in a bad spot, though I know the woman likes to keep her son, a lowly deputy town marshal, in his place."

"I don't think so good when I'm having my horns swoggled." Yakima stared absently over at the gold-filled saddlebags, then returned his gaze to the marshal. "Why don't you think he could have killed her?"

Burkholder leaned forward in his chair and spoke slowly, as though trying to impart complicated information to a child. "The boy thought he loved the girl. All he really loved was her tits and her accent, but for a kid like Darling, born and raised here by a ma like Miss Venora, polishing off beer bottles and whiskey shots around that place when he was ass-high to a muskrat—shit, man, beddin' Miss Fabienne was like beddin' somethin' wild and . . . *strange*! A girl from another world."

"So I must have done it in a drunken haze," Yakima growled.

"Nah. I don't believe that no more. Miss Fabienne was seen emptyin' her chamber pot around ten thirty last night. Told Miss Venora she had a headache and was retirin'." Burkholder grinned. "You musta really played her out." When Yakima just stared at him, blank-faced, the marshal cleared his throat with cha-grin, and said, "McMasters said he seen you asleep in your horse's stable about the same time, when he went out to check on the horses."

"Did you talk to the other men in the saloon last night? I'd like to know where—"

"My deputy was right here all night, on duty from seven to seven, guardin' your money."

"How do you know?"

"All I can prove is that he made his usual rounds, because several people seen him. He was in the Wild Coyote around ten. That's when he found out you'd been upstairs with Miss Fabienne. His ma barred him from climbin' the stairs, and she had Tully and two of the customers—friends of Darling's, the two you met this morning—holdin' him back and settlin' him down." Burkholder gave a wry wink as he drained his whis-key. "He left soon after that and no one saw him around again."

"That doesn't prove he didn't sneak in the back way. No one saw me leaving, so it's damn possible no one saw him coming. Or leaving after he slipped into her room and shot her out of jealousy."

"Doubt it," Burkholder said, splashing more whiskey into his cup. "The teacher summoned him just after he left the Wild Coyote. Miss Kane's a might on the nervous side, don't ya know? A female thing. . . . Anyway, she thought she seen or heard someone sneakin' around her house, and came over to fetch Shade, to look around. He was over at the school for a good half hour, settling Miss Kane right down."

Yakima finished off his own whiskey shot and set the cup on the marshal's desk. He sniffed and ran a hand across his mouth. "I understand your wantin' to protect your deputy, Burkholder. But you don't know when Fabienne was shot."

"Couldn't have been much after ten. As soon as her son left the building, Miss Venora went up and locked Miss Fabienne's door. She locks all the girls' doors when they're done workin' for the night. They can unlock the doors from the inside, but they're under strict orders to not do so for anything except a fire. Under no circumstances are they ever to open their doors to any man after Miss Venora has closed them down for the night. She musta been dead when Miss Venora locked her door, though the madame must not have checked on her, just assumed she was asleep."

"Figures," Yakima said. "That way they can't do any business on their own, and their customers are always screened by the madame. All right, you sold me that it's unlikely Darling shot her. Not impossible, but unlikely. Anyone else in town have reason to kill her?"

"How would I know? Never knew the girl. Too damn young and purty for this old bag of bones. A girl like that'd make a fool out of me. When I need a girl . . . and feel up to it . . . I usually go for the older Injun girl, Gladys Red Bird. Haven't seen even ole Gladys in a month of Sundays."

Burkholder flushed and brushed a hand across his nose, embarrassed. "Whores . . . shit, they can piss a man off seven ways from sundown and no one but the man would ever know about it. A man's relationship with a whore—even though she's public party—is a private thing. You savvy?"

"I reckon that's what got your deputy's tail in a twist over Fabienne." Yakima stood and grabbed his rifle. "What I'd like to know is who else—?"

There was a muffled thud on the jailhouse stoop. Yakima swung around as the door opened, and Tully, the Wild Coyote bartender, poked his head in the door. He wore a rabbit skin hat with earflaps tied beneath his chin. His broad, cinnamon-bearded face was red, his blue eyes rheumy from the cold. He'd opened his mouth to speak but stopped when he saw Yakima standing before him. He slid his incredulous gaze from the big half-breed to Burkholder, and his eyes glazed slightly, as though he'd suddenly forgotten what he'd come here for.

"Well, spit it out, Jim. I believe you two already been introduced."

Tully glanced once more at Yakima, then lifted his

chin at the lawman, his gold eyetooth flashing in the lamplight. "Best come over to the saloon, Marshal. Your deputy . . ." He shook his head darkly while snow swirled into the room from behind him. "Miss Venora's beside herself."

Burkholder wrinkled his brows impatiently. "About what?"

"Shade . . . Someone blew him clear out the back wall of the privy." Again, Tully shook his head. "He's alive, but just barely. And unless the doc can get all his guts shoveled back inside him, he won't be alive much longer."

Chapter 15

"This don't make no sense," someone was shouting above the wind. "It just don't make no damn sense at all!"

There were several men gathered behind the privy that flanked the Wild Coyote from about twenty yards away, near a woodshed and snow-covered clumps of scrub brush. Two handheld lanterns jostled uncertain light and inky shadows. The light reflected off the privy's back wall, which bore a large, ragged hole. The light threw the men behind the privy in eerie silhouette.

On the other side of the privy from the group, a woman was screaming hysterically and crying. Yakima couldn't see much as he trudged through the deepening snow behind Burkholder and Tully, approaching the privy, but two or three people appeared to be half dragging the screaming woman, who was obviously Miss Venora, through the snow toward the saloon's open back door through which umber light flickered.

"My boy!" the woman screamed, fighting to free herself of the others' grip. "My boy! My boy!"

And then they managed to wrestle her through the open doorway. Someone slammed the door, and her screams faded beneath the wind and the snow pelting the building.

"Step aside," ordered Burkholder. "Step aside there, Murphy. Bud—you, too—let me through!"

Yakima stopped a few feet away from the group and watched as the marshal dropped to a knee beside the figure stretched out on the ground in the circle of men behind the outhouse. There was another figure kneeling beyond Burkholder. Yakima recognized the doctor though the man was swathed in fur. He was crouched low over the fallen man's chest, and the light from the lanterns reflected off the silver-chased earpieces of a stethoscope.

When the doctor raised his head and straightened his back, Yakima saw the open, death-glazed eyes of Shade Darling and the bandage of the nose that Yakima had smashed a few hours ago. The deep purple bruise from around his nose reached up around his eyes. The deputy's mouth was open wide as though still in a death struggle, lips stretched back from his teeth in a painful grimace. The man did not wear a coat but a blue work shirt to which his star was pinned. At least, Yakima thought it was blue. It was hard to tell amidst the blood soaking it.

The deputy's guts were spilling in ragged curls out onto the deep snow around him. Steam slithered around them. His pants were pulled down to his ankles, and his legs looked pale and thin and ghastly in the unforgiving light of the jostling lanterns. Yakima could see one of the man's silver-spurred boots, but the other was covered by his denims.

"I'm sorry, Dusty," Howe said. "There's nothing I can do for him. He's gone."

Burkholder, his back to Yakima, just knelt there beside the dead deputy, staring, working his jaws. The men in the group around him stood in silence now, the lanterns lowered as though to give the dead man some privacy.

After nearly a minute, Burkholder turned his head toward the gaping hole in the privy's back wall. The two men carrying the lanterns lifted the lamps now to reveal the ragged hole through which Darling had apparently been blown while he'd been sitting on the privy hole.

"It don't make no sense!" This, again, from the leprechaun-like gent whom Yakima recognized as the Wild Coyote's piano player and whom the sheriff had called Murphy. "It just don't make no damn sense, Sheriff! Who the hell would shotgun Shade Darling through the privy like this?"

Burkholder straightened and looked around at the other men. They looked back at him and then one by one, they shifted their gazes from the marshal to Yakima flanking him. The lanterns came up. They were held by the leprechaun called Murphy and one of the other two men Yakima had beaten up that morning, Eldon Potts, who had a thick bandage over his right ear and one arm in a sling.

When all faces had turned toward Yakima, who couldn't see much of anything now except silhouettes because of the lanterns aimed at him, the half-breed eased his Yellowboy off his shoulder to let it hang down low by his right side—ready.

Burkholder followed the other men's stares to Yakima, then returned his gaze to the group. "He was with me," he said loud enough to be heard above the wind and blowing snow raking the outhouse. "The breed's been over to my office for the last half hour. Whoever killed Shade—it wasn't him. Now, everyone get on inside. Tully, you and Murphy haul Shade inside. Get Saul Abernathy to buildin' a wooden overcoat. Then come on back over here. I want to talk to everyone who's been patronizing the Wild Coyote for the past hour or so."

When Tully and the man called Murphy had hauled the body off, the crowd filed through the saloon's back door. Yakima lingered around the privy, inspecting the hole through the back wall.

He went around to the front and looked at the door. It was still attached to the frame by the locking nail, but there was a wagon wheel–sized hole in the middle of it. Whoever had killed him hadn't wanted to wait till he'd come out, but had blasted him through the door.

That meant a double-barreled shotgun probably loaded with double-ought buck. The last time Yakima had seen a gut-shredder like that was in the hands of the barman, Tully. There'd been at least seven men out here scuffing around in the snow, so he doubted he'd be able to pick up the killer's tracks. The wind and falling snow was filling in even the recently made footprints. Still, couldn't hurt to sniff around.

Shouldering his Yellowboy, he looked carefully around the privy. He glimpsed a faint set of older tracks that were merely blue streaks in the pale snow. They led around the west side of the Wild Coyote, through a break between the saloon and a boarded-up barbershop beside it. He couldn't see much in the break on account of the near-total darkness, but when he reached the street at the far end, he picked them up again as they angled west of the alley mouth, across the boardwalk fronting the barbershop, then back into the street.

When Yakima was halfway across the broad main trace, the tracks gave out completely, leaving only the sugary snow that was piling up faster and faster, the wind blowing harder as the last light leached out of the sky.

He continued across the street and looked up at the Canon House Hotel. There was a light on in the downstairs windows, so he tramped on up the front stoop and pushed one of the winter doors open, a bell over his head jangling to announce his presence. The bell served only to cause the man sleeping in the armchair to his left to break off his snores and snort a few times, the old Laramie newspaper stretched biblike across his chest rustling softly.

Yakima closed the door and opened it again, swinging it quickly and causing the bell to ring more raucously. The oldster in the armchair lifted his head, blinking his eyes mantled by a thick wave of blue-gray hair. "Huh . . . Wha-what the hell?"

Yakima closed the door and stomped his boots on the hemp rug beneath him.

The old man looked chagrined as he turned to Yakima, then closed his paper and sat up straighter in the chair. "Don't know where the time goes. Just before

I figured I'd close my eyes for a bit, it was still light out there. Cloudy light, but light. Christ Almighty—what time is it?"

"Around seven," Yakima said, glancing out the window. "Looks later on account o' the storm."

"You lookin' for a room?" The old man raised his voice louder than he needed to, which meant he was probably hard of hearing or nearly deaf. Yakima was likely wasting his time here. If anyone had passed the oldster's window, he wouldn't have seen him because he'd have been sawing logs in earnest, and his hearing was so bad, no sounds on the street would have roused him.

"Maybe."

Yakima stared at the narrow, carpeted stairs rising at the lobby's rear, beyond a potbelly stove and a desk fronting a mess of empty pigeonholes and key rings on the right. He was thinking about the men who'd bushwhacked him. "Who you got up there, old-timer?"

The old man stood, his old joints popping, and raised his voice in irritation. "The name's Crandall. Percy Crandall. And I only got two boarders—prob'ly the last two of the season. Caught in the storm, don't ya know?" Crandall chuckled as he tossed his newspaper onto the chair he'd vacated. "Got so busy gamblin', they didn't leave before it was too late."

"They tried to get out of the valley?"

The old man nodded. "Came back lookin' like snowmen."

Yakima kept his voice low. "They up there now?"

"Either up there or over to the saloon." The old man scowled and thumbed his rawhide suspenders out from his potbelly. He wore a robe over threadbare long-handles, red wool socks, and deerskin slippers. "Why? If they owe you money, I don't want no trouble on the premises. If you start any trouble, I'm gonna send for Marshal Burkholder and Deputy Darling."

"What room?"

"Huh?"

"I said what room?" Yakima repeated, raising his voice slightly.

"You deaf, young man? I done just told y—"

The old man cut himself off when Yakima turned to him holding two gloved fingers to his lips. The old man just stared at him, his brown eyes rheumy from sleep and age, the whites as yellow as flypaper. Yakima strode quietly past the stove that, judging by the chill in the room, had all but gone out while Crandall had napped.

He looked over the scarred oak desk, saw that the only brass ring not sporting a key was the one marked 2. He turned to warn the old man with his eyes, then mounted the stairs, taking the steps two at a time but walking on the balls of his feet and wincing when the old steps creaked beneath his weight. A minute later he stopped in the dark, cold second-story hall, the plank-board door before him sporting a hand-painted number 2.

No light shone beneath the door or around the sides. No sounds within. The two boarders might have heard Yakima downstairs, and blown out their lamp to wait for him, guns ready, on the other side of the door.

He placed his left hand on the doorknob, keeping the right one wrapped around the Winchester's neck, his thumb on the hammer, his index finger gentling the trigger. He was mildly surprised when the knob turned and the door creaked away from the frame.

Half concealing himself behind the wall to his left, he gave the door a shove and tightened his finger on the Winchester's trigger as the dark room opened before him. The air pushing against him was cold and rife with the smell of stale tobacco and a sour corn-shuck mattress. A cheap blue curtain was drawn over the room's single, small window.

There was a charcoal brazier against the wall to his right. It was cold and dark. A pair of duck trousers was draped to dry over the back of a chair in front of it. The stove hadn't been lit in hours.

Yakima moved on into the room. The room's single bed sporting two pillows was mussed, some of the covers hanging nearly to the floor. A pair of saddlebags lay on the bed, another on the floor beside the washstand. A razor and a cake of lye soap lay atop the stand, beside a cracked china bowl and ewer.

The men who'd rented the room were still claiming it. Which meant they were somewhere in the town, or in the canyon nearby. Probably, as the old man had said, they were at the saloon. Yakima wondered if they were the killers and, if so, why?

Fabienne and the deputy had an obvious connection. But why had they bushwhacked Yakima as though to kill him and then spared him when they had him dead to rights?

He went out, closed the door, and headed downstairs, where the old man was waiting for him, looking owly at the bottom of the staircase, one horny hand on the newel-post.

"I run a tight ship here, damn it," Crandall barked. "Folks who rent from me do as I say or leave!"

"Don't get your bloomers in a twist," Yakima said, brushing past the old man to the door. "I'm leavin'."

"And don't come back!"

Yakima didn't hear that last, as he'd already slipped back out in the wind and the blowing snow. It was nearly good dark, but the snow offered enough light that he could see up and down the street for about fifty yards. There were a few lamplit windows up and down the street, as well.

Soon, he'd head over to the Wild Coyote, but first he'd walk around a little more. The footsteps of the deputy's killer—or what he'd taken for the killer's sign—had led toward the Canon House. If the man hadn't gone inside, maybe he'd gone on around the place and was holing up somewhere behind it. This time of the year, there were plenty of empty cabins in Dead River.

Pulling his collar high, he walked out back of the hotel and into the shrubs and rocks behind it. He was looking for more tracks in the snow or lamplight that might indicate an occupied cabin. A few minutes later he'd found nothing but dark hovels with shuttered windows and coffee tins overturned on their chimney pipes, or boards weighted down with rocks atop the stone chimneys, keeping animals and weather out.

He was moving past a mud brick stable when something shifted ahead of him about fifty yards, visible against several lamplit windows he hadn't seen until now. As he stepped out past the stable, the muzzle of a double-bore gut-shredder was pressed against the side of his head—so cold it made his teeth ache.

A woman's voice: "One more move, you son of a bitch, and I'll blow your head off!"

Yakima swept his rifle straight up. The woman squealed. The squeal was clipped by the thunder of the shotgun's blast.

Out the corner of his right eye, Yakima saw the streak of flames slanting skyward. The shotgun smacked the stable wall and fell. At the same time, moving instinctively, Yakima pivoted, drew his left hand back behind his shoulder, and let it fly, connecting soundly with the face of the gray silhouette before him.

The woman screamed as she flew sideways and hit the ground hard, skidding several feet, snow flying up around her. Her scarf fell away from her face. Her knit cap tumbled off her shoulder. Brown hair cascaded down her shoulders. She tossed it back and drew a hand to the cheek that Yakima had just tattooed. He couldn't see her face clearly in the snowy darkness, but he could see enough of her that, coupled with her voice, he knew she was Ramsay Kane—schoolteacher and mayor of Dead River.

Yakima stared down at her. She stared back at him, holding her hand to her face. He couldn't see her expression, but he sensed her fear.

He sucked a breath and spoke against the moaning wind. "What're you doin' out here with that cannon, Miss Kane?"

"I was about to ask you the same thing, Mr. Henry."

"Ain't that a coincidence?" Yakima stooped and pulled the shotgun out of the snow, brushed the snow off its barrel, inspecting it closely. "Lookee here—a long-barreled, double-bored shotgun. Just like the one that was used to blow the illustrious deputy town marshal of Dead River off his throne."

She sounded incredulous. "What're you talking about, Henry?"

"If I look in here and find it's loaded with double-ought buck, Miss Kane, I'm gonna be real disappointed in you."

As she lay there, one leg curled beneath her, he clamped his rifle under his arm and tripped the shotgun's breeching lever.

"Hold it!" a wind-torn voice shouted.

Ramsay Kane gasped and jerked her head to her right. Yakima lifted his own head up to see a figure moving toward him, crouched over the rifle he held in both hands before him, the barrel aimed at Yakima. Yakima froze, the shotgun in his hands hanging open, the barrels pointed at the ground.

"Just hold it right there, mister!" He detected a Southern, possibly Texas, accent. It sounded familiar, but he couldn't place it.

The man moved up on him. He walked with a limp that Yakima hadn't noticed before. He was clothed in a fur coat and high-topped fur boots, with a shaggy, peaked muskrat cap on his head. As he stopped several yards behind the woman, Saul Abernathy said, "What's goin' on here?"

"Hold on."

"Seen you cross the street, mister," he said, shifting his weight nervously from foot to foot. "What was that blast about?"

"It's all right, Saul," the teacher said. Turning her head toward Yakima, she added, "I think."

"What's that supposed to mean?" asked the carpenter.

Another, smaller, bulkier figure moved up behind him, trudging through the snow—this one a woman, her black wool skirt buffeting about her legs. She was dressed in so much black that Yakima could just barely make out her silhouette, but he could see her gray hair blowing in the wind. She looked like a large, old bird grounded because of the wind.

"I seen you!" she shouted, pointing, her voice like a mad grackle's. "I seen you in a dream I had . . . ridin' a black horse and bringin' trouble to Dead River!"

"Mama," the man called Saul shouted, but keeping his eyes and his rifle aimed at Yakima, "go on back to the shop. I got it under control!"

"Doin' evil out here," the old woman shouted. "Up to no good, sneakin' about in the storm where you thought humanly eyes couldn't find you! You and *Miss Ramsay Kane*!"

"Mama!"

"Saul, put the gun down!" demanded Ramsay Kane, pushing onto her knees, her hair blowing wildly.

A muffled blast sounded in the distance.

A man screamed. Yakima couldn't tell for sure what direction the sounds had come from, as the wind had swirled and obscured them. They seemed to have originated from the southwest side of town—the direction of the marshal's office.

Saul Abernathy and Ramsay Kane both turned their heads in that direction.

Yakima dropped the shotgun. Lifting his rifle, he bolted forward and rammed the stock against the side of Abernathy's head, dropping the man where he stood.

His mother squealed, lunged for Yakima, and fell in the snow.

Another scream, thin with distance, rose.

Yakima ran.

Chapter 16

Snow blasting him, Yakima ran across the main street and down the side street where the marshal's office and McMasters's livery stable sat amongst several boarded-up businesses. He couldn't see much except the snow blowing from a gray sky.

Ahead were a couple of flickering lights. He could see the gauzy outlines of the buildings to his right and left, and when he was about fifty yards away, he saw the marshal's office.

That's where the lights were flickering.

On the office porch steps, a figure lay sprawled.

The half-breed slowed his pace, looked around carefully. He continued to the figure, dropped to a knee, took his Yellowboy in his right hand, and rolled the man over with his left.

"The bank money," Marshal Burkholder rasped, his long body convulsing, legs stiffening. "They . . . got the bank money!"

"Who?"

The light left the man's eyes. His head fell to one side. His body relaxed. His gloved hands fell away from the gaping wound in his belly. His chest rose, fell, and did not rise again.

Yakima rose and stumbled up the snowy steps to look through the gaping office door. The flickering lantern on the marshal's desk was the only light, so he couldn't see anything clearly. As he walked inside the office, he saw that the door of the cell that had been housing the stolen Douglas bank money was standing wide.

Inside, there was only the vacant cot.

The saddlebags were gone.

Yakima cursed, wheeled, and went back outside. At the bottom of the porch steps, he looked around. The snow was scuffed all around the building, but two distinct sets of tracks that were filling in fast with fresh snow led off across the street, angling gradually toward the town's center.

Yakima levered a round into the Winchester's chamber, lowered the hammer, and jogged across the street, following the tracks across a vacant lot on the other side. The two men were running hard. Yakima saw a broad scuffed and packed mark where one had tripped over a snow-buried rock and fallen. The two had continued between two stables. Yakima followed. Judging by the freshness of the tracks, he wasn't far behind them.

His heart thudded. He raked cold breaths in and out of his lungs. He leaped snowy sage and small cedars and occasional piles of trash or boards. Ahead, the rear of several Pine Street business buildings loomed.

A light flashed in the gauzy darkness. A crack sounded on the heels of another flash. Yakima felt a burn across his left cheek. As he threw himself forward, another bullet ripped like a knife across his upper right arm, tearing his coat.

Warm blood oozed under his shirt.

He cursed loudly, rose to a knee, and began firing at a rear corner of a building thirty yards ahead and on his right, from where the gun had flashed. He heard the muffled thuds of his slugs chewing into the building's rear wall. Bounding off his heels, he ran forward.

In his haste, he tripped over several chunks of scattered firewood. They rolled under the soles of his boots, and with a grunt he fell facedown on the ground, banging his head against the pile of wood that the other split logs had tumbled from.

He groaned, blinked—dazed.

As he rolled onto his back, the logs turning and sliding beneath him, he saw a dark figure moving toward him from his back trail. The figure was holding a long gun across its slender body.

He'd dropped his rifle, but he grabbed it now. As he started to bring it up, the figure stopped abruptly, and Ramsay threw up her hands.

"Henry—no!"

He lowered the Winchester and twisted around to look at the place from where the shots had come. Then he turned to the woman again. "Get down!"

Awkwardly, she dropped to her knees and looked around. Yakima fired several more shots at the rear corner of the building. The slugs blew up snow puffs and hammered the wooden wall with dull thuds. There was no return fire. The wind howled, and the snow swirled.

He lowered the rifle. The marshal's killers were

likely gone. They wouldn't get far. He'd finally found one good thing about this damned snowbound valley—your enemies would be here until you found them again, or they found you.

"Are you hit?" The woman set her shotgun down and crawled toward him.

"No." He was thumbing cartridges from his shell belt through the Winchester's loading gate. "What the hell you doin' out here? Tryin' to get your fool head blown off?"

"I followed you. I saw the marshal. Your head's bleeding." She grabbed his arm. "We'd best . . . good Lord—you've been shot!"

"It's just a burn. I'm gonna get after those sons o' bitches." Yakima let her help him to his feet, but when he pulled away from her, he found the snowy night pitching around him and a bell tolling in his head.

He stumbled, almost fell.

"Like I was sayin'," the woman said, crouching and tugging his left arm around her shoulders and wrapping her right arm around his waist. "We'd best get you back to the marshal's office. You're gonna need some tending. Those men will still be in town tomorrow. Where the hell else are they gonna go?"

"I can make it."

She held on to him and began leading him back the way they'd come. "Be quiet, Mr. Henry."

"Why're you doin' this, Miss Kane?"

"Burkholder sort of thought you were cleared of Fabienne's murder. And you're about the last man in town capable of protecting the rest of us from those savages. I saw what they did to the marshal. If they killed both lawmen, God only knows what they have in mind for the rest of us."

As Yakima stumbled along beside the woman, his feet uncertain and his vision slightly blurry—the recent braining on the heels of the two he'd had early in the day had left him reeling—he said, "What were you doin', skulkin' around outside with that barn blaster?"

She paused, glanced behind her. "Oh, no—I left it back there." She started forward again. "Never mind. I'll retrieve it in the morning. It's my only gun except for an old cap-and-ball pistol my father gave me. To answer your question—I heard something outside my window. Or . . . I thought I did. It might have been the wind, but I'm pretty sure I heard something and even saw a shadow through my curtain. The men in town will tell you I'm hysterical at times, which is bullshit. Anyway, I must have seen those killers walk past my house after they killed Shade Darling, because a shadow did indeed pass by my window!"

They crossed the vacant lot and were heading across the street, arm in arm, staggering drunkenly. Occasionally a blast of wind would send them stumbling to and fro until the woman got her feet set and was able to steady Yakima.

"Oh, Lord," she said, gagging as they stumbled up the jailhouse steps together, looking down at Burkholder's partly snow-covered body. "I think I'm going to be sick!"

She whipped away from Yakima, who grabbed a roof support post to steady himself. He could hear the woman retching behind him as he pulled himself up the stoop, then got the office door open and stumbled inside. He closed the door to keep as much of the snow and cold as possible outside, and walked heavily toward the chair fronting the marshal's desk.

He dropped his hat on the floor, bit off his gloves, then leaned back in the chair and probed his aching forehead with two fingers. They came away a little bloody but not bad. He looked at his upper right arm, saw the blood staining his coat around the ragged three-inch tear.

"That's a good coat you tore, you son of a bitch," he grunted, working the mackinaw's bone buttons back through their rawhide loops and shrugging out of the coat, letting it sag against the chair back.

He looked at the tear in the bloodstained sleeve. Through it, he saw the pink furrow the bullet had carved across his upper arm, over the top of his iron-hard biceps. It wasn't much of a burn—just enough to nettle him. The blood in the pink groove was liver-colored, and it oozed a little when he squeezed his biceps.

The door opened, and Ramsay Kane walked in on a gust of windblown snow. Her eyes and cheeks were wet, her hair flecked with snow. She closed the door, hesitated there, one hand on the door, the other on the frame. Her shoulders quivered.

"Why?" she said, her voice pinched with emotion. "He was a good man. He's been a good marshal here for many years." She turned away from the door. "Why is all this happening?"

"You tell me—I don't live here."

"It's funny, don't you think, that this all started after you came?" She hardened her jaws a little. "With that money."

Yakima looked at her.

"Everyone in town knows about it. I don't know

who told whom. Deputy Darling probably told his pals, and word spread like a wildfire."

"You think he and his friends intended to steal it, and they got crossways with each other?"

The man who'd bushwhacked him on the pass hadn't looked like either of Darling's pals that Yakima had sent to the medico that morning. But Darling might have had more friends than those two. And who knew how many men might have set their sights on the Douglas bank loot?

"You tell me," she said sarcastically, crossing her arms on her cape. "I don't live in that world."

She glared at him. Suddenly, her lips rounded, and she shook her head. "My nerves are shot. Seeing the marshal lying out there like that . . ."

She went to the wood supply box by the potbelly stove, grabbed a chunk of split cordwood, and opened the stove's door. She stirred the glowing embers around inside the stove until she had a few flames leaping, then tossed the chunk on top of them. She added a couple more logs, then closed the door and turned to Yakima.

"Let's get you onto Burkholder's cot, and I'll tend those wounds."

Yakima heaved himself to his feet. He wobbled a little, and she helped him over to the cot on the far side of the room from the desk.

The marshal had set up a makeshift sitting area here, with a cot boasting several blankets and a bobcat hide as well as a corn-shuck pillow covered with blue-striped ticking. There was a braided, oval rug on the floor, a rocking chair, two tomato crates spilling old books, brittle newspapers, and yellow-backed dime novels. Beside the crude bookshelves, against the outside wall, stood a washstand with a tin pitcher and washbowl.

Yakima sat down on the edge of the cot.

"It'll take a while to heat water," she said, walking back toward the marshal's desk. "I'll clean those cuts with whiskey. Dusty usually kept a bottle in his drawer here. Always gave me a shot or two during our so-called council meetings, which usually only involved my giving him a reading lesson." She grabbed the bottle out of a lower desk drawer, popped the cork, and walked back over to the cot. "He said he wanted to be able to read Mr. Emerson before he kicked off."

Tears glazed her eyes. She swiped them away with the back of her wrist. Yakima stared at her, felt a warmth of appreciation for the woman's beauty. She was gray-eyed and even-featured, with a straight nose and a strong jawline. There were streaks of gray in her hair, and her skin was not smooth but blemished in several places. It was tanned and weathered.

She no longer owned the beauty of youth, but the richer beauty of a mature woman. He could tell that her years had not been easy. He could also tell that the body beneath her coats and skirts would be a full, supple one.

"Don't stare at me like that, Mr. Henry," she warned as she lifted her skirts to tear the hem off her petticoats. "Or I'll leave you here to do this yourself."

"You ain't married?"

"No," she said firmly, giving him a direct look and then pouring whiskey into the wadded-up scrap of cotton in her right hand. "Neither am I wanton."

"That's one up on me."

"So I heard," she said with a schoolmarm's disapproval. But he thought he saw the corners of her mouth give a little upward quirk. "First thing you do when you ride into town is sleep with the town's most alluring young lady of the evening . . . heedless of Deputy Darling's warning against such a coupling."

"I'm not good with authority."

"Would you like to remove your shirt or shall I cut off the sleeve?"

"Hell, no need to cut off the sleeve!" Quickly, he pulled his shirttails out of his buckskin trousers, and started unbuttoning it. "That sleeve can be patched."

"It's bloodstained."

"As much as needs to'll come out with a good soak in a pot of snowmelt."

She helped him take his shirt off, held it up as though it were a dead snake, then dropped it onto the floor. He unbuttoned his long-handles top, which clung to him like a second, pink skin, and peeled it down his arms until it lay bunched at his waist. She flinched a little at the scars on his hulking torso, hammered and shaped like a silver concho, his weathered red neck rising from his shoulders like a sandstone knob of rock.

"Good Lord, Mr. Henry—you've been around. And that's putting it delicately."

"Hasn't been an easy life," he said, wincing when she touched the whiskey-soaked cloth to the bullet burn, "but it's been a life. More than some of my dead friends can say."

"I won't ask you what you do for a living," she said, moving her face up close to his bulging biceps and gingerly dabbing at the wound.

"I'm not a pistoleer, Miss Kane." He was watching her work. "And I'm not a regulator."

"What are you, then?"

"I guess you could say I'm a professional grub-line rider." Yakima winced again, chuckling. "I've done some ranch work, railroad work, stage-line work. Just about any work you can name . . . I've done it."

"How'd you throw in with Sheriff Kelly?"

"I was in his jail."

She lifted her eyes to his, turning her mouth corners down.

"In bed with the wrong woman . . . again?"

"Nope." Yakima grinned. Having her here, this close to him, ignited a warm passion in him. He wrapped a hand around her arm, gently pulled her to him. "The right one, I reckon."

Frowning, she pulled away from him. "I told you, Mr. Henry, I may be unmarried, but I am not a brazen hussy."

"Gonna be a long, stormy night," he said. "I see no reason why we shouldn't make a time of it."

He pulled her toward him again.

She didn't resist this time.

Just as she let him press his lips to hers, the door flew open and slammed against the wall as two men, bristling with drawn weapons, stormed into the marshal's office on a chill wave of wind and snow.

Chapter 17

With a startled scream, Ramsay Kane pulled away from Yakima and, straightening, swung around toward the two fur-clad figures standing just inside the office's open door.

Yakima's right hand dropped to his pistol butt, and held there. Both intruders were holding guns on him—the tall man on the left, a rifle. The shorter man, Eldon Potts, aimed a cocked Remington straight out from his right shoulder. Both were the friends of Deputy Darling, who'd attacked Yakima that morning, and they wore the bruises and bandages to prove it.

The tall man had a bandage wrapped scarflike around his head beneath his round, fur hat, holding his broken jaw closed. The short Potts had a stout leather brace, like a horse collar, around his neck. Their air frosted visibly in the air around their heads.

"Get out of here—both of you sons of bitches!" demanded Ramsay Kane.

The tall man bounded forward, raising his rifle and narrowing one fierce eye, his hawk nose flaring. "Look at what we done found, Eldon." Spittle bubbled through his long yellow teeth and out the corners of his mouth as he spoke—or tried to speak, rather, the bandage holding his jaws taut. "Our purty little mayor makin' time with the half-breed. With the marshal lyin' dead out on the porch steps!"

He sucked a liquid breath through his teeth.

"I told you to get out of here, Boz," Ramsay ordered, her brittle voice quavering with emotion. "None of anything happening here is any of your business. Stay out of it!"

"Oh, you'd like that, wouldn't you?" said Potts. He stepped forward now, too, waving his cocked pistol around. "How long you two been in cahoots, anyways?"

"What the hell are you talking about?" Yakima said, his hand still wrapped around the horn grips of his holstered Colt.

"Don't slap me on Thursday an' tell me it's Friday!" bellowed the short man, the confining neck brace making it hard for him, too, to speak clearly. He looked at the cells at the back of the dimly lit room. "Where's that Douglas bank loot?"

Boz took another jerking step forward. "What'd you do with it? We know now you two done killed the marshal and took it. Plannin' on holin' up here for the night, ruttin' like a coupla minks, then lightin' out somewheres as soon as the weather clears."

"That's ridiculous!"

"Shut up, Miss Mayor." Potts walked up to Ramsay and aimed the gun at her face from two feet away. "We know where you come from—what kinda woman you are. A goddamn yellow-livered Reb from Arkansas—you and your pa and your brother, Elm. Southern outlaws—all of you! Now that your pa and your brother's gone, you just been waitin' to find a way out of here—a way out of here loaded to your pretty little gills with a tidy little sum of stolen gold!"

"We ain't gonna let that happen," Boz said, spittle dribbling down his chin. "That money's ours. We ain't sayin' it's right. No, sir, we ain't fool enough to think stealin's right."

Potts said, "But we're done tired of ole Dead River, and we aim to get out of here, same as you. Only it's gonna be us totin' that gold, not you. You, Miss Kane— you and the half-breed's gonna be feedin' the hungry wolves that prowl around here of a winter." He laughed and turned stiffly to his partner. "Ain't that right, Boz?"

"Thanks for killin' Shade fer us," Boz said, his flat brown eyes on Yakima. "That saved us havin' to split the gold three ways." A bizarre grin sliced across his long, horselike face, making his eyes glow.

"Where is it?" Potts lowered his pistol to Ramsay's belly. "Where is it, Miss Mayor? Maybe, if you tell us quick, we'll share a little of it with you . . . if'n you're real good to us."

He lurched forward, intending to nuzzle Ramsay's neck. She gave an enraged scream as she reached up and raked her right hand down his face, carving three bloody lines in his round, weathered face starting at his right eye.

He gave a shrill scream, triggering his pistol into the wall behind and between Ramsay and Yakima. As he stumbled back, slapping his left hand to his bloody eye, Yakima bounded up from the cot and grabbed Boz's rifle with his left hand. He shoved the rifle straight up. The carbine thundered, the slug hammering into the ceiling.

Yakima lurched forward, ramming his sore head into Boz's forehead. The tall man howled and stumbled backward toward the open middle cell. Yakima moved with him, wrenching the rifle free of the man's right hand with his own left, raising his right and jabbing it twice against the sharp point of Frank's chin.

His lower jaw made the same cracking sound it had made earlier, turning cockeyed inside its brace.

"Ungh," Boz moaned, his face going as white as the bandage trying to hold his jaw in place, his eyes glazing as he stumbled straight back into the cell wall. As tears oozed from his eyes, he fixed Yakima with a harrowing stare and reached for the .45 holstered on his duck-clad right thigh.

Yakima swung the man's own rifle butt against the side of Boz's head. As the tall man dropped like a fifty-pound sack of corn, Yakima whipped around, racking a fresh cartridge into the Winchester's chamber.

Potts was screaming as he stumbled against the office's front wall, clutching his bloody eye with one hand while sliding his pistol around as though trying to draw a bead on Ramsay, who was screaming and flopping around on the cot, covering her head with her arms.

In Yakima's hands, Boz's carbine roared three times, the cartridge casings clinking off the iron-banded cell door behind the half-breed's right shoulder. Potts slammed back against the room's front wall. He dropped his pistol and threw his arms up above his head before falling to his knees and hitting the floor in a growing pool of his own blood.

He shuddered as though lightning-struck, boots tapping the scarred floorboards like a telegraph key. Ramsay lowered her arms and lifted her head. She looked at the still quivering but lifeless form of Potts, then shuttled her shocked gray-green eyes to Boz, who lay on the floor in front of the middle cell, blood oozing from the back of his cracked skull.

Yakima could tell by his still form that the tall man was as dead as his partner.

"Sweet Jesus," Ramsay said, breathless, her face as white as the snow on the floor in front of the still open door. She looked at Yakima, her eyes widening. "What kind of a man are you?"

Yakima ejected the third spent shell from the carbine's breech. It hit the floor with a dull clang. "One who just saved your hide."

He leaned the carbine against the cell and walked over to the front door. He meant to close it but then saw Burkholder outside on the steps, the man's boots nearest the building. The marshal was nearly covered in snow. Only the toes of his boots and the tip of his nose poked above the swirling white powder.

Yakima went down two steps, picked up the lawman's ankles, and, wincing against the burn in his arm and the sundry aches in his skull, dragged the man into the office. He laid him out against the front wall, kicked the door closed, and walked over to the cot where Ramsay now sat, leaning her back against the wall.

She had both her knees drawn up to her chin, the soles of her fur-lined leather boots wedged against the cot's edge. She was just sitting there, breathing heavily, as though she'd run a great distance, staring at Yakima with a faintly befuddled expression.

"They were planning on taking the money," she said, a bewildered tone in her voice. "They and . . . Shade Darling."

"Reckon this town was starting to nettle 'em some. I know how they feel." Yakima reached down for the whiskey bottle that was still standing on the floor where Ramsay had left it. He handed it to her. "Have a drink on Burkholder."

She grabbed the bottle, slowly brought it to her lips, closed her lips over its mouth, and tipped both her head and the bottle back. She took two swallows, then lowered the bottle and smacked her lips. If the who-hit-John had burned going down, she didn't show it. She was obviously accustomed to strong hooch.

She extended the bottle to Yakima. He took it, tipped a long pull, and squatted on the floor in front of her. "I was ambushed up the eastern pass earlier."

"You're getting right popular," she breathed, still staring with that dazed, torn expression.

"Two men. At least two. One had a nose like Boz's over there, and a brown plaid mackinaw and a bullet-crowned hat. I didn't get a look at the other one."

He took another pull from the bottle and looked at her again. She was still staring at him as though trying to see through dirty glass. "I don't know who you're talking about."

"I'm thinking whoever they are, they took the money. Don't ask me why, but why not? Anyone else still around capable of all this . . . and stealing stolen bank gold?"

"Well, I wouldn't have said Shade Darling was capable of such a misdeed. I guess I was wrong." He'd handed her back the bottle, and now she took another pull as if it were her lifeblood. "You think that's why they killed him?"

"I don't know." Yakima looked at Potts, who had finally stopped shivering. "Somehow, all this has to be related."

"And the girl?"

"Maybe she and Shade were planning on running away together, after they'd taken the money." Yakima shook his head. "We hadn't been in town long enough—Kelly an' me—for anyone to cook up some elaborate plan to steal the loot they might have known was in the jail for maybe an hour, two at the most."

"I have to get out of here." Ramsay dropped her feet to the floor and, wincing, heaved herself to her feet. "I can't take being around these dead men. I don't know how you live like you do."

"Hold on," Yakima said, straightening, holding the whiskey bottle by its neck. "I'll walk you home."

"I'm not a schoolgirl who needs protection from the likes of you, Yakima Henry." She was a little wobbly on her feet as she made for the door.

Yakima stood near the cot, staring at her. She looked at Marshal Burkholder, then closed her hand over the doorknob. She stared at the door for a time, and then she swung her head to Yakima and hiked a shoulder. "I reckon it couldn't hurt."

He quickly wrapped a bandanna around his arm, buttoned his long-handles top, and pulled on his shirt. When he'd pulled his coat on, donned his hat, and grabbed his rifle, he led Ramsay outside, looking around carefully to make sure he wasn't about to get them both dry-gulched. He doubted that the men who'd stolen the loot would hang around to kill him, though. Whoever they were, they were likely holing up somewhere, counting their plunder.

Yakima would find them. He might even find them tonight. After he dropped Ramsay off at her house, he intended to head back to the Canon House, see if the men had returned to their room. Getting the loot back, and finding the killers, might be doable by midnight.

As he moved along the side street toward Pine Street, unseen in the snowy darkness, he glanced over his left shoulder. Ramsay was following him from only a few feet away, a tenseness in her body, her head turning slowly from left to right warily.

He thought he heard her say something. He slowed to let her catch up to him. When she was walking just off his left shoulder, he said, "What's that?"

"It's too early in the year for a storm like this."

"What's that mean?"

"Maybe old Ma Abernathy was right about you. Maybe you brought trouble with you . . . you and the black horse she saw in her dream."

Yakima looked at her. Her hair blew wildly in the wind. She turned to him, pinned him with her dark gaze.

Cradling his rifle in his arms, he continued toward Pine Street. "Yeah, maybe. Maybe it was waitin' on me."

Chapter 18

Yakima paused in the street before the Wild Coyote.

Most of the windows of the three-story building were lit, turning the snowflakes swirling before them into wind-jostled fireflies. The piano, however, was silent. There was only the moaning wind and the jangling of shingle chains up and down the stormy street.

Something moved a block away to the east.

Yakima tightened his grip on the Yellowboy, then relaxed as he watched the dark canine form—a coyote, fox, or dog—slink across the street and slip into a break between a boarded-up land office and a harness shop.

He glanced behind him. Ramsay Kane stood just back of his left shoulder. "I don't know where you live," he told her.

She looked around warily, her hair sliding across her face, then stepped out in front of him and angled toward the dark Canon House sitting kitty-corner from the Wild Coyote. Following her, Yakima kept his eyes on the hotel, wondering if the two men he was looking for were up there in their room. Where else would they go on a night like tonight? They likely weren't too worried about getting caught, as they'd killed both the town's lawmen. Now there was only him—Yakima—to run them to ground.

As he followed Ramsay through a break between buildings, heading toward the northeast, where no lights shone in any of the shacks around them, he wondered again why the men had bushwhacked him and then brained him later, and let him live.

Damn curious. Maybe old Ma Abernathy was right. Maybe he and Wolf had started all this inexplicable, nonsensical trouble. Wouldn't be the first time, he thought with a barely suppressed snort.

Ahead of him, Ramsay walked up the snowy porch steps of a neat, brick, square-shaped house with a narrow, unpainted porch. A light shone in a window behind a flour sack curtain. Beyond the house, sitting at an angle to it, was the school—it was shaped like a church but boasted a bell tower instead of a steeple. It was a small building sheathed in snow-mantled piñons, a large, wind-bent tamarack, two small outhouses, and a sprawling woodpile flanking it.

Ramsay fished a key out of her pocket, opened her door, and went in, stepping aside and holding the door, looking at Yakima with an eyebrow arched. After her demeanor earlier, he was a little surprised she'd let him in.

He shook his head. "I'm takin' a walk."

"No," she said abruptly, shivering as she looked into the stormy night behind him. "Cold out there. . . ."

Again, he shook his head. "There's a place I want to check out, before the killers' trail goes completely cold. I'll be back to check on you before I head back to the jail."

She nodded, furling her brows, and closed the door. She glanced out the door's curtain, then pulled her head back and let the curtain fall back into place across the pane in the door's upper panel.

Yakima moved on off the porch, following his and Ramsay's tracks that were quickly filling with fresh snow. After a time, he diverged from the tracks and soon found himself at the back door of the Canon House.

He pulled the handle, but the door wouldn't budge. It was a stout-timbered door fitting taut in its wood frame. Likely barred on the inside. He tramped down the gap between the hotel and another, smaller building on its north side and up the porch steps.

Slowly, chewing his bottom lip, he turned the knob of the front door. He heard the latch click. Even more slowly, he opened the door, biting his lip harder when he heard the faint tinkle of the bell overhead. He continued to inch the door forward, the bell ringing softly, making really more of a grating sound, until he stepped inside.

Then he closed the door just as slowly.

He turned around, saw that there was a single lamp lit—no, not a lamp, just a candle in a stone jug atop the old man's small desk. The draft from the door had nearly blown it out, but now it was sizzling as it sputtered back to life and dribbled wax down the jug's narrow mouth. The old man himself was sitting in the chair as before, to the left of the foyer. A cat was curled on Percy Crandall's lap, atop a knit afghan that reached from the old man's ankles to his neck.

The old man's head was turned toward Yakima. Snores rose. The cat was just a curled silhouette on his lap, with two pulsing yellow eyes that followed Yakima as he made his way, walking on the balls of his feet, along the foyer and past the ticking stove and the desk. He mounted the stairs, chewing his lip again as every other step gave a groan. He kept his hand off the rails to either side, because they were even creakier than the stairs.

When he finally found himself in front of room 2, he doffed his hat and tipped an ear to the door. He heard no movement from within. There was only the distant mewling of the wind and the creaking of the hotel's ancient timbers. No light shone beneath the door. There was no light at all except the ambient snow light from a window at the end of the hall.

Holding the Yellowboy in his right hand, the barrel inches from the scratched door panel, he closed his left hand around the knob and turned it. Just like earlier in the day, it clicked. The dry hinges groaned as the door sagged inward.

Yakima stepped behind the door casing and gave the door a hard nudge. The rectangular opening was as black as velvet. No guns flashed and popped at him from inside. The air in the room was as cold as that in the hall.

Yakima lit a match, held it high as he stepped into the open doorway. He couldn't see much by the light of the match, so he went over to the wobbly dresser with a cracked mirror and lit the candle lamp on top of it.

He held the lamp high and looked around.

The room looked as it had before . . . only the saddlebags and sundry other possibles were gone. The room had been vacated.

Yakima blew out the lamp. Quickly, no longer caring how much noise he made, he clomped down the hall and down the stairs. The cat leaped out of Percy Crandall's lap with an indignant meow, and Crandall grunted and chuffed, swinging his head around.

"What in tarnation? Who's there?"

Standing by the desk, Yakima held up the jug with the candle in it. "Me."

"Who's me?"

"Where'd your boarders go?"

"Who?"

"The men you had upstairs. They cleared out. Where'd they go?"

Crandall was twisted around in his chair, glaring owlishly at the half-breed. "I don't know. They just came by about an hour ago and cleared out. Didn't say where they was goin', and I ain't in the habit of askin' folks their business, just as I don't go nosin' around in theirs!"

"What'd they look like?"

"You're askin' a helluva lot of questions for a damn Indian!"

Yakima slammed the jug down. Again, the candle almost went out. It sputtered to life again as Yakima cast his broad shadow over the old man, who sagged down warily in his chair.

"What did they look like?"

Crandall snorted, raised and lowered his hands on the arms of his chair. "One was tall—sorta tall like you. Dark-skinned, too."

"He have a nose even bigger than mine? And a brown plaid coat?"

Crandall nodded. "The other was just as tall but rangy. Had glasses and a spade beard."

"What were their names?"

Crandall wrapped a fist on the chair arm. "Hell, I don't even recollect what I had for supper!"

"They sign a register?"

"Hell, I don't keep a register. What's the damn point of a register? As long as they pay me, that's all I ask."

Yakima gave a frustrated snort and went out, letting the bell clang raucously above the door. He shivered as the sharp teeth of the wind sawed into him and battered his face with snow blowing down over the roof's edge.

A weariness like an ox yoke weighed down on him. He was light-headed from too little food. He'd been here two days, and this town that had killed its own lawmen and a beautiful prostitute—and swiped a cache of stolen gold he'd sworn to protect—was killing him, as well. If he could, he'd mount his black horse and ride the hell out of here and leave the town's miseries to itself.

But he couldn't do that.

And he wouldn't do it even if he could.

But, for some reason, and for one moment, believing he would took the edge off his pain and fatigue.

He stumbled down the Canon House's porch steps. He started back in the direction of the marshal's office, where he intended to sleep, but, remembering Ramsay Kane, he swung northward and retraced his steps to the porch of her house, feebly lit against the storm.

"Everything all right?" he asked as she pulled her door open.

She was dressed in a plain but neat and clean gold-brown day dress, with fur slippers on her feet. Her hair was down, and it shone from a recent brushing in the lamplight.

Nodding, she pulled the door open. He doffed his hat and walked in, drawn by the warmth of a fire and the smell of roasting meat.

"Are you hungry?"

He nodded.

She took his rifle and leaned it against the wall by the door, then helped him out of his coat. She hung the coat on a peg in the wall, then led him into a small kitchen where a square, oilcloth-covered table sat against a curtained window. There were two place settings on the table—cracked stone mugs, chipped china plates, and tarnished silverware.

Yakima sagged into a chair, making it creak beneath his weight. She filled his mug with coffee from a small black pot. There was a bottle on the table, and she splashed a good amount of hooch into the mug, then went to the range from which she lifted an iron skillet.

She forked a thick steak onto his plate, then one onto her own plate, and from another skillet she shoveled out fried potatoes and green beans from an airtight tin. Neither spoke as they ate hungrily.

Yakima finished before she did, and sat back in his chair, sated at last. His fatigue pressed down on him, but it was a good feeling now. He would sleep well, letting go of all his cares for a short time before morning.

"There are more potatoes," she said as she continued eating and sipping her coffee.

He shook his head. He took a sip of his own coffee.

He'd never tasted coffee so good. The whiskey in it eased the dull throb in the back of his head and in his temple and bullet-furrowed arm. When she finished her own meal, she cleared the table and then refilled their coffee cups, splashing more whiskey into each.

She sagged down across from him, leaned back in her chair, and lifted the smoking mug to her lips. A wind gust sprayed snow against the window, like sand, rattling the pain.

Yakima sipped his own coffee. "You're from the South. . . ."

She frowned over the rim of her mug. "Does that matter to you?"

Yakima laughed. "No."

Her cheeks colored slightly and she lowered her eyes to her coffee, blowing on the surface, then taking another sip. She set the cup down on the table. "My family fought in the war—my father and my brothers. They rode with Quantrill, robbed several banks in Missouri and Arkansas after the war. The North hunted them like dogs. That's why we came here."

She looked at the curtained window. "I'd promised myself to a boy who died in that war. I came here full of hate for the North. We found that half the little settlement of Dead River—it wasn't much more than a gold camp then—was populated by several families from the North. Feuds boiled, of course. A few people died because of the old hatreds. Gradually, as the population dwindled, the feuding died. Now it just festers now an' then, like it did earlier."

"That what makes you"—Yakima looked at the nearly empty bottle on the table between them—"nervous?"

"I reckon you'd leap at shadows if you'd ever been raped, Mr. Henry."

He looked at her.

She kept her eyes on her coffee mug. "Two years ago, a man broke in here. I'd just come in with an arm-load of wood, hadn't closed the door tight. When I turned after dropping the wood in the box, a man was standing in front of me. Wearing a flour sack mask." She lifted her eyes to Yakima's. "Did you notice Saul Abernathy's limp?"

Yakima didn't say anything.

"I grabbed my daddy's old cap-'n'-ball and shot the rapist in the calf as he was leaving. Still don't know if it was Saul, but he disappeared right after the 'incident' and when I started seeing him again, he was favoring that right leg."

"What'd the marshal do?"

"I never told him."

Yakima waited.

"I always hoped he'd try it again, Saul. That old Greener lays down the law way better than any law dog ever done."

She smiled, her gray-green eyes flashing a little from the hooch and likely giddiness from the cold and the topsy-turvy day. She leaned forward, pressing her mouth against the top of her wrist. "Forgive my Ozark grammar and my ideas about justice. Both come back when I drink."

"We'd best get that popper back."

"Tomorrow." She pushed off the table rising. "Now . . . time for bed."

"I'll be goin'." Yakima drank down the last of his coffee.

"No point." She looked down at him, still sitting his chair, and blinked slowly. "I got me a big, lonely bed, Mr. Henry," she said, letting the words roll off her tongue like the velvety petals of laurel sliding down the slopes of an Ozark Mountain riverbed.

She gave him a lingering, beckoning stare, then walked out of the kitchen.

Chapter 19

Yakima woke the next morning feeling sated by the woman's cooking as well as her body. He'd slept hard enough to temper the pain in his head, and the furrow across his arm burned only slightly.

He sat up, dropped his bare feet to the floor, rested his elbows on his knees, and lowered his head to his hands, digging his fingers into his scalp. Behind him, Ramsay groaned. It was like one of the love cries she'd given the night before as they'd buried themselves beneath the sheets and heavy comforter made from deerskins and fleece, burrowed down in the cornshuck mattress, and entangled themselves in each other's bodies, moving, rocking, and toiling together, warmly oblivious of the cold night outside.

She groaned again.

He turned to her—a long, slender shadow against the pale light of the window on the bed's far side. She was turned away from him, her face hidden, her hair sprayed invitingly across the pillow. The cold room seemed to push him back toward her, but, fighting against it, he shucked off the comforter, stood naked, stretching, then went out into the cabin's tiny parlor and lit a fire in the hearth.

He hurried back into the bedroom and rolled into bed beneath the thick, soft comforter, turned to Ramsay, and spooned his body against hers. Wrapping his arms around her, he cupped her heavy breasts in his hands. Instantly, the nipples pebbled, and she opened her mouth slightly, drawing a long, deep breath.

She reached behind the swell of her rump, found him ready, and pulled him inside her. She pressed her cheek to the pillow as he thrust against her. A few minutes later, she was pulling at the pillow with her fists and grunting loudly at the wall as he bucked against her hard, holding her hips, finishing.

When they'd quivered together, spending themselves, she hooked her arm behind her shoulder and splayed her hand across his head. She turned her own head and kissed him wetly.

"Still think I'm an evil spirit?" he muttered into her neck.

"Mister," she wheezed, "I don't care *what* you are."

He lay behind her for a time, pressed hard against her, letting his blood settle, nuzzling her neck. She lay warm and pliant in front of him, breathing regularly, drifting back into sleep.

Reluctantly, he pulled away from her, crawled out of bed, and washed himself at the basin atop the marble washstand, which, with a small dresser and narrow armoire, were the room's only furnishings. The walls were unadorned, whitewashed pine planks; no tintypes hung on them—only one small, cracked mirror.

Outside, he couldn't hear the wind or the snow. Maybe the storm had died.

"I'll make some breakfast," she said in the room's misty silence, stirring.

"No need. I'll be goin'."

"What's the hurry?"

"If the snow's let up, those killers might get ideas of trying to drift out of the valley."

"The passes won't be open for days, and that's only if it warms up and the sun shines." She sat up in bed, let the covers fall from her breasts, and stretched. "But have it your way. I'm going with you."

He chuckled as he stepped into his balbriggan shorts. "No, you're not."

She swept the covers off her, and stood—a woman-curved, long-haired shadow in the room's dim light, her full breasts jostling as she strode to the washbasin. "I'm the mayor. And if you know anything at all about the hierarchy of a town's government, I'm the chief law enforcement officer . . . not to mention the only one left."

"Christ," he groaned, scooping his buckskins off the floor.

"Where to?" she asked fifteen minutes later as they walked out the front door and into the cold, gray dawn.

The wind had nearly died, and the snow had dwindled to a few thin strands stitching the blue air. The area around the cabin was blanketed white, a mist of wind-tusseled snow swishing over the sugary surface.

Yakima moved down the three steps and into the yard, looking around, thinking. "How many houses still occupied here in town, you think?"

She looked off, considering. "Let's see—Miss Venora and Tully live over in the Wild Coyote. Old Lucky Ryan has a cabin behind his harness shop, but you'll find him mostly in the Wild Coyote with everyone else . . . except the preacher and the Abernathys, of course. They live in a lean-to addition behind their furniture shop.

"McMasters lives in his barn. Percy Crandall mostly sleeps in his lobby chair in the Canon House. When I was over at the Coyote, I saw a couple of drifters who were too deep in poker to leave before the storm struck. They're likely holed up over there. Of course, there's the wolfer, Thunder Dodd. He has a cabin up on the western pass, but he'll be spendin' the winter in the Canon House, most likely, as Miss Venora won't allow him upstairs with the girls. Foul man." She paused, considering. "Those are the only folks left in town. With the girls at the Coyote, that wouldn't make twenty, I'd guess."

She looked at Yakima with a vague question in her eyes.

"Nice to know who's accounted for," he said, buttoning his mackinaw's top button, "and who's not."

"I heard Alta Banos is back . . . without Christian."

"You know her?"

"She was one of the reverend's pupils . . . until she eloped with one of the older boys at the school and they left to start their own spread."

"Well, they started it," Yakima said, grimly. He thought about Alta, and that led him to wondering about Kelly's condition. He'd check on the sheriff again later. "Let's walk the town," he said. "Keep an eye out for tracks in the snow, and smoke lifting from chimneys. I'm thinking our killers must have holed up in an otherwise vacant shack."

"I could take one side of the town," she said, moving down her porch steps and pulling her second glove onto her left hand. "But I'd just as soon we didn't split up. I'm the *chief* law enforcement officer. I leave the dirty work to the men who work for me."

"Do I work for you?"

"It seems you volunteered for the job."

He gave a grim smile and let her lead the way around her cabin, the snow crunching beneath their boots. They walked about halfway between Pine Street and the south edge of Dead River, where they could see most of the shacks in the town's small area. Ramsay told him there were a few more, original mine shacks farther out, along Dead River itself, but she couldn't think of one that wasn't dilapidated to the point of being unlivable.

"When a cabin's vacated," she explained, "most everything that's usable, including the doors and windows, are scavenged and used elsewhere. My own parlor window came from such a shack on the south fork of the river. My school bell came from an old Spanish church east of town."

They reached the west end of the town, crossed Pine Street, and circled around to the north, seeing only crows and two coyotes that had come in to scrounge the trash piles. A tabby cat sat on a snowy corral rail, huddled into itself, its fur like a thick coat, and watching Yakima and Ramsay with cautious interest. A magpie cawed from a low, sod roof, and the cat lifted its yellow eyes and gave its tail a predatory flick.

Ramsay retrieved her shotgun from where she'd set it down the night before, and used her skirt to brush the snow off it. She breached it to check the heavy, brass loads, then carried it cradled, childlike, in her arms.

The only tracks Yakima found after they'd passed the rear of the Wild Coyote and its privy, from which Shade Darling had been blown in a spray of wood slivers and red viscera, were those of a mountain lion that had apparently taken a walk through a corner of the town just before dawn. It had been dragging something dead, judging by the blood—probably a domesticated cat or a dog.

Yakima walked with Ramsay back to the main street, the buildings on both sides looking like gray-brown watercolor against a gray-blue canvas peppered with the white of zigzagging snowflakes. The mayor canted her head capped in knit red wool toward the Wild Coyote. "Drink?"

"Nah, think I'll . . ." He let his voice trail off as he looked toward the church and Preacher Ekdahl's lodge, which flanked the church on its right and behind it about fifty yards. A bulky horseback rider was coming along the snow-covered trail, the lodge behind it, the church to his right. A black leather bag flapped down his horse's right shoulder.

Yakima let the doctor ride up into the street, and then he and Ramsay stepped forward. Doc Howe reined the white-socked dun gelding up and glanced at the pair regarding him curiously. "The boy died."

"What boy?" Ramsay asked.

"Alta Banos's boy—Christian."

A stone dropped in Yakima's belly. "How?"

"A lingering pneumonia caused by lungs that hadn't fully developed. I examined the child day before yesterday, and his heart sounded weak. Didn't wake up this morning when Alta tried to feed him."

"Oh, no," Ramsay said.

The doctor sighed and shook his head. "I don't know what gets into those people. She never should have made the trip here with a child so young. She knew he was ill." He looked pointedly at Yakima. "You know about the marshal? Christ, his office is a damn morgue!"

"Don't know who killed the marshal," Yakima said. "But I shot the other two."

"In self-defense," Ramsay added. "Let's discuss this later, Doc. I'll be calling a town meeting soon, in the Wild Coyote. Now, though"—she glanced at Yakima—"I'd best follow you over to the preacher's."

"Miss Banos and Ekdahl are in the church," the doctor said. Spurring the gelding forward, he muttered, "I'm gonna tell Saul to build a little box, and then I'm gonna fetch a drink."

Lifting her skirts above her boots, Ramsay tramped off through the snow, following the doctor's horse tracks. Yakima walked beside her, feeling hollow, numb. There'd been several killings in Dead River since he'd arrived—and he'd done some of the killing himself—but the news of little Christian's death had rammed an especially sharp knife in his gut.

He followed Ramsay up the shoveled church steps. She leaned her shotgun against the wall, beside the door. Inside, the air was dark and smelled of candles, sweat, and varnish. Yakima doffed his hat, swiped it across his thigh. A woman stood just inside the door, facing the front of the church, her hands folded in front of her.

Ma Abernathy turned her wicked, wrinkled face to Yakima and Ramsay and blinked, aghast. The old woman was dressed entirely in black, including a black cape and a black wool scarf, her pewter hair pulled back severely. She looked every bit the haunted and hateful old crone.

She said nothing, but her yellow-gray eyes blazed at Yakima.

Ramsay glanced at Yakima, then walked past the old woman, striding down the aisle between the pews, through murky light angling down from two long stained-glass windows in each wall. At the head of the church, a tall, silver-haired figure and a short, dark-haired figure knelt at the altar rail, their backs to Yakima and the old woman who continued to regard Yakima with unabashed disdain.

The heads of Preacher Ekdahl and Alta Banos were bowed in prayer. Just beyond them stood a stone altar held together with gray mortar and fronted with a large cross formed by two peeled pine poles and a carving of the crucified Christ. On the altar lay a very small, blanket-wrapped bundle.

As Ramsay approached the altar rail, Reverend Ekdahl looked at her, grim-faced. She muttered something, and he rose slowly, his long legs clad in black duck cloth unfolding, and turned toward the front of the church, his blue eyes finding Yakima standing with Ma Abernathy, and blinking slowly, almost bemusedly.

He glanced at Alta, who remained kneeling with

her head bowed, and then began walking up the aisle toward Yakima. He held a broad-brimmed, low-crowned black hat in his hand. His unbuttoned buffalo coat hung slack from his shoulders, revealing the white clerical collar. One elbow of the coat was nearly worn through.

"Now, Mrs. Abernathy," the preacher said with gentle admonishment as he approached her and the half-breed, "everyone is welcome in God's house."

"Why . . . this is a heathen, Reverend," the old woman hissed, then jabbed her acrimonious stare toward the front of the church. "That . . . *Mexican* is one thing, but—"

"We have all sinned." Ekdahl turned to Yakima, and blinked, his eyes glowing in the light from the stained-glass windows. "The doctor tell you?"

Yakima nodded. He wasn't paying much attention to either the preacher or the old lady who kept drilling into him with her pious, angry gaze. He was watching Alta. Although he could detect no outward display of grief in the young woman's set shoulders or unmoving back down which her blue-black hair fell, limned in silvery light from the windows, he knew the horrors racking her. They were the kind of horrors that nothing could abate except time, and maybe a god if you had the luxury of one.

Yakima looked at the preacher, whose silver soup-strainer mustache rose as he offered a gentle smile. "Come on in, if you'd like. Have a seat, Mr. Henry."

Yakima looked at the woman, whose eyes seemed to burn with an even more heated fury. The half-breed gave a caustic grunt, swung around, and headed back outside. The preacher followed him out and stood beside him atop the shoveled steps, Ekdahl running a hand through his hair as he set his hat on his head.

"How'd it happen?" Yakima asked him.

"Alta went to wake him this morning, but the boy wouldn't open his eyes. What a horrific scream it was that woke me." Ekdahl stared off toward the stormy heart of Dead River and sighed. "I dressed and fetched the doctor myself. The boy was dead, of course. There was nothing Howe could do. There is nothing now that anyone can do, except for our Lord and Savior, of course."

He turned to Yakima and gave his condescending smile. "You likely wouldn't understand God's grace, Mr. Henry. Given time, however, I'm sure you could be brought to understand it. You have it, even if you don't know it."

"Does Alta have it?"

"Of course she does. I raised her here myself. Myself and Mrs. Abernathy . . . when my house of God was open to many others just like her—the homeless, the lost, the wretched . . ."

"That's good enough for me, then," Yakima said, and began moving off down the steps.

The preacher touched his arm and followed him. "I heard from Mr. McMasters that the marshal was found dead this morning in his office. Two other men, as well. I also learned that Shade Darling was killed in a most ungallant way last night. What in God's name is happening here, Mr. Henry?"

He looked genuinely perplexed, maybe even a little afraid.

"Your guess is as good as mine, Preacher. When I

find out anything, I'll let you know." Yakima turned away from the man and began walking back toward the sprawling lodge flanking the church.

The preacher said nothing, just stared after him stonily as Yakima walked off along the buried trail that skirted the church's fenced-in graveyard, the snow-mantled stones pushing crookedly, cold as bones, above the drifts.

Chapter 20

Yakima had no sooner opened the door of the preacher's house of God than a boom like a thunderclap sounded, making the windowpanes rattle and the mantles of the gas lamps chime.

Closing the door, Yakima looked at the ceiling. "Kelly?"

There was a muffled cry. Yakima racked a round into his Yellowboy's breech and set off to find his way up to the preacher's attic. He missed a turn and had to backtrack down a dim corridor, then mounted the narrow stairs to the children's room.

Kelly's door was closed. Thuds and grunts sounded from inside. Yakima rapped on the door. "Kelly—you in there?"

He opened the door and stumbled in to find the sheriff dressed and on all fours, the man's back facing Yakima. He was shaking his head as though trying to clear it, and clutching his wounded side. His hat was on the floor.

Yakima looked around, then, seeing that the young sheriff was the only one in the long, narrow attic room, leaned his rifle against the wall and dropped to a knee beside Kelly, who was cursing and groaning and continuing to shake his head.

"What the hell happened?"

"Tried . . . to get the hell outta here. Musta fell and hit my head on that damn bedpost." Kelly dropped back on his heels, sitting up and holding one hand to his side, the other to his right temple. "Damn!"

"Where the hell were you tryin' to go? The doc said you needed bed rest." Yakima grabbed the man's arm and began to pull him off the floor. "Let's get you back in the mattress sack."

"Ah, Christ, Yakima—I heard what's goin' on out there." Halfheartedly, the young sheriff let Yakima guide him back to his cot. He dropped down on the edge of it, his hair badly mussed, his face flushed. "Burkholder dead. Darling Dead." He looked up at Yakima, eyes as befuddled as the preacher's. "What in God's name . . . ?"

"Somethin' tells me He don't have anything to do with it." Yakima dropped down on the cot across from Kelly's. "And that ain't the half of it. The money's gone."

The sheriff only blinked and stared at him through rheumy eyes, as if this additional bit of information was too much to fathom.

"Whoever took it shot Burkholder. I think they also shot Darling and the whore, too, though I haven't quite savvied the connection. As soon as I find 'em, I will."

Kelly continued to stare uncomprehendingly at Yakima. Finally, he sagged back against his pillows, lifting one leg onto the cot, leaving the other dangling over the edge. "Christ! I gotta get that money back to Douglas. It's real damn important I get it back!"

"You'll get it back. Those two who stole it have to be around Dead River somewhere." Yakima rose, walked over to one of the two small, rectangular windows, and stared out through the frost-starred pane. "Both passes are closed and won't be open again until spring or we get a good . . ."

He frowned as he stared off over the brow of a hill directly behind the lodge and the stable and corral that flanked it. He wasn't sure, but he thought he'd glimpsed a thin strand of smoke rising from the other side of the hill to disappear against the rocky, pine-stippled ridge flanking it and the low, gunmetal sky from which more snow was beginning to fall.

"A good what?" Kelly said, canting his head to look up at Yakima. "A good melt?"

"Yeah." Yakima backed casually away from the window, not wanting Kelly to know he'd seen something out there. The young sheriff had to stay in bed, or he'd likely bleed to death. "A good melt. Never know—could happen."

"I'd say there's a fifty-fifty chance we're socked in here till spring."

"Yeah, maybe." Yakima drew a deep breath and hooked his thumbs in the side pockets of his mackinaw. "You get a good rest, Kelly. I'll find out who killed Burkholder and the others, and I'll get back to you."

"The doc told me Alta's boy died." The sheriff merely shook his head in mute awe at all the bad things that had happened here. He looked up again at Yakima. "I reckon I'd best deputize you."

"No need. The mayor of Dead River already done that."

"Mayor, huh?" Kelly winced as he squirmed down a little lower in the bed. "Who is the mayor, anyways? I don't recollect this town even havin' one."

"Fella named Kane." Yakima gave a wry snort, walked over to the door, and picked up his Winchester. "Remind me to introduce you sometime."

He ducked through the doorway and headed down the stairs.

Yakima slogged through snow-weighted piñons and buried bramble a couple of hundred yards behind Ekdahl's place. Breathing hard from the climb through the snow that had drifted nearly knee-deep in places, he hunkered down behind a boulder at the top of the ridge. He doffed his hat, dropped it into the snow beside him, and edged a look around the boulder's right side.

On the other side of the bluff lay a broad creek bed. Apparently, there had been a small mining community here at one time, as there were three cabins and a large tailing pile on the slope above them, with a hundred-foot Long Tom stretching down the slope and into the wash. The Long Tom was mostly covered in snow, but Yakima could make out the line of the long series of sluice boxes beneath the sugary covering.

Off to the right, along the narrow, ice-glazed creek that flowed at the base of Yakima's bluff, were several dilapidated communal stock pens.

The roofs of two of the cabins were caved in. The cabin farthest right and nearest the stock pens was mostly intact though its windows were missing shutters, and there was a ragged hole in the far left side of its brush roof. There was no front door, only a black, rectangular hole.

A rusted tin chimney pipe protruded from the right side of the roof, and from his vantage the half-breed could clearly see a thin tendril of smoke unfurl from the pipe and wave like a flag before licking down over the edge of the roof to obscure the front door.

It was cold out here. Cold enough for a fire much larger than the one the cabin's occupants were obviously maintaining. Which meant they intended to keep the fire small and endure the cold swooping in through the cabin's windows and open door, and not risk their smoke being spotted.

The air was so quiet, with only the hushed whisper of the light snow falling and landing in the drifts around him, that Yakima could make out the muffled voices emanating from the shack. He looked around. The men probably had horses out here somewhere. If they were holing up here, they'd want their horses near.

Yakima donned his hat, crawled down the bluff a few feet back from the boulder. Then, looking around cautiously, not wanting to spook the men's horses, he began trudging along the side of the slope, about twenty yards below the crest, out of sight from the shack on the opposite side, heading east.

When the ridge started to curve back away from the village, Yakima walked up and over it, then ran, crouching, through a stand of pines down the other side toward the creek. Halfway down, his right boot caught on something beneath the snow. He hit the ground hard, wincing as rocks ground into his knees and thighs. He managed to hold on to his Winchester, and as he got up, cursing and spitting snow, he glanced back to see what had tripped him.

A small pile of rocks with some weathered gray wood showing beneath, where his boot had displaced the stones. Yakima rose to his knees, brushed snow from the other rocks, removed some of the rocks until the lid of a small gray box stared up at him.

The letters *U.S.* had been stamped into the wood. Age had deteriorated them so they were only a vague outline. Yakima had seen such boxes before—they were ammunition boxes the U.S. Army provided its soldiers. Many soldiers kept them after they mustered out of the service and used them as footlockers of sorts.

Yakima ran his hand along the edge of the lid, until he found the hasp on the side farthest away from him. He paused to look around him, making sure he was alone. From his vantage here on the side of the ridge, he could just make out the roof of the shack he was headed for, just barely see the white smoke curling up from its chimney pipe.

Yakima leaned the Yellowboy against the tree fronting the cairn. Removing several more of the stones, he found the rawhide handles on either side of the box and lifted. One of the handles broke free, but the other held, and the half-breed managed to lift the box up from its resting place and swing it around toward him so it was resting unevenly atop the snowy rocks, its front side with the hasp facing him.

There was no padlock. A three-inch stick had been thrust through the hasp, securing the lid to the box.

Yakima removed it, opened the lid, the rusted steel hinges of it pulling free of the rotted wood.

Yakima stared down into the box, blinking, pulling his head back slightly.

Inside the box lay a small, blanket-wrapped bundle, the leathery crown of a doll-sized skull showing through a fold. Attached to the leathery brown head were several sandy blond hairs thin as an old woman's mustache. There was the faint pungency of rot. Wrinkling his nose, steeling himself against what he knew he was about to find, Yakima peeled the blanket open with his gloved fingers, until the decomposed skeleton of a small child, an infant—maybe even a fetus—stared up at him through eyeless, button-sized sockets.

Yakima removed his hands from the rotting blanket and leaned back on his heels, studying the dead child for a time, frowning at it, repelled by it but at the same time feeling an age-old sadness tug at his heart. Why here? Why'd they—or she—bury her child out here in an old army ammo box?

Why not in the cemetery?

But he knew why. It was the timeless story of unholy love—a night of romantic bliss not unlike the nights Yakima himself had spent with Fabienne and Ramsay Kane—only to be followed by an unwanted pregnancy and . . . this.

A child buried in an ammo box.

He shuttled his gaze from the dead child to the canyon below. Then he slid his eyes to his left, to the roof of the house he was headed for. Had the mother resided there? Maybe in one of the other two shacks. Or maybe she'd lived in Dead River. In the preacher's house of God, say?

She'd probably buried the child here on the side of this ridge, close to where she'd lived, so under cover of darkness she could shed a few tears on these rocks, pay her respects to the fruit of forbidden love, to an innocent child she couldn't keep.

Yakima wished he hadn't opened the box. Carefully, he folded the blanket closed on the tiny body, replaced the lid on the box, and mounded the stones back over it.

He grabbed his rifle, pushed a pine bough out of his way so he could look back toward the cabin, then ran crouching down the hill. He crossed the creek at a beaver dam, strode a hundred yards up the other ridge pocked with boulders, stone knobs, and stands of pine, then made his way along the ridge until he was directly behind the windowless shack. There was a small, dilapidated stable back here, and he could see two horses milling about inside.

He felt fortunate that at least one window of the shack still bore its shutters—the rear one. The shutters were closed, which should increase his chance of approaching the shack without being seen.

As long as the horses, both staring toward him and flicking their ears, didn't give him away.

Slowly, taking his rifle in one hand, he made his way down the snowy slope. The footing was slippery beneath the sugary snow, and twice he fell—once hard, and he grunted as his butt hit the sloping ground. Tensing, he shot a cautious glance at the cabin. It was so quiet out here he thought he would have been able to hear the footfall of a deer half a mile away, which meant his grunt might have been heard from inside the shack.

He waited, watched the cabin. The voices inside had died, but no one came out to look around and no one opened the rear window shutter. With painstaking slowness and quiet, he heaved himself up out of the snow, regained his feet, and began walking even more cautiously than before down the hill. After fifteen minutes that seemed like a couple of hours, he passed a dilapidated privy, then pressed a shoulder against the shack's rear wall, canting his head to listen.

Nothing.

He frowned as he stared at the weather-silvered log in front of him that bore the initials TM, but he heard nothing at all but the breeze lightly combing the brush roof above his head. He pulled away from the wall and took one step forward before he heard a rasp behind him.

A wooden bark followed and he'd just turned his head in time to see the shutter fly out from the window from which a rifle barrel jutted, like the tongue of a giant, striking snake.

A face appeared above and behind the barrel—round and red with blue eyes wide and wild behind round, steel-framed spectacles—and then the man howled raucously as smoke and flames stabbed from the rifle's maw.

At the same time, Yakima threw himself back against the rear of the cabin. The slug puffed snow about a foot in front of where his feet had been set. As the shooter's victorious howl died and a look of cow-stupid befuddlement clouded the ambusher's raw features, Yakima pushed off the wall, pivoting toward the cabin and raising his Winchester while thumbing the hammer back.

The shooter's mouth formed a near-perfect O as h
screamed and jerked his head back behind the wall
Yakima's rifle thundered, the slug chewing a larg
dogget of splinters from the window casing and miss
ing the shooter's face by a hairbreadth.

Snow crunched nearby, the sounds growing loude
with each running footstep.

Ejecting the spent shell casing over his right shoul
der and seating a fresh round in the Winchester'
breech, Yakima pivoted to his left. A man appeared of
the cabin's rear corner—the tall, black-bearded mar
with a bullet-crowned hat and wearing a brown mack
inaw whom Yakima had seen in the woods. He held
carbine in his hands. He stretched his lips back from
his teeth in an angry grimace and swung the carbin
down, thumbing the hammer back.

Chapter 21

Yakima's rifle leaped and roared.

The man grunted and fired a round into the wall of the cabin. He dropped the rifle and, grabbing his bloody left cheek with both hands, twisted around and staggered off through the snow, slipping and sliding and dragging his boot toes.

Yakima ran around the cabin to the front. He did not pause as he bolted around the front corner, diving through the open door while casting a concentrated gaze into the room before him. The bespectacled man was standing, crouched over a Spencer repeater, to the left of the rear window, an anxious look on his haggard face sporting several days of beard stubble beside a thin, tobacco-stained goatee.

The Spencer boomed. Flames flashed.

Yakima hit the floor on his forearms, lifted his Yellowboy, took hasty aim, and drilled the haggard man with the Spencer through the center of his quilted deerskin coat. The man screamed, dropped his rifle, and clutched his chest where blood began to form a large dark brown stain.

His lids fluttered over his eyes. His knees hit the floor, and he fell forward onto the shack's dirt floor on his face.

Yakima racked a fresh round into the Winchester's breech and stepped back, seeing the other man through the window in the east wall of the shack, beyond a few ribbons of remaining sackcloth curtain clinging to the frame and fluttering in the snow-stitched breeze. The man was on his knees, facing away from Yakima, and spitting blood into the snow beneath him.

Yakima raised his rifle, planted the stock on his shell belt, and strode out of the shack and down the side, stopping ten feet away from the bearded man on his knees and spitting scarlet gobs of blood into the snow, where it steamed. He wore a brown plaid coat and a red neckerchief. He had longish, greasy hair. His thick black beard was blood-matted.

He turned his pocked red-brown face toward Yakima, brown eyes pain-racked and bright with fury. He gritted his large yellow teeth beneath the ax-handle-sized nose that Yakima had seen on the eastern pass just before the other man had laid him out with a pistol butt, and cursed.

"You shot me in the face, you dog-eatin' son of a bitch!"

"Want another one?"

The angry spark in the man's eyes dulled. Clamping a bare hand over his bloody left cheek, he looked at the repeater the half-breed was aiming at a downward slant from his right hip.

"Where is it?" Yakima said, his voice taut, looking around in case there were any other ambushers drawing beads on him. He didn't think there were, but it paid to be careful.

"Where's what?"

"You know what." Yakima took one step forward, thrusting his Winchester barrel at the man's right cheek in mute menace.

The man studied Yakima for a time. Blood dribbled between his thick fingers and down his knuckles and into the dark hairs on his wrist, thinning and branching out as it continued into his coat sleeve.

"If you mean that loot—we didn't get it. We was too late."

Yakima stepped back. "Get up and get inside."

The man stood slowly, keeping his hand pressed against his cheek. His voice was slightly garbled from the pressure against his face, as he said, "And we didn't kill Burkholder, neither. We found him that way—Pink an' me."

Yakima followed the man into the cabin. The man stopped just inside the door, no doubt staring at his friend, Pink, who lay facedown on the floor in a pool of his own blood. His glasses lay nearby, one lens cracked. Yakima used the stock of his rifle to push the bearded man farther into the cabin and out of his way as he looked around for the saddlebags.

There was nothing inside the cabin except a rusted-out, sheet-iron stove, one kitchen chair missing half its back, and two saddles, two saddlebags, two saddle blankets, and two bedrolls. A couple of food tins lay on the hard-packed dirt floor beside the stove that had no door. Inside, flames licked up from two floury white pine logs with blackened ends. There were only a few more chunks of dry wood on the floor with the discarded tins.

Yakima looked at the man in the brown plaid coat. He was now holding his neckerchief to his cheek and looking at Yakima darkly, his broad, pitted nostrils flaring as he breathed, his chest rising and falling.

Yakima said, "What's your name?"

"Jordan Tyree."

Suddenly, before he could so much as blink, Yakima rammed the butt of his Yellowboy into the man's solar plexus. Tyree dropped to his knees with a thud and a deep, raucous groan of expelled air. He hung his head low, his long, stringy hair hanging down over the crown of his skull to the floor.

"Why, you savage son of a bitch!" he managed after nearly a minute of trying to suck a breath back into his chest.

"I was just tryin' to refresh your memory, Tyree."

"Christ . . . I done told you the *truth*!"

He grunted and groaned for another minute, then lifted his head by inches. When he was sitting up straight and leaning his butt back against his heels, he licked his thick, chapped lips and lifted his painracked eyes to Yakima.

"Like I said, we got there too late. We was standin' out on the far side of the jailhouse, waitin' for Burkholder to open the door. The marshal walks up from the side street and mounts his porch. The jailhouse door opens, and a shotgun blasts him back down his steps."

Yakima slid his eyes around the room. He'd forgotten that Burkholder, like Darling, had been killed with a shotgun. There was no shotgun in the cabin. That didn't mean these two didn't have one, but it gave the man's story some credibility.

"You must have seen who shot him, then."

Tyree hiked a shoulder. "I seen him walk out of the office with the saddlebags draped over his shoulder, carryin' a shotgun. It was dark and there was a light behind him. Me an' Pink didn't hang around there long. We wanted nothin' to do with killin' a lawman. All I saw was a man, about my size, a little shorter, in a heavy coat and a hat. He moved off down the porch steps, and me an' Pink waited to see which way he was headed. Then we lit straight out across the street into that vacant lot."

"Which way did the killer head?"

"Turned left when he left the office, sort of slunk around the building, stayin' close to it, so his shadow would blend in with that dark wall, I reckon. I didn't pay much attention after he left the porch."

"Why'd you shoot at me?"

Tyree stared in mute exasperation at Yakima for a moment. "'Cause you was comin' after us, and for all we knew you was the killer. Figured you spotted us and wanted to hush us up about the marshal's killin'."

Yakima studied the man. He didn't like him, but he was believing him. He tapped his thumb on his Yellowboy's hammer. "Why did you ambush me on the pass, and why're you holin' up out here?"

"Ambushed you by mistake. Figured you was Darling. He beat us at cards two nights goin', and we owed more money than we figured we could win at the tables and wheel, the way our luck was holdin'. We thought we'd try to get over the pass before the storm settled in. Didn't make it. Couldn't see shit, and the horses were fallin'. When we was comin' back down, we seen you . . . thought you was Darlin' followin' us. He'd have killed us if he knew what we was up to."

Tyree compressed his lips. "Merciless son of a bitch . . . We're out here till the passes open up—all winter, comes to that."

"Suppose you didn't kill him, then?"

The skin above the man's hawk nose wrinkled. "He's dead?" His eyes lighted hopefully.

Yakima said nothing. He'd heard the man's story and he believed it. He didn't want to believe it, but he did. It kept everything complicated.

Who was the killer? Where was the money?

He could see killing the lawmen if he was after the stolen Douglas loot, but why had the killer killed Fabienne?

"You mind if I get up?" Tyree asked. "Get a shot of whiskey? You done did a nice job on my cheek."

Yakima lowered the Yellowboy, stepped back. He looked around the cabin once more, wanting to see some clue here that might implicate Tyree and his dead partner in the murders and thievery. But he saw nothing. Likely, just a pair of stupid, grubline-riding saddle tramps who were only a little more desperate than most everyone else in Dead River.

"Do yourself a favor, Tyree," the half-breed said, heading for the shack's door. "Stay out of my sight. And if I do see you again, it'd better not be with a gun." He glanced back at the man who'd dug a bottle out of a saddlebag pouch and was holding the bottle halfway to his mouth while regarding Yakima with dull-witted skepticism.

"I stay out here alone, I'll freeze to death!" Tyree complained. "I'm outta wood, an' this cheek grieves me bad!"

Yakima walked out away from the shack, heading for the creek and the ridge beyond it. He found a shallow ford, then climbed the ridge, slogging through the deep snow. But he wasn't thinking about the snow. He was thinking about Burkholder and the stolen loot, and ticking off the faces he'd seen in the town in his mind. Likely, he'd met up with the killer here, somewhere. He'd seen him either in the street or in the Wild Coyote. The man had the loot stashed somewhere.

Where?

Anyone in town was likely capable of stealing the stolen loot. But how many would be capable of bloody murder? Whoever had killed Darling had done so with passion. Without passion, it's damn hard to kill a man while he's sitting in an outhouse, his pants bunched at his ankles.

You have to do more than just want a man out of your way to do that. You have to really hate a man to do that.

Yakima was so deep in thought that he wasn't aware he'd walked back into Dead River until he heard voices on his right, and found himself tramping out of the snow-covered shacks and brush and pushing onto Pine Street. He turned to see the preacher and Ma Abernathy walking toward him on his right, from the direction of the church and the reverend's house.

"Surely you don't intend to have the child buried in the *church* cemetery," the old woman was saying, her head turned toward the preacher, whose own head was canted down toward the freshly fallen snow. "He wasn't *baptized*!"

"But the mother was," the preacher said, his deep voice carrying in the quiet, snow-laced air. "And I think for my dear Alta, we can make an exception."

"Oh, but, Reverend—I don't mean to sound uncharitable," complained Mrs. Abernathy, "but the girl is . . . she's a . . . *Mexican*!"

Just then, when she and Preacher Ekdahl were about thirty yards away from Yakima, the old woman lifted her crowlike head. Her eyes widened, and her lips bunched in brash reproof. Ekdahl saw Yakima then, too, and while the preacher slowed his stride, the old woman branched away from the reverend, walked wide around Yakima, and, nose in the air, headed for her and her son's furniture shop under Dr. Howe's office.

"Mr. Henry," the sky pilot said by way of greeting, giving his smile that he might have meant to be affable but which only betrayed the man's condescension. "I trust you found the sheriff in good spirits, despite the depravity that's been occurring in his jurisdiction of late. I understand the money that he and you brought here for safekeeping has been stolen."

The man looked at Yakima with open suspicion.

Yakima glanced at the church behind Ekdahl. "How's Alta?"

"As well as can be expected."

"Out there . . ."

Yakima glanced back toward the ridge he'd just left,

seeing Jordan Tyree riding toward him on a saddled horse—a speckle gray with dark brown legs. The man held a hand to his cheek as he rode slouched and sullen in his saddle, just now following Yakima's own ragged tracks between two slumped, white ponderosa pines.

"I come upon the grave of a small child." Ignoring Tyree for the time being, the half-breed returned his own accusing stare to the preacher. "And I'm just wondering how many more are out there. How many more weren't fit to be buried in your consecrated ground yonder?"

"What're you talking about?"

"You likely wouldn't know, would you?" Yakima felt an old anger burn. "You put up your church and your school, and you say you include all, but whether you know it or not, you exclude most."

The preacher blinked indignantly. "You're mad!"

"Go to hell, Ekdahl." He swung around and tramped off toward the church, following the preacher's and the old woman's tracks through the blue-shadowed drifts.

More snow was coming down now. The breeze was picking up and swirling it. From a long ways off, above the wind, came a coyote's mournful yammer.

Yakima pushed through the church gate and walked up the shoveled stone path. He climbed the steps, opened one of the timbered doors, and stepped into the dingy church, its cold, still air smelling of candle wax pushing against him.

He rested his rifle on his shoulder as he walked up the aisle. Alta was standing at the front of the church, her back to Yakima, moving her hands over the altar upon which her dead child lay.

He stepped over the low communion rail and walked up beside the girl. She was dressing Christian in a knit wool bodysuit.

"I don't want him to get cold," she muttered.

Yakima placed his hand on the back of her neck, felt her coarse hair slide against his palm. She turned to face him now, eyes wide and shiny, lips parted. "I caused this."

"Nah."

"I shouldn't have brought him here. I didn't want to stay alone at the ranch. All winter. I didn't want to stay alone and . . . I knew that . . ." She turned her shiny eyes, tears falling like gold dust from her lashes and down her mahogany cheeks, back to the child lying inert upon the altar, on a small, tattered brown deerskin. "I knew he was sick. He couldn't breathe at night. . . ."

"You did the best you could."

She shook her head slowly as she pulled the tiny suit up the baby's waxen, stiffening body. "It's all right," she said, breathing heavily, shaking a thick tangle of black hair from her eyes. "He is with his father now."

Yakima squeezed her neck sympathetically. "I'll help you bury him."

"I will bury him."

"I'll dig the hole."

She shook her head as she wrapped the skin around little Christian and lifted the dead child to her chest. "The reverend said he will speak over him." She smiled, her eyes bright and teeming with sadness but also with what appeared a victory of sorts.

Yakima brushed his hand over the dead child's head.

Then, leaving the girl to her boy, he tramped heavily back to the front door and outside. He looked at the two stretches of timbered or brick buildings facing the wide white street before him. The sputtering snow was a veil hanging over them.

Rocky, pine-studded ridges rose all around the canyon the town sat in. The tops of the ridges were lost in the low clouds and the falling snow.

A cold, lonely place. No place to spend the winter. He felt a sudden, intense jealousy of those who'd left before the storm had struck. If only he could leave, head to Arizona, maybe deep into Mexico, where the sun shone.

Where was that goddamn money?

He needed a drink. . . .

He moved heavily down the steps and started down Pine Street, blinking against the feathery snow pelting his eyes. Footsteps sounded behind him. He turned to see the barman from the Wild Coyote, Jim Tully, and a man just as large but older and with a broad face with a badly scarred upper lip step out from the side of the church. This was one of the regulars at the Wild Coyote—the wolfer, Thunder Dodd.

Tully held a shotgun straight out from his right hip. Dodd wore patched buckskins and a shaggy bear coat and round fur hat. An untrimmed salt-and-pepper mustache mantled his lip. He aimed a Civil War model Spencer .56 repeater from his shoulder at Yakima. He smiled menacingly through his mustache.

Both men moved slowly toward the half-breed.

Tully said, "Sheriff Kelly's waitin' for you at the Wild Coyote. First, drop them guns."

"Kelly?"

Someone else stepped out from behind the church. Ramsay Kane held her own shotgun cradled across her breasts. Her wool skirts buffeted in the wind. She blinked snow from her lashes and studied Yakima grimly for a few seconds before she said, "McMasters found the saddlebags. They were in the stall with your horse, Yakima."

She compressed her lips until they were outlined in white. "Drop your weapons, before I gun you where you stand!"

Chapter 22

Yakima bent his knees and set his prized Yellowboy repeater gently in the snow. Even befuddled by the orders and the information about the saddlebags, he resented having to turn the rifle over to the elements, as the snow would not only stain the fine walnut stock, but it would seep into the receiver and foul the action.

Straightening, shifting his eyes among the faces of the three holding guns on him, he reached under his coat and unbuckled his shell belt. The belt and holster and stag-gripped .44 he also eased into the snow beside his rifle. He looked at Ramsay Kane, who stood cradling her shotgun and regarding him stonily.

"The pigsticker, too," she said, glancing at his shoulder.

He reached up and removed the Arkansas toothpick from its sheath and dropped it in the snow with his guns. "You're buyin' that lie about them saddlebags?" he asked Ramsay.

"Don't matter what she buys," said the wolfer, Thunder Dodd. A white frontiersman with a lifelong aversion to Indians, he still wore his cunning grin; he was delighting in this favor he was doing for Kelly. "Fact is, Kelly wants to see you. So, move. March, dog eater!"

Ramsay glared at the man. "That's enough, Dodd!" Then she looked at Yakima, commanding him with a dull, sad gaze.

The half-breed turned around and began walking along the street, angling gradually toward the right, to where the Wild Coyote sat, drab, gray, and silent, snow piling up on its mansard roof and on the balcony on which he'd first seen Fabienne, like frosting on an elaborate wedding cake. There were several coffins propped on sawhorses outside the large front window, right of the door. The furniture maker, Saul Abernathy, was planing one now as Yakima approached, the wood curling up at the end of the plane, his eyes regarding the group before him warily.

Yakima slowed his steps. Whoever had planted the saddlebags in Wolf's stall had obviously been trying to frame him. Anger seethed in him. Suddenly, when he saw the shadow of one of the men behind him, he swung around quickly, knocked Tully's shotgun aside with his left arm, then hammered the man's face with a slashing right fist.

Thunder Dodd yelled, but before he could level his Henry on the fast-moving man before him, Yakima danced, swung around, and smashed his right boot against the backs of the man's knees. Dodd's legs buckled.

The Henry barked. The slug chewed into the Wild Coyote's front wall, just above the window. Yakima pivoted again, lofting himself several feet in the air, kicking his right leg, then slamming his left boot against the side of Dodd's head.

The man folded up as neatly as a jackknife, snow closing over him like water.

Tully had bounded off his heels. Glowering, red-faced above his cinnamon beard, missing his hat, the barman came at Yakima with both fists moving up around his neck. Yakima feinted, caused the man to swing heavily, then rammed one jab past the man's other fist and into his chin. As Tully staggered backward, trying to set his feet, Yakima's second fist struck the man's high left cheek with a solid thud.

Tully screamed, twisted around, and fell. He lay on his back, hands at his sides, staring up at the sky through unblinking eyes. His breath puffed in the air above his mustache-crowned mouth.

Both men were down and out of commission. Ramsay stood before him, about ten feet away, her boots spread a little more than shoulder width apart.

"I'm about two seconds away from shooting you," she said.

"If you really believe I took that loot, trip those triggers."

Yakima gave her nearly a full minute. She just stared at him, her eyes beginning to show some uncertainty. He swung toward the Wild Coyote and went on inside.

There were several nude, dead bodies laid out atop tables at the back, and the girls of the place were cleaning them up and dressing them for burial. Darling was there with Burkholder and the two men Yakima had killed in the marshal's office.

The dead men were pale and hairy, but somehow

they looked as though they could get up off their tables and order a drink. Other townsmen, including Percy Crandall, owner of the Canon House, sat at other tables around the room, nursing beers or shot glasses and sucking cigars or cigarettes with a solemn air. The leprechaun, Murphy, wasn't playing the piano, but stood behind the bar, a loosely rolled quirley smoldering between his lips and a badger coat draped over his shoulders.

Miss Venora sat near the body of her son, drinking whiskey from the bottle and now directing her hard, drunken gaze, bleary-eyed, at Yakima.

One of the girls wrang out a cloth in a tin basin. The tinny sound of the water and the ticking of the potbelly stove were the only sounds in the place. That and one of the other drinkers spitting a quid of chew into a sandbox near his table.

Sheriff Kelly was sitting alone at a table near the front window. He had his ankles crossed on a chair, and he was aiming a carbine atop the table before him at Yakima one-handed. The carbine was propped atop the bags of stolen loot. There were still a few stalks of hay protruding from the lumpy pouches.

"That make you feel better?" he asked, glancing out the window at the two men Yakima had taken down.

Yakima balled his hands into tight fists at his sides. "I'd be one dumb savage to hide those saddlebags in my horse's stall. What is this, Kelly?"

"I just know what I heard."

The young sheriff, who looked pale and gaunt but better than he had when he'd first arrived in Dead River, glanced at the liveryman, who sat a couple of tables away, his thick arms extending across his table as though to guard the heavy schooner of ale between them. He had his head turned to one side, sliding his bright, drunken, delighted gaze between Yakima and the sheriff and back again.

"What Mr. McMasters told me, I didn't want to believe," Kelly added, uncrossing his ankles and dropping his boots to the floor. "Still don't. But I reckon it was just too big a temptation, wasn't it?" His chair creaked as he rose from it, wincing a little at the stitch in his side. Wincing again, he draped the saddlebags over his shoulder. "It's prob'ly my own fault—lettin' you out of jail to posse up with me. I should have left you there, where you'd do your time, then move along."

"Look . . ."

Kelly shook his head out of sadness as well as to forestall further argument. He glanced into the dingy depths of the Wild Coyote, past the faro layout and the roulette wheel, at the dead men laid out like giant landed fish. "Why'd you kill old Burkholder, for chrissakes? That truly does astonish me. I never figured you for that."

Yakima said nothing. He was staring at the young sheriff moving slowly, painfully around the table, but he could feel all eyes in the room on him. Anger, frustration clamped his jaws together. He balled his fists, heard his own breaths rasping in and out of his nose.

Someone here had taken the bags and hid them in Wolf's stall. Why would they set him up? Or had the stowing of the bags merely been a stupid move, the setup unintentional? It didn't make sense. The puzzle of it tolled in Yakima's ears like a church bell.

Jack Kelly stopped ten feet from Yakima, at the edge of the half-breed's kicking range. He loudly racked a shell into the carbine's breech and curled his gloved index finger over the trigger. His eyes were cool, his lips curved down in disappointment. He waved the gun at the door.

"Let's go. I'm lockin' you up, takin' you with me back to Douglas when the pass opens." His voice was low, soft, pitched with a fateful reluctance. "Go peaceful, now, Yakima. You had me believin' I could trust you, and I don't want to have to drop this hammer on you. Christ, you saved my life! But if you try doin' again what you did out there, I will."

"Have it your way."

Yakima turned and pushed through the door and onto the boardwalk. Ramsay stood there, facing the street. She didn't look at Yakima. Tully and Dodd were just now gaining their feet, beaten and bloody and giving their darkly furious gazes to Yakima.

"You fellas had better go on over to the doc's, get yourselves checked out," the young sheriff advised.

"Maybe you'd better have a hand, there, Sheriff," suggested Thunder Dodd, spitting blood in the snow.

"I'll be all right. See the doc. Then have a drink on me."

The saddlebags draped over his left shoulder, Kelly followed Yakima up Pine Street, in the direction of the marshal's office.

While the half-breed had little doubt he could take the young man, he wouldn't. Couldn't. There was still something in Kelly that Yakima was fond of—a naïveté in striking contrast to the rough frontier he'd grown up on. An almost foolhardy defiance of corruption that had made him teeter over the edge of reason.

At the moment, it made him overly gullible, to Yakima's detriment, but he'd soon see that the half-breed had not taken the loot. He just needed time to reason it through.

Yakima would give him that time.

Yakima said nothing as he turned down the side street on which the marshal's office sat. Kelly said nothing, either. The wind was picking up, the snow coming down so hard at times that the buildings on the far side of the street disappeared in a white fog. Yakima could hear the young lawman's footsteps behind him, crunching softly in the fresh snow. He glimpsed Kelly in the periphery of his vision as they filed along the side street, then up the snow-covered steps of the jailhouse.

Yakima opened the door, moved on inside.

There was a sepulchral chill and dinginess to the earthen-floored building. The stale smell of blood, wood smoke, tobacco smoke, and sweat filled the air.

Kelly stepped wide of Yakima and waved his carbine at the first cell closest to the dead marshal's cluttered desk. "In there."

Yakima moved into the cell. Kelly took the key ring off the peg protruding from the center post, thrust the door closed, its rusty hinges squawking fiercely, and tried it. The bolt had locked. The door did not come open.

Yakima stood looking through the bars as Kelly set his carbine and saddlebags on the desk, then sagged wearily down in the marshal's swivel chair. Kelly said nothing. He kept his hat on as he hiked a boot on his knee and laced his fingers behind his head, staring straight across the desk at the closed door.

The wind howled. Snow ticked against the plankboard walls.

Yakima wrapped his gloved hands around the iron bands of the cell door. "If you're gonna keep me here awhile, how 'bout a fire?"

Kelly said nothing. Yakima stared at him, his heavy brows ridged, his green eyes dark beneath them. Kelly's shoulders moved. After a time, a sound came from the man. Soft chuckles rose from the direction of the desk. Yakima's battered, befuddled brain was slow to realize they were coming from the young lawman himself.

"What's funny?" he growled at last, hoping that the sheriff had thought it through and was just now realizing the error of his ways.

Kelly's chuckles grew a little in pitch and volume. He leaned farther back in his chair and flexed the fingers that were entwined behind his head, just beneath the brim of his soiled Stetson.

"I'm surprised at you, breed," the young lawman said in a sneering voice, glancing sideways at Yakima, his eyes bright with mockery. "Would have reckoned you'd have it figured by now."

Yakima didn't say anything. He stared darkly through the cell's doors, suddenly feeling like a caged lion. His heart hammered slowly against his breastbone. He felt as though every muscle in his thick body had turned to granite.

"Got old Burkholder out of the way, got you out of

the way." Kelly patted one of the saddlebag pouches. "Only had to part with my babies here for a little while. Long enough to implicate you." He heaved himself out of his chair, grabbed the saddlebags, which he draped over his left shoulder, then sauntered past Yakima to the jail's middle cell. With a wince against the pain in his side, he dropped the bags onto the cot, then stepped out and closed the door.

Yakima kept his eyes on him. The half-breed's face was implacable. Kelly stepped up in front of Yakima. With that sneer on his face, he looked like Kelly's impostor.

"Been waitin' a long time for such an opportunity."

"You were intendin' the whole time to steal the loot yourself?" Yakima's voice was so low as to be nearly inaudible beneath the wind's keening outside.

Kelly nodded. He gently padded his lower right side through his buttoned coat. "Hadn't planned on takin' the bullet. Wasn't about to let that stop me, though. Just glad I had sense enough to sign you to my posse. Them others weren't much help, but I figured they wouldn't be. You turned out to be more help than I could have imagined. Got me here, got the gold here. Only problem was, once I had you and the gold here, I had to get rid of ya. Oh, once or twice I considered askin' you to throw in for a percentage."

Kelly shook his head slowly as he stood staring at Yakima from only a few feet away. "I just knew, though—I got a pretty good sense about men, you see—that you wouldn't go for it. A lowly half-breed, fed slop your whole life, not wanted anywhere but a federal prison eventually . . . but you wouldn't go for a deal like that. What's the old expression? Honest to a fault. A white knight. Or should I say a *red-skinned* knight?"

Yakima made a lunge for him. The young outlaw must have sensed it coming. He lurched back, just inches beyond Yakima's flexing hands, the half-breed pressing the side of his face up hard against the iron cell door bands. He grunted, enraged, wanting nothing more than to wrap his hands around the thieving killer's throat and squeeze the life out of him.

"You yellow-livered bastard," Yakima said, unable to fully comprehend the severity of the young man's betrayal. "You killed Burkholder—now you're tryin' to stick me with it!"

"No, no," Kelly said, showing all his teeth beneath his thin mustache as he grinned. "I didn't kill the marshal. My . . . what do you call it? My accomplice did that. I wasn't up for too much movin' around just then, so I had to find me a friend. Found me an' old one, in fact."

"Who?"

"Why should I tell you?"

Yakima just stared at him, squeezing the cell's iron bars in his fists.

"Ah, hell. Why not tell ya?"

Kelly walked back to the desk, lifted his carbine off it, and planted the butt against his hip as he moseyed back toward Yakima's cell.

"You ain't gonna be alive for more'n another minute, anyways." He grinned again, dimpling his cheeks. "Mrs. Abernathy's boy, Saul, ain't near the good boy his ma thinks he is. In fact, Saul and me used to ride together, a few years ago. Till his ma got her wicked old talons into the poor bastard again. Not for long, though. Saul's gonna help me get outta here, soon as the pass opens. He won't get much beyond the pass, though. See, that there's a lotta money in them pouches, but it's gonna have to take me all the way to Mexico and keep me there a good, long time."

"Why kill Fabienne?"

"Oh, I didn't do that!" Kelly said quickly, indignantly. "No, no, no—I didn't kill the girl. Someone else done that. Didn't bother me none, though, sorry to say. I figured that little incident might get you out of my way, figured maybe Deputy Darling would have you stretchin' hemp on Pine Street." Kelly scowled. "No, you slipped slick as shit outta that one. Can't say as I know who killed the girl, but you know how a whore's got more enemies than a chicken-stealin' dog-fox."

"Deputy Darling?"

"I reckon that was Saul, all right. I didn't order him to do it, but I would have. Reckon ole Saul was just thinkin' ahead." Kelly gritted his teeth and closed his eyes. "Enough talk, goddamn it. My side's beginnin' to grieve me again. I believe I'll head on back to the preacher's place. That Alta Banos—she's got a mother's touch!"

Kelly winked.

"Not anymore," Yakima said. "Her boy's dead."

"Pity. But I reckon you're right." Kelly turned away from the cell and walked over to the front window right of the door. Stooping, he looked out. "I'd move on over to the Wild Coyote, but it wouldn't look right for an upstandin' county sheriff to mix with fallen women.

Hope the storm blows itself out soon. I'm gettin' right randy—thinkin' about all the Mexican tail that gold's gonna buy me."

He sauntered with a menacing expression back toward Yakima's cell, leveling the carbine's barrel. He grabbed the key ring out of his pocket and aimed the Winchester at Yakima's belly.

"Get back against the wall."

"Why?"

"Do it or start dyin' right here an' now . . . slow."

Yakima backed up to the outside wall. Kelly poked a key in the cell door's lock, winced a little as he jerked it this way and that. Finally, the bolt clicked. Kelly drew the door wide and kept the carbine aimed at Yakima.

"Too bad you tried to escape." The killer's fist tightened around the neck of the Winchester's stock. His eyes flattened out beneath sandy brows. "Here's where we fork trails, partner."

Chapter 23

Yakima stared at the killing, thieving young lawman, narrowing his eyes, his heart thudding in fury and frustration.

"Need me out of the way for good, huh?"

Kelly grinned with menace. "Let me apologize in advance."

His finger began pulling back on the carbine's trigger.

Boots thudded on the porch steps. Snow squawked under a heavy tread. Kelly turned as the door opened, and Jim Tully poked his broad red face under a thick rabbit skin hat into the room. The man's watery eyes beneath snow-dusted lashes slid between Yakima and the sheriff.

"Trouble, Sheriff," the barman said, giving his head a single, fateful wag. "Just found Saul Abernathy dead in his shop with a hole in him this big!" The man spread his hands to indicate a shotgun blast.

Yakima looked at Kelly, whose face had gone as white as the storm raging outside. The half-breed laughed.

Kelly slammed the cell door and raised his carbine.

"That's terrible news," he said, recovering his earlier composure—the serious demeanor of a respectable county sheriff. He cast a quick glance at Yakima, another glance at the money pouches on the cot in the middle cell, then began striding toward Tully. "I'm right behind you, Mr. Tully!"

He set his carbine on his shoulder, dashed out the door, and pulled it closed behind him. His and Tully's boots thudded on the porch and crunched off through the snow.

Yakima stared at the door, his mind reeling. He could come to few conclusions about anything here in this crazy town, except for two things:

He had to find a way out of the cell.

And he had to kill Sheriff Jack Kelly.

Fury fairly popped and sputtered in his bloodstream. He walked to the front of his cell, grabbed the bars, and gave them an enraged jerk, making the entire cage ring. Frowning, he looked at the lock. He thought he'd detected a loose sound in the locking bolt. He remembered that Burkholder had had trouble with the door when Yakima had first arrived with the stolen loot.

His heartbeat quickened hopefully as he stepped back, jumped up, and wrapped his hands around two bars in the ceiling. He swung his body backward and forward, like a trapeze artist. When he'd built sufficient momentum, he thrust himself forward and slammed his boots against the door with a savage grunt.

The door rattled in its hinges but held fast.

Clinging to the ceiling bars, he began swinging again.

When he'd built up enough momentum, he slammed

his heels against the cell door with more violence than before. The door leaped in its frame, the lock making a *ching*ing sound like coins being dropped on a floor.

Bunching his lips, his face brick red, purple veins swelling in his forehead, he again swung himself back and forth from the ceiling. He cursed loudly as, with every ounce of energy he had in his two-hundred-plus pounds, he hammered his boots against the door.

It popped open with a metallic bark and slammed against the door of the cell with the loot in it. The entire building jumped. A chunk of the rusted locking bolt skidded across the floor before resting up against a leg of the cold woodstove.

Yakima looked around for a weapon. All he could see was a badly rusted Dickson Nelson Mississippi rifle, likely without a patch box, and an octagonal-barreled Sharps carbine with a stock wrapped in rawhide chained to the gun rack on the wall over Burkholder's desk. The chain was thick, the padlock stout. No point in trying for either weapon.

Yakima looked through the desk, rummaging around but finding nothing but empty bottles, ancient wanted circulars, court and tax registers, cigar stubs, a mummified mouse, and other bits of the dead marshal's past. There were a few cartridges of various calibers, but no pistols.

He had a clear mental image of his own Colt and Yellowboy lying out in front of the church. There was no way they were still there. Tully or Thunder Dodd had probably retrieved them. Or . . .

A little nerve of hope sparked in Yakima's heart.

Had Ramsay gone back to pick them up, to keep

them from being buried under a foot of fresh snow? The woman obviously knew the value of good weapons, and there were likely no better-quality or -maintained firearms in Dead River. If she hadn't retrieved them, someone else likely had.

There was only one way to find out.

He opened the jailhouse door and peered out into the storm. The afternoon was waning. The fading light and dancing snow curtains made it impossible for him to see more than thirty yards beyond the jailhouse porch. He shuddered to the wind's cold lash and stepped outside, drawing the door closed behind him.

Continuing to look around, he trudged down the snow-mantled steps and turned right, jogging through a large drift. He didn't know the town well enough to travel very efficiently in a near whiteout at times, but after several minutes of blind fumbling through the knee-deep snow, and falling twice after tripping over buried trash and firewood, he found himself hunkered low against the west wall of the Wild Coyote, between the saloon and the harness shop beside it.

Lights fell from the saloon's big front window onto its front gallery, faintly illuminating the street. Abernathy's furniture shop—where Saul had also apparently built coffins and likely served as undertaker, as many carpenters did—sat across the street from the Coyote, and about fifty yards in the opposite direction from Yakima.

The half-breed kept his head low as he started toward the furniture shop and the several shadows jostling through the buffeting snow veils, heading toward the saloon. They were mere ghostly figures for nearly a minute. As they came closer, Yakima could see two men working their way through the snowdrifts while hauling a body between them.

They moved nearly side by side, one fur-clad figure carrying the arms of what had apparently been Kelly's accomplice, Saul Abernathy. The other man had hold of the dead man's ankles.

Behind them came several more figures. One Yakima recognized as Kelly in his blue wool coat and Stetson, which he'd tied to his head with a red knit scarf. The other, walking a little behind and to one side of the rogue sheriff, was a shorter, bent figure obviously in skirts. That would be Ma Abernathy, Saul's pious mother and not-so-adept keeper of her wayward son's soul.

As Yakima watched, the woman dropped to a knee in a drift. The wind tore a wail from the woman's lips—an agonized outburst against the weather as well as her son's murder. Kelly swung around, helped the woman to her feet, and began guiding her by an elbow on over to the Wild Coyote, which had become the town's morgue in the wake of so many murders.

As the body bearers and the old woman and Kelly mounted the saloon's steps and drifted on out of Yakima's view, the half-breed was struck by the sudden realization that another murder had been committed. When he'd first heard Tully tell Kelly that Abernathy had been killed, he'd been so thrilled at having escaped imminent death at the maw of the rogue sheriff's carbine, and amused at the irony of Kelly's cohort's demise, that he hadn't stopped to marvel at the news.

Kelly's confession had seemed to clear up the

killings. Abernathy had done the dirty deeds. Now, however, in light of the carpenter's own murder, it seemed likely he wasn't the only one slinging lead around the storm-battered town of Dead River.

Yakima ran a snowy sleeve across his face, as though to clear his mind of its deep befuddlement. Too many questions for an unarmed man on the run. He had to focus on staying ahead of Kelly until he could get his hands on a weapon or two, then go stalking the sheriff as the sheriff had stalked him.

He stepped out from the gap between the buildings, then, angling left, jogged heavily through the deepening drifts to the other side of the street. Once there, he headed down a break between the dark Canon House and the low building beside it and, ten minutes later, jogged up to Ramsay's small, neat shack, the walls of which creaked like the hull of a clipper ship in a storm-tossed sea. Several curtained windows on the bottom story shone with saffron lamplight.

Yakima took the steps two at a time. He'd just gained the porch when she shouted behind him, *"Hold it right there!"*

Yakima stopped, turned slowly. She stood near the bottom of the steps in her heavy, snow-laden coat and buffeting skirts, her red cap on her head. Her hair blew around her head and shoulders in the wind. In her gloved hands was her double-barreled shotgun. The fingers on her right hand glove had been removed to make it easier to shoot.

Yakima stared at her, sliding his gaze between the pale, grim oval of her face beneath the hat, to the gun she held unwaveringly in her strong arms. He felt himself gulp against a burst of buckshot he suddenly felt was imminent.

Just as Abernathy and maybe Sheriff Darling had in their last eye wink of life?

Was Ramsay Kane the shotgun murderer?

Slowly, his heart thudding, Yakima raised his hands to his shoulders. "I'm not armed."

"How'd you get out of jail?"

Yakima blinked, glanced at the gun she held so firmly in her hands despite the wind, then lifted his gaze once more to her calm, long eyes—a predator's eyes. "Where you been?"

"Never mind where I've been. How'd you get out of jail?"

He suddenly felt a wave of dark apprehension. Maybe coming here hadn't been such a good idea. . . .

"I busted out. Kelly was gonna kill me. To keep me quiet about the stolen Douglas bank money he intended to hightail it to Mexico with all along. He had Burkholder killed." Yakima paused, the skin over his belly prickling, because that's where the woman was aiming the shotgun. "Saul did it. He threw in with Kelly."

Had Ramsay bought chips in the same game?

She shook her head once, slowly. "I don't believe you."

"Why not? Because McMasters found the loot in my horse's stall?" His frustration was tempered by wariness and the harrowing expectation of seeing flames blossom from her gut-shredder's barrels. "Hidin' it there would only stamp me a thief and a killer. That's why it was planted there. By Abernathy. So he and Kelly could lock me up with nobody around here getting suspicious about who the *real* thieving killers were. So they could get out of the canyon scot-free." Yakima paused, added tightly, "And keep me from huntin' 'em."

Yakima watched her, feeling like a bug on the end of a pin. She kept the shotgun on him. Around her, the storm raged. What was going through her mind? Maybe she was weighing the risk of her blast being heard against allowing him to live and possibly giving her and Kelly away to the others.

What others?

With Burkholder and Darling dead, who else in town would buck Kelly? Except for the mayor herself . . . unless she'd dealt herself into his game.

Suddenly, she lowered the shotgun halfway. Yakima released a half-held breath. She looked around cautiously, then jerked her chin at the front door. "Go on inside, and I'll study on it. But don't come near me. So help me, you do . . ." She raised the double-bore popper again, hardening her jaws.

Yakima turned and pushed the door open, stepping inside and pounding his boots off on the stout hemp rug before the door. He glanced behind, saw that she'd mounted the steps but had slowed down to wait for him to move on into the house. He did, tramping into the slight gap between the parlor and the kitchen area. He turned toward her, again raising his hands.

She came in, took the gun under her right arm, and closed and locked the door. Yakima felt a surge of hope sprout in him when she pulled the shade down over the window in the door's upper panel. That must mean she'd help him stay ahead of Kelly—if she found herself believing his story, that is. If not, he might get led back over to the jail at the end of her Greener.

Or maybe she'd kill him in here and call it self-defense. Who wouldn't believe her? Kelly would be as happy as a kitten with a fresh bowl of milk to see Yakima turned under.

She held the shotgun on him, wagged it toward the sparsely but homily furnished sitting area on his left. "Get in there . . . by the stove."

Still wondering where she'd come from tonight, he moved over to where a black potbelly stove shone in the light of two guttering candle lamps. The warmth emanating from the slightly ticking stove was welcoming in spite of his apprehension. "You didn't happen to fetch my guns out of the churchyard, did you?" he asked, remembering what he'd come here for in the first place.

"Do you think I'd give them to you if I had?"

"You would after you realized I hadn't taken that money."

"You can predict the future now?"

He grunted his frustration and turned to the woodstove. The heat pressed against him, instantly turning the snow on his coat to water. He unbuttoned the mackinaw, shrugged out of it, and tossed it over a chair back near the stove.

Behind him, Ramsay said, "What am I supposed to tell Kelly when he comes looking for you—which he'll no doubt do as soon as he realizes you broke out of his jail?"

"I reckon you'll tell him what you want."

He used his right boot to lever out of the heel of his

left one. He kicked the boot off, then used his cold, wet stocking foot to lever out of the other boot. Behind him, he heard a thud, like that of a gun butt being set down, and then he heard her footsteps behind him.

"Oh, Yakima!" She snaked her arms around him from behind, and he felt her body still cold from the storm press up against him, her soft cheek grinding against his back, between his shoulder blades.

He stood stiffly, facing the stove, as she pressed her hands flat against his belly. "This mean we're friends again?"

"Ah, hell," she said. "What do I care if you took the money? Look at me." She pressed her supple body harder against his. "I'm just the teacher of a dying little mountain town, and I don't even have any students to teach most of the year. As you can imagine, being mayor doesn't require a lot of my time."

There was a loud knock on the door.

Yakima jerked with a start. Ramsay jumped, dropped her hands to her coat pockets.

Yakima turned to her, grabbed her shoulders. "That's Kelly. What're you gonna do?"

She backed away from him, regaining her cool reserve. She nibbled her upper lip, swallowed, then canted her head toward the bedroom door. "Get in there. I'll get rid of him." She stared up at the half-breed, her wary eyes searching his. "I will. I'll send him on his way. Then you and I—we'll think of something."

Yakima squeezed her shoulders. "You're thinkin' with your head now, right? Not with what might or might not happen in there later?" He tipped his head toward her bedroom door, then narrowed a hard green eye at her. "The heart—or anything south of it—ain't something a soul can bank on."

The knock came again, harder this time, rattling the glass in the door's upper panel. Kelly's muffled voice: "Miss Kane!"

She curled her upper lip. "You get on in there and don't count your chickens before they hatch." She started toward the door, glanced back at him. "And leave the shotgun where it is."

Chapter 24

In his stocking feet, Yakima moved into the bedroom that, since its door had been closed, had not benefited from the woodstove's heat. A wash of blue-gray light seeped through the room's single, curtained window. He left the door open a crack, heard the front door open, even felt a draft, before Kelly's voice said, "Sorry to disturb you, Miss Kane."

"Sheriff, what on earth are you doing out in this weather?" the school-teaching mayor asked convincingly. "Come in so I can close the door!"

Yakima heard the thuds of several sets of boots, felt the reverberation through the floorboards beneath his cold, wet stocking feet. Kelly had a couple of men with him. The door closed with a thud.

"Got a problem," Kelly said, only about fifteen from Yakima now, who kept his head back behind the door as he eavesdropped. "That half-breed I rode into town with, Yakima Henry . . . he escaped from the jail. 'Fraid he's on the loose."

"Oh, no."

"Me an' Tully and Mr. Dodd here just started

scouring the town for him. Hard to track in this wind, but I did see some fairly recent tracks out front of your place. . . ."

"That was me, Sheriff. I was out trying to shovel my walk, get a handle on the snow, before I saw that it was only getting worse instead of better. I also made a trip to my shed for meat and firewood."

"No sign of Mr. Henry, then, ma'am?"

"No, I haven't seen him. And I certainly hope I don't."

That, too, was damn convincing, Yakima thought.

"I feel like such a fool," the rogue lawman said, not as convincingly. "Bringin' a man like that to this little town an' turnin' him loose. Like a damn wolf—if you'll pardon my French."

"He didn't kill Marshal Burkholder. I heard the shot that killed the marshal, and Henry was with me when I heard it."

Kelly said, "How can you know for sure that was the shot that killed Burkholder?"

Jim Tully's voice: "Who else? Done shot him through the brisket when he stole the sheriff's gold."

"The bank's gold, Tully," Kelly corrected in a voice so somber and serious that Yakima nearly snorted. "The gold of the good citizens of Douglas. Thank God I got it back. The half-breed is obviously a dangerous man, however. We have to find him or more people will die, I'm afraid."

"Wasn't him that killed Abernathy," said Dodd. "He was locked up!"

Unless she was a very polished actress, there was genuine shock in Ramsay's voice as she said, "Saul is dead now, too?"

"'Fraid there might be two killers on the loose," Kelly said.

"Sheriff, you're frightening me a little."

"Maybe you'd better come on over to the Wild Coyote," offered Tully. "Most folks are gathered there out of the storm. Miss Venora's fryin' up some elk steaks—you know, just tryin' to keep her mind off Shade."

Thunder Dodd said, "That dog eater blew him right out of the privy!"

"That's enough, fellas," Kelly gently admonished his new posse. "Miss Kane is frightened enough. We'd be happy to escort you over to the saloon. . . ."

"No, thank you. I'll be fine here. I have supper cooking, and I have my shotgun. No one gets through that door unless I say so. But thank you, men, for the offer."

The door clicked open. Yakima heard the wind, felt the icy draft. Boots thudded and the floor creaked.

Yakima glanced through the crack in the bedroom door in time to see Kelly's shoulder slip out the front door as Ramsay closed it. She threw the locking bolt and froze, facing the door, as Yakima said softly, "Best go on into the kitchen, make some coffee or somethin'. I'll stay in here for a minute, make sure they're gone."

She nodded and then casually swung away from the door and went over to the hulking black range. Yakima pulled his head back from the two-inch crack in the bedroom door, crouched down, and pressed his back against the wall, facing the gray splotch of the window on the far side of the bed that took up most of the room. As he'd expected, a shadow moved beyond the window, and suddenly the unshaven face of Jack

Kelly appeared as he removed his hat, then pushed his face closer against the glass.

Yakima dropped farther down, so that the bed concealed him. When he lifted his head again, edging a look over the bed, Kelly was gone. Yakima gave a grim smile, brushed his hand against his right thigh where his Colt revolver would normally have been.

Desperation raked him. He needed a rifle or a pistol. Anything . . .

When he figured that Kelly, Tully, and Dodd had had a good look through all the windows, he rose and went out into the main sitting room. Ramsay turned from the range where she was tending a sputtering frying pan. She said nothing as Yakima crossed the cabin to the front window behind a rocking chair and edged the curtain away from the glass with the back side of his hand.

Beyond the frosted window, three vague figures retreated through the blowing snow, the stuff on the ground bounding up against their knees as they headed back in the direction of the Wild Coyote.

"They gone?" Ramsay asked.

Yakima turned from the window. "For now."

"For what it's worth . . ." Ramsay flipped a couple of steaks in the frying pan. "I believe your story."

"What changed your mind?"

She wiped her hands on an apron she'd tied around her slender waist and full hips, and pulled two stone mugs down from a rough wooden shelf over the range. A coffeepot was simmering on the warming rack. She picked it up, filled the mugs, brought one into the sitting area.

"Kelly's not a very good actor." She came up to Yakima, extended the steaming mug to him. "That's been on the stove for a while, probably strong enough to melt a wheel hub, but you look like you could use it." She glanced at the brocade-upholstered rocking chair with oak arms carved into the shapes of rams' heads. "Have a seat. Get those wet clothes off. We'll dry them here by the stove."

As she turned toward the kitchen, Yakima grabbed her wrist. "I want to ask you a question."

She looked at him with wry expectance. He wasn't sure how to form the question so as not to offend her. Her brows furled slightly, and then she turned to look at the shotgun leaning against the kitchen wall. When she turned back to Yakima, her lips shaped a smile and her long, hazel eyes blinked.

"No, it wasn't I who killed Saul Abernathy. I've had plenty of opportunities over the past two years. I wouldn't wait to do it during the worst storm we've had this early since I came here."

She pushed her warm body up against his, rose on her toes, and pressed her lips against his. "I didn't kill Deputy Darling or any of the others, either, though I wish I had."

"Why's that?"

"Because there's a killer running around here somewhere. If not me—who?"

"You don't seem worried."

"Why should I be? I have you here." Her mouth corners lifting another oblique smile, she walked away and came back with the shotgun. She thrust it sideways at Yakima. He took the gun uncertainly, weighing it in his hands.

"There—that's proof I'm not a cold-blooded killer, isn't it?" Ramsay asked.

She turned away and walked back into the kitchen, leaving Yakima standing there holding the two-bore in his hands, feeling only a little better now about his situation. "Go on," Ramsay said as she turned the steaks once more. "Get out of those clothes. Then we'll eat and drink something and huddle away from the storm."

She turned her head to smile at him with faint flirtation. Yakima leaned the rifle against the wall, glanced out the window once more, and began shucking out of his cold, wet clothes.

Outside, the storm raged on.

Ramsay's bedroom was warm. The small stove ticked and crackled. Occasionally wood fell in the grate with a soft thud.

She straddled him atop the bed, a bobcat robe draped over her shoulders. Her hair fell down, framing the pale oval of her face. He massaged her breasts and groaned as, straddling him, impaling herself on him, she rose and fell on her knees.

Her warm, sweat-damp breasts were heavy and sloping, gently jostling as she made love to him. As she moved faster, sighing, shuddering, she clamped her own hand over one of his on her breasts, pressed one against his throat so hard that he could barely get a breath down his windpipe, then tipped her head back and gave a long, ululating moan of fulfilled desire.

After a time, she sagged onto the bed beside him and lay curled against him, soft and silent as a cat. He knew she wasn't asleep, because he could feel the gentle brush of her lashes against his side, beneath his armpit, when she blinked her eyes.

He lay as silent as she, listening to the storm. The glow of the coals was a restful umber light around the edges of the stove doors. Still, a faint apprehension clawed at his spine. Not altogether an unpleasant feeling. Thrilling, in an odd, carnal way. He touched his throat, wondered in the back of his mind if, in the back of her own mind, she wanted to kill him.

The shotgun leaned against the wall near the stove, about the same distance from each one of them.

Yakima sat up, dropped his feet to the floor, and walked over to the window, parted the curtains, and looked out at the storm-tossed gray-black night.

"Come back," she said, rolling onto her side, facing him, and resting her head on the heel of her hand. "I'm cold."

"I doubt that."

"Lonely, then."

Staring out at the storm, he could vaguely see the window lights of Preacher Ekdahl's lodge. The gusts wiped them out, like the lights of a ship rising and falling on sea swells. "Tell me about that school over there. Ekdahl's School for Wayward Children, or whatever it is."

"What do you want to know?"

"How'd it get started? How come it's not still going?"

"Oh," she said in mild surprise. "I guess you know nothing about it."

Yakima turned to her, saw the ambient light from the window touch her light gray eyes in the darkness there amidst the quilts and animal skins. "Ekdahl started it close to twenty years ago now, before my father, brothers, and I came to Dead River. When Dead River wasn't much more than a handful of mining cabins, tent supply shacks, and the Wild Coyote."

"The saloon's been around awhile, I take it."

"Oh, yes. The original building was closer to the creek, where most of the activity occurred before the gold gave out. A big, sprawling place, long since burned down, taking a lot of the girls with it. Miss Venora made it out alive, and rebuilt it here, sort of making it the cornerstone of the new town.

"But back before it burned down, it was twice as big. At one time, Miss Venora had thirty girls working for her—Russians, French girls, English, Chinese, Mexicans. And as you might expect, some of them—quite a few, actually—found themselves in the family way. Soon, our fair town was overrun with fatherless, and mostly motherless, children.

"That's when Preacher Ekdahl, who originally came here to prospect for himself and hold Sunday services out of a tent shack down along the creek, was informed by his Lord and Savior that he should build a school for these children, and the citizens of Dead River should pay for the school as well as the church with a special 'fornication tax.'"

"Huh?"

Ramsay gave a wry chuckle. "The city council approved the fornication tax, and the lodge was built. All the bastard children of the upstanding men and the low-standing whores of Dead River were sent there to be taught in the ways of Christianity by Preacher Ekdahl and Ma Abernathy."

"Ma worked with the preacher?"

"She cooked and cleaned for him and the children for several years."

"So, what happened to the school?"

Ramsay rolled onto her back with a sigh. "The population dwindled, as it's still dwindling. When most of the children reached a certain age, they simply left. Then, as of about three years ago, there were no more children."

"Were you ever one of those children?"

"No. I lived down by the creek with my father and my only brother who made it home from the war, until my father died of a heart stroke and my brother, Elm, turned his wolf loose, as they say on the frontier." She drew a deep, plaintive breath. "Haven't seen hide nor hair of him since he left, which leads me to believe he's either dead or in prison."

A brief pause.

"I took up school teaching to get by, though there aren't many students anymore. Haven't been for a couple of years. Became mayor just last year, and that brings in ten dollars a month, though something tells me the town is right now on its very last legs."

"Don't tell me you're a soothsayer, like Ma."

"Ma's full of shit. She doesn't like Mexicans or Indians or even Irishman or men with mustaches. Only her depraved son, who I hope is right now burning in the everlasting butane flames of hell, and Preacher Ekdahl."

Yakima snorted. He thought through all that he'd

heard, and then he asked, "Alta Banos was one of those children at the school?"

"That's right. She left with Christian Banos a couple of years ago. Quite a few of the girls and the boys from the school paired up—in spite of the reverend's best efforts at keeping them apart. Christian had been abandoned at the church by a Mexican sheepherder whose wife had died. The boy couldn't have been more than five. Even after joining the school, he ran around town, delivering newspapers and running errands for the shopkeepers."

Yakima went over to the stove and opened its single, square door. Staring in at the glowing coals, he said, "I found a grave on the northern ridge yonder. Above those three cabins."

"Good Lord, what were you doing up there?"

"I found a baby in an ammo box. A very small child. I said 'a grave' but it was only covered up with rocks. A cairn, I guess."

"That's probably not the only one out there."

Yakima took a small shovel and scooped some coal into the stove. He watched the fire flame up, then returned the scoop to the coal box and closed the door. He sagged down on the edge of the bed, staring at the ticking stove, remembering Alta stealing away through the cedars to the other grave behind the preacher's lodge.

"I bet it ain't."

Neither he nor she said anything for a time. He heard her move a little behind him, the bedcovers rustling slightly. Her voice was very low, pensive. "Every town has its secrets."

"Like kids buryin' their own kids in the hills here an' there?"

"Darker secrets."

Yakima glanced at her behind him. She was sitting up in the bed now, her blankets drawn up to just above her breasts. She had her arms outside the covers, one hand pulling at the index finger of the other.

"There was a rumor many years ago that some of those babies buried here and there about the hills were . . ." She let her voice trail off so that all Yakima could hear now was the crackling inside the iron stove and the windblown snow. He waited.

Ramsay's voice was low, with a hard edge, as she said, "That they were fathered by old Ekdahl himself."

Yakima stared at her. He felt something drop in him, like a stone shifting at the bottom of a quiet lake. He looked toward the window, saw the distant lights of the preacher's lodge through the curtain. He only vaguely saw the lights, however. In his mind, he was watching Alta Banos walk out to the little mound in the pines far back of the church.

It took Yakima a few moments to digest that additional bit of repelling information. "So, the son of a bitch wouldn't allow even his own children be buried in the churchyard. . . ."

"Wouldn't allow them even to get born."

Yakima felt his chest rise and fall slowly as he watched Ramsay's silhouette against the plain pine headboard.

"Ma Abernathy was a real hand at that sort of thing."

"At what sort of thing?"

"At making sure none of the seed that was planted at Ekdahl's lodge—be it by the preacher or any of the other males about the place—ever came to fruition."

A scream rose in Yakima's ears.

No, not in his ears. From outside.

Outside, someone was screaming.

Chapter 25

Ramsay said in a hushed voice, "What was that?"

Yakima held his breath as he pricked his ears to listen, wondering if what they'd both heard had only been a trick of the wind.

The scream came again. It was more like a loud sob from far away, wind-obscured and pleading. He ran over to the window and looked out, unable to see much of anything but darkness and the paleness of snow on the ground and in the air. The lights of the preacher's lodge appeared even fainter than before.

Yakima grabbed the shotgun, paused at the bedroom door. "This loaded?"

Sitting straight up in bed, holding the covers over her breasts, Ramsay nodded. Yakima dashed out through the open door. His clothes were draped over the backs of two kitchen chairs fronting the woodstove. He set the shotgun down and stepped into his long-handles, socks, and boots, then grabbed the shotgun. Ramsay stood in the bedroom doorway, a lion skin wrapped around her naked body.

"Be careful," she said in a thin, breathless voice.

Wishing like hell he had his Yellowboy, Yakima unlocked the front door, opened it a crack, and peered out. He couldn't see much more than he'd seen from the bedroom window. He went out into the snow that had piled up on the porch and pulled the door closed behind him. Slogging through the calf-deep snow, he moved down the porch steps and out into the yard, looking northward, in the direction from which the screams had come—if they really had been screams, and not the wind.

As his eyes became more accustomed to the darkness, he thought he saw something in the snow about fifty yards ahead of him. It looked like a small figure in silhouette against the snow. It didn't seem to be moving.

Looking around cautiously, hefting the shotgun in both hands and thumbing both hammers back to full cock—whatever was happening out here could be a trap that Kelly was setting for him—he moved slowly ahead, lifting one boot at a time and setting it down firmly in the sugary powder before lifting the other one. Beyond the slumped, dark figure, the lights of the preacher's lodge winked dully behind the blowing snow veils, like matches snuffed and then lit again. The slanting, driving snow gave them the illusion of movement.

Yakima was ten feet from the figure when he saw the long black hair blowing in the wind, the end of the blankets wrapped around the young woman's body flapping like bird's wings.

"Alta!"

His own voice sounded like someone else's, far away, as he dashed to the girl. As he dropped the shotgun and placed his hands on her shoulders, he felt a cold wetness against his right palm.

"Alta," he said again as he gently lifted her.

She tensed her shoulders as he scooped her out of the snow. She muttered something he couldn't hear. Awkwardly, his boots slipping and sliding, he managed to snake his arms beneath her and, cradling her against his chest, turned and began walking back toward the house.

The cold wind battered him, bit him bone-deep. It ripped the breath from his lungs. As he slogged through the snow, Alta's hair blew against his face, and inexplicably he found himself remembering the slightly gamey, alluring smell of her from the night they'd spent together—that long, long-ago night—on the floor of her shack before the fire.

He mounted the steps. The front door opened, and Ramsay stepped back in the dark house as she held the door wide. Yakima stumbled through it.

"My God—who is it?"

"Alta."

"Jesus, she must be frozen!"

"I think she's got bigger problems than that."

Ramsay closed the door and hurried around Yakima toward the bedroom's open door. "Bring her in here. I'll light a lamp."

Yakima eased Alta, who was moaning and slowly shaking her head, onto the bed. "I left the shotgun outside," he said as Ramsay lifted the mantle from a candle lamp on the room's small dresser. "I'm gonna fetch it."

"What was she *doing* out there?" Ramsay exclaimed from the bedroom as Yakima headed for the front door.

Yakima moved outside once more, stopping at the bottom of the porch steps and looking around. All he could see were the shifting shapes of the school and a few abandoned shacks around Ramsay's house. And the mysteriously shifting lights of the lodge.

He dug around in the snow where he'd found Alta, and finally wrapped his hands around the shotgun. He depressed the hammers, looking around once more, icy fingers of apprehension raking his spine, then returned to the house. Inside, he leaned the shotgun against the living room wall, near the stove, and then went into the bedroom.

The lamp shone on the dresser, its watery light flickering throughout the room. Ramsay wore only the skin over her otherwise naked shoulders as she sat on the bed beside Alta, whom she'd rolled onto her side. She was peeling the sleeve of Alta's cream, muslin day dress down off her right shoulder. The dress was slick with fresh blood that glistened in the lamplight.

Alta shivered and groaned, turning her head from side to side painfully.

Ramsay glanced at Yakima. "Look at this."

As she pulled more of the dress down Alta's back and arm, Yakima saw the several pellet-sized wounds in the back of her arm and across her right shoulder blade.

"Shotgun," Yakima muttered. He glanced at the double-bore he still held in his hands.

"She's in shock. We have to get those pellets out and get these wounds dressed."

"Should I fetch the doc?"

Ramsay shook her head. "In this weather, it would take too much time. I'll try my hand at it, and we can bring him in when the storm breaks." She looked at

Yakima again. "Will you build up the fires and put water on the range? I'll get these clothes off her and try to get her warm."

He hurried out and built up the fire in both the parlor stove and the kitchen range, scooping water from a wood bucket into an iron stewpot and setting the pot on the range. As the water began to heat, he looked out the kitchen window toward the lodge. Thoughts swirled.

What the hell had happened up there?

Who had shot Alta? Why?

He wanted to backtrack the Mexican girl, but first he had to help Ramsay get those pellets out of her back.

Ramsay called to him. He went to the bedroom, where the mayor of Dead River had finished stripping Alta, who lay facedown on the bed now while Ramsay inspected the dozen or so bloody pellet wounds extending down toward her right buttock.

"She said something about the reverend," Ramsay said, casting Yakima an anxious look while Alta's blue-tinged lips moved as she muttered and flickered her eyelids.

"No, Preacher!" Alta said now, in a fear-pitched voice, shaking her head, her face toward Yakima on Ramsay's pillow.

Yakima dropped to a knee beside the girl, placed a hand on her head, smoothing her hair back from her round, pale cheeks. "Alta, what about the preacher? Did he do this to you?"

Her eyes opened suddenly. They blazed fearfully at Yakima, but then the lids narrowed slightly, and her breathing grew more slow and regular. She clenched one small brown fist tightly in front of her chin.

"Yak . . ." She seemed too weak and chilled to continue.

"That's right, Alta—it's me, Yakima." He continued running his hand over her hair, now damp after the snow in it had melted. She was shivering, blue-brown lips quivering. "What happened up at the lodge? Who shot you? Was it Ekdahl? Was it the preacher?"

She stared at him, but it was as though she no longer saw him. Suddenly, her eyelids drooped down by small increments over her eyes.

Yakima touched her shoulder, gave her a little shake. "Alta?"

Ramsay placed a hand on the back of his neck. "She's in shock. I don't know if it's from the wounds, the cold, or what she saw up there."

Yakima stared down at the girl, who had fallen into what appeared a deep slumber though her shoulders continued to quiver as she made small groaning sounds through her twitching lips. "I'm gonna have to go up there."

"What about Kelly? If you run into him . . ." Ramsay let her voice trail off, then frowned. "You don't suppose he has anything to do with this, do you?"

Yakima sighed and rose heavily, numb with confusion and rage at whoever had done this to Alta. Whoever had shot her had obviously done so from a fair distance, because of the broad pattern of the pellets, and while she'd been trying to get away.

"I wouldn't put anything past Kelly," Yakima said, running a frustrated hand through his hair. "But you heard her as well I did—it was Ekdahl's name she was sayin'."

Ramsay wrapped an arm around his waist. "I think you should wait till the storm clears."

Slowly, Yakima shook his head. "Whoever did this might be gone by then. Or holed up. Time to end this thing—whatever the hell is goin' on around Dead River—and Kelly, too, if he's a part of it—right now. Tonight."

He left the house while Ramsay was plucking buckshot out of Alta's back, having forced enough whiskey down the girl's throat to dull the pain and keep her out. Against Ramsay's objections, he'd left the shotgun with her, in case the killer or killers got past him and came to the house.

Now as he moved off the snowy porch steps, he shoved the woman's old Rebel-model cap-and-ball revolver into his coat pocket and headed northward, following Alta's ragged but quickly disappearing tracks through the fresh powder. As he walked, he looked around him carefully and kept his ears pricked, though in this wind he doubted he'd hear anyone stalking him until they were nearly on top of him.

At the edge of town and on the buried trail to the lodge, he glanced over his right shoulder.

The only lights in the town were the glowing front- and second-story windows of the Wild Coyote. The other buildings were black and forlorn looking in the howling storm. Ahead, the preacher's lodge's windows shimmered through the ruffling veils of falling snow.

Yakima continued forward, following Alta's tracks

until they disappeared just past the dark church, whose bell he could hear clanging dully in the bell tower. Hunched against the wind, he stopped to dig the gun out of his pocket and look around.

Nothing but the stormy darkness again.

Ahead, the lodge was a blocky, velvet outline punctuated by rectangular yellow-red lights. As he moved closer, he could hear its timbers creak, hear the snow pelting its walls like sand.

Slowly, he approached the sprawling building, not so much stepping through the snow now as heaving his legs through it. It made for slow, hard going, and by the time he'd gained the top of the porch steps, he was out of breath, his lungs burning as though he'd swallowed fire.

He pressed a shoulder against the wall left of the heavy timbered doors, and leaned forward, hands on his knees, sucking deep lungfuls of air. When his heart had finally slowed its hammering, he tripped the heavy latch and was only mildly surprised to feel it give easily, to hear the latch click, and the door to move inward against his gentle thrust.

Holding the revolver up close to his chest, barrel raised, he stepped slowly inside the big house's broad foyer and quickly closed the door by its carved wooden handle, easing the latch home. He didn't know why he'd taken care with the latch, because anyone near would know the door had come open by the draft and the sudden loudening of the wind's howl. But he felt the need to be as furtive as possible.

He stood in the broad foyer with its heavy ceiling

beams, listening. Down the hall ahead, a light shone from the right. The walls creaked and he could hear the muffled gusts and eerie mewls of the untethered wind, like enraged, unearthly monsters flying about the town. Fear clawed at the half-breed, for he sensed something beyond the usual norm of wickedness here in Dead River. And from what he'd seen so far, much of the evil originated here in this big, empty house.

He walked slowly down the hall, wincing at the soft thuds of his boots on the floor. There was a closed door at the hall's far end. On the walls around him were game trophies including elk and mountain goats, and over the broad open doorway that led to the house's big parlor area, a grizzly bared its savage fangs.

Yakima clicked the pistol's hammer back and turned into the doorway, extending the pistol out in front of him. The big room with all its heavy leather and oak furniture, and the countless shelves slouching under the weight of many tomes, appeared empty. But a half dozen gas and candle lamps were lit, and a fire blazed in the hearth.

Keeping his thumb on the old pistol's cocked hammer, he entered the long, L-shaped room, walking straight ahead past a map table on his right and the giant, crackling stone hearth on his left. When he came to the base of the L, at the room's far end, he saw a balcony above him, and several doors—some open, some not.

The balcony and the doors didn't interest him half as much, though, as did the man hanging from the balcony rail.

Chapter 26

The rope's end was tied around the base of the rail, the noose at the other end digging into Preacher Ekdahl's weathered neck and cutting off the blood supply to his head. He was dressed as Yakima had seen him before—a ratty, ankle-length buffalo robe over a black shirt and white collar, with wash-worn broadcloth trousers, their knees so worn they appeared yellow, cuffs tucked into the tops of lace-up boots.

The man's neck appeared broken, as his head was tipped at an odd angle. He turned very slowly from left to right on the faintly creaking rope. There must have been some life left in the man, because his boots were twitching just enough to give his long, gaunt body some bounce at the end of the rope, and to keep him turning.

When he'd turned a full circle and was once again facing Yakima, the man's eyelids fell halfway down his eyes and stopped. The light reflected from the half dozen bracket lamps in the room lost its sharpness. His left boot toe rose and fell and grew still.

There was a chair on the floor beneath Ekdahl—one

of those strange chairs with an S-shaped back and in which two people could sit at the same time, facing opposite directions. It lay on its side, only one of its two spruce green brocade-upholstered seats facing up.

Yakima looked up at the balcony again, with its pine-paneled walls and several doors. Was the killer in one of those?

He glanced back the way he had come, then looked at the two closed doors beyond Ekdahl, and then at the balcony once more. He ran his tongue across the underside of his upper lip and then called, "Kelly?" His voice echoed weirdly in the high-ceilinged, two-story room.

Only the creaking walls and crackling, wheezing fire answered.

He figured the stairs beyond the closed door at the end of the foyer would take him up to the balcony, as they also led, by a twisting route, to the two dormlike rooms in which the preacher's orphans had been sequestered. But the two closed doors ahead of him seemed to beckon him, so he continued forward, ducking beneath the preacher's nearly still boots.

He turned the knob on the right-side door and opened it. He paused for a few seconds. Then, when no shotgun blasted from within, he stepped inside and put his back to the left wall. He looked around the room—an office, with a big, hide-covered desk—lit by several more lamps, including a green-shaded Tiffany lamp on the desk itself. There were more books in here, all of a religious nature, judging by the gold- or silver-embossed titles on the spines.

There was more of the same furniture as that in the

parlor, only less of it, but with a long leather sofa along the wall on the room's far side, under a large oil painting of a naked Mother Mary with a halo around her head, and the naked baby Jesus in her arms. Several hide-and-fur-covered pillows were arranged on the couch, and three colorful afghans were draped over the scrolled mahogany back.

The afghans and everything else in the room were dull with dust and tattered with age. Cobwebs hung from the antlered elk head mounted beside the window flanking the desk on which only the lamp, a penholder, an inkbottle, and a carved cherry cuspidor sat.

Yakima took in the room in less than a minute, deeming it empty. But then he gave the brunt of his attention to a wooden ladder angling up through an open trapdoor in the ceiling on the room's far left side. Slowly, keeping a cautious eye on the rest of the room, Yakima walked over to the ladder.

With his pistol in one hand, he placed both hands on the ladder and gazed up into the open door, unable to see anything but darkness. In the room to which the door led, no lamp had been lit. The smell of dust and pent-up air emanated from the hole, as though it had been closed for a long time.

Until now.

Yakima grabbed a hurricane lamp from a bookcase and held it high against the ladder. The light caressed a low, steeply pitched ceiling bearing what appeared to be carved initials and pine knots. He tested the ladder. It creaked but seemed steady enough. Holding the lamp in one hand, the old Colt in the other, he climbed the stairs, wincing a little as he raised the lamp and his head up through the door.

He stopped at the top of the ladder and looked down a long room with a good dozen bunks and the spitting image of the room Kelly had occupied. Or maybe this was the same room. Was Yakima only seeing it from a different vantage?

Again, he called Kelly's name. Receiving no reply, he climbed off the ladder and into the room, ducking his head beneath the steeply pitched roof. Holding the lantern in one hand, the pistol in the other, he walked down the narrow center aisle between the twin rows of cots, a sick feeling, as though he'd chugged a quart of sour milk, building in him.

No, this wasn't the same room that Kelly had been holed up in. This had to be the one opposite that room— the girls' room.

The trapdoor led up from the preacher's office to the girls' room.

Christ, what in God's blue hell has been going on here?

Yakima walked down the middle of the room, swinging his head from side to side, inspecting the cots that were all made up with wool blankets and quilts and corn-husk-filled pillows covered in blue-striped ticking, though none of the cots had apparently been slept in for a long time.

Dust lay over everything. The wind gusts from outside permeated the cracks in the walls and the ceiling, and churned the dust so that Yakima felt it tickle his nose. There was the smell of old sweat, piss, and mouse droppings.

Hanging cobwebs jounced. He felt them sticking to

his face and neck as he walked, burning against the lantern he held high in his left hand.

Halfway down the room, he stopped and peered into the shadows at its other end. The door to the hall at the top of the stairs was half-open. Raked with apprehension, anticipating a gun blast at any time, Yakima stared at the half-open door. He had the feeling he'd been led up here for some reason. Either into a trap or . . . maybe he was being given a tour of the preacher's diabolical world.

Slowly, he shoved his head through the door. The hall outside was empty. The stairwell dropped to his right into dangerous darkness. Yakima stepped out of the girls' room and into the hall, and held the lantern out over the narrow incline of the stairs, the fluttering, red-pink illumination tumbling like water onto the landing about ten feet below.

No one was there. Yakima saw a mouse scuttle against the landing's far wall and pull its wiry tail into a hole. He heard it scratching around in there, and then, except for the wind outside and the ceaselessly complaining timbers, silence.

The door on the opposite side of the hall was half-open—again as though someone were inviting Yakima inside. He swallowed, swung the pistol toward the opening, and then stepped through, lifting the lantern high. His throat was dry with apprehension.

He could be walking into an ambush; anytime, a gun could flash in front of him. But he was too deep in the house, too enmeshed in its grisly secrets, to stop now. Besides, whoever was beckoning to him was likely the person who'd shot Alta. And likely others . . .

He stopped at Kelly's cot. The only sign of Kelly was the recent indentation in the first of the two pillows propped against the wall at the head of the cot. The blankets were thrown back, the blood-spotted sheets beneath them mussed.

Kelly's gear was gone.

Yakima raised the lantern again and turned a full circle to scrutinize the room, the lantern's light shouldering shadows across the low-ceilinged space. Yakima's breath puffed in front of his face. Even with heat rising through the steel grate in the floor, it was damn cold up here. The kids that had been sequestered up here must have been awful cold in the winters.

Imprisoned and likely terrorized by the crazy preacher stalking around in the house below them, making his forbidden forays into the girls' room. For what? Yakima heard himself blow a bitter breath through his nose.

What other reason could there have been?

Yakima was about to head back to the hall door when something about ten feet beyond Kelly's cot captured his attention. He walked over, lowering the lantern. He crouched beside the open trapdoor, the door itself lying flat against the floor to the left of the opening. A ladder angled into the dark room below the square hole.

Yakima's heart fluttered.

He dropped to both knees, lowered the lantern through the opening in the floor, seeing only a rug and wainscoted walls below. He looked around the room he was in—the boys' dormitory. The sick feeling returned in earnest, and his heart hiccupped, hammered his breastbone for several beats.

"What in Christ's name . . . ?" he heard himself whisper.

The scent of smoke touched his nose. The fire in the hearth? No. This smoke wasn't carrying the smell of burning pine, but more of a stench, like burning trash. It was the smoke of burning varnish and fabric. And it seemed to be getting stronger, making Yakima's eyes burn.

He lowered the lantern through the hole and looked around the room below the boys' dormitory—a large room outfitted with a bed, several dressers, a standing mirror, and a stout armoire.

The preacher's bedroom.

The lantern light flashed in the mirror and glistened off the open door at the room's far end, near the big bed covered with curly mountain goat hides and fronted by a scrolled wooden headboard carved with the figures of winged angels.

The room appeared empty.

Yakima dropped down the ladder into the room and walked toward the front door, seeing the ghostly wisps of smoke drifting through the opening to be burnished by the lantern's light. Holding the lantern high, he moved slowly through the open doorway.

He found himself in a broad hall. To his right was a painting of a gray-bearded man in a white robe holding a gold staff while smiling down on children and newborn lambs and spotted calves—all lounging together in a jade green field with mountains all around.

Yakima, getting his bearings, recognized the door beyond the painting as the entrance to the preacher's office. The preacher himself was hanging about thirty feet beyond Yakima, though all the half-breed could see of the man were his lower legs clad in shabby broadlcloth, and his scuffed, lace-up boots that had finally fallen still.

The smoke was getting thicker. It seemed to be coming from several directions.

Yakima hurried ahead, ducked beneath the preacher's boots as he strode into the L-shaped parlor and turned the corner toward the lodge's front door. He stopped suddenly.

A big figure stood before him, at the other end of the room. Flames leaped around the man, and now Yakima could smell the stench of burning kerosene, see the fire dancing above the sheen of liquid on the floor near the big man's boots.

The man was silhouetted against the flames though Yakima could see the fire's reflection in his eyes.

The man's shoulders jerked. He raised something in his hands. Yakima dove to his own left as the shotgun boomed, angry flames jabbing from its twin maws. The half-breed felt the bites of several hot pellets in his right side as he hit the floor, his head glancing off a stout table leg.

The impact aggravated the other sundry bruises his skull had endured over the past couple of days. Pain chewed into his jaws and down his throat. The floor beneath him swam. Groaning, he rolled onto his back, wincing against the renewed pain in his head as well as the hot bites of the buckshot in his side.

His eyelids fluttered until they opened halfway. He stared straight up to see the shotgun's twin maws drop down toward his face. He could smell the cordite and the hot iron. The maws, only inches from his face now, were as large as twin indigo mountain pools.

He slid his gaze up along the double-bore's tarnished barrels to see thick hands in fingerless wool gloves gripping the stock. A bearded face loomed above the hands, near the neck of the scratched walnut stock. The cinnamon beard spread, opening the thick red lips. Yellow teeth glistened in a malignant sneer. A gold eyetooth flashed.

Yakima tried to reach for the shotgun, but his arms felt like lead.

Then his eyes closed. The back of his head hit the floor. Just before spiraling into unconsciousness, he was aware of a vague satisfaction at not giving his killer the pleasure of his being conscious for his own murder.

Chapter 27

A thunderous explosion told Yakima that he'd been conscious for the shotgun's detonation, after all. Intense heat beat against him. There was the breathy roar of leaping, prancing flames.

Was he in hell?

Coughing on the fetid smoke that filled his nostrils like dirty gauze, he lifted his head and opened his eyes. No, he wasn't in hell unless hell was the preacher's sprawling lodge that had been a hellish prison for "wayward" children not so long ago. Tully must have figured he was dead or wanted to leave him a painful, fiery death in the lodge. The explosion he'd heard was a ceiling beam falling at an angle to land about six feet away from him, flames leaping all around it, smoke broiling toward the ceiling.

The smoke was so thick that it caused tears to stream from Yakima's eyes. He tried to suck a breath, but his lungs were pinched and burning. What had saved him from asphyxiation, he absently realized, was having been passed out on the floor where the last bit of oxygen in the room was still lurking. But it was burning up fast.

His battered head pounding, Yakima heaved himself onto all fours. He grabbed his hat and began crawling toward the preacher's office, seeing the shadow of Ekdahl himself dangling from the balcony rail over the doorway. Yakima glanced up as he approached the man. The man's white collar glowed brightly. Red flames danced in the man's dead eyes.

Yakima crawled into the preacher's office just as one end of a broad beam ripped out of the ceiling and slammed into the floor, making the whole house jump. The balcony rail gave way; the rail and Ekdahl tumbled into the flame-engulfed parlor. Flames like glowing orange snakes coiled and uncoiled along the beam's upper edge. The entire second story of the place must have been engulfed in the fire that the bearded man had set. That's all he been able to tell about the man—that he was big and bearded.

A curtained window showed in the wall beyond the preacher's desk. Yakima grabbed a chair and, gritting his teeth, slammed the chair through the window. Glass clattered. Instantly, he felt the draft of the storm. Like maniacal giants, the flames behind him howled as they sucked at the fresh oxygen for strength. They grew by leaps and bounds and came roaring toward Yakima like a locomotive on a steep downgrade.

Yakima leaped onto the preacher's desk and dove through the window, tearing through the curtains and the remnants of glass clinging to the window's edges. He hit a steep drift, and instantly his world turned from the burning butane bowels of the preacher's hell to the deep, penetrating freeze of the polar ice cap, snow slithering up his coat sleeves and down his collar.

He shuddered and sucked a breath and gagged on the snow filling his nostrils and plugging his throat.

He bounded up off his heels, spat snow from his throat, and drew a breath as he staggered out away from the house while twisting a look behind and up at it.

The entire sprawling place was ensconced in jutting, slithering, licking flames. They stood out in stark contrast to the dark mass of the wood and stone and the multitiered shake-shingled roof. Where boards had already disintegrated, he could see the glow of the fire that had worked its way into the house's bowels, gutting it ruthlessly and totally.

The red glow made the sky above it look even blacker than before. It made the swirling snowflakes glow like sunlit dust motes. The heat now pressed against Yakima, and he realized that the deep drifts rising to his knees were acquiring a slushy crust.

A shutter broke loose from one of the upper-story windows, came flapping down, buffeted by the wind, and landed with a crackling, burning thud in the snow near Yakima. The half-breed moved out farther away from the house, sucking breath through his gritted teeth against the pain of the several buckshot wounds in his right side and down his right leg, and circled around the place to the front.

He grabbed his right leg high up near his hip, felt the oozing blood and burning pain. Looking ahead toward the town, he wondered where the shooter was. And then he remembered that he'd dropped the old cap-and-ball revolver in the preacher's parlor.

He glanced back at the lodge that was now fully engulfed and roaring like a hundred angry lions, more shutters and timbers falling to steam and sizzle in the snowdrifts.

Again, he looked ahead. The church was lit by the fire's glow. The fire lit up the snow, and its reflected light made it even harder now to see the town beyond the church. He could, however, see dark tracks angling away from the lodge and following the snow-covered trail into Pine Street.

Would the killer try to lose himself amongst the others once more?

Yakima started forward, trudging painfully through the deep powder. A figure moved ahead of him. He stopped, flinching. Then he saw the blowing hair and buffeting skirts, and as Ramsay made her way toward him through the snow, she called his name though it sounded little louder than a chime against the wind and the fire's roar. She held her shotgun in both gloved hands and used the heavy gun to balance herself in the precarious footing.

Yakima continued forward.

"Are you all right?" she yelled, breathless, as she approached him.

"Go on back to the house!" he said, continuing forward, slightly dragging his right foot and holding his gloved right hand against one of the buckshot wounds, feeling the wetness even through the glove.

"What happened?"

"Killer's on the loose. Hanged Ekdahl. He's around here somewhere."

Trudging clumsily along beside him, she met his stare. "Kelly?"

"No." Yakima shook his head as he and Ramsay

passed the church and started down Pine Street. "No . . . wasn't Kelly. I don't know who in the hell it was." He remembered the flash of the eyetooth in the bearded face. He'd seen it before. His was too battered for the memories to come. He felt drunk. . . .

Yakima looked down the broad, snowy thoroughfare of Pine Street and the false-fronted buildings on either side. The fire reflected dimly off the gallery posts, shingles, and facades. Stormy darkness pooled beside them, hovered over them.

A million different places for the killer to hide. Yakima grabbed the woman's shoulders. "Ramsay, go on back to the house, lock the door, and stay there!"

Something sounded beneath the howling wind. Ramsay had heard it, too. She turned her head eastward along the street, her eyes narrowed against the swirling snow.

The sound came again. It sounded like a drum.

Only it wasn't a drum.

It was the killer's shotgun.

Yakima cast his gaze toward the Wild Coyote. It was too far away to see clearly in this weather, but he could see its lit windows, downstairs and up in both the front of the place and the side facing Yakima. He pulled away from Ramsay and, forgetting himself, began running toward the saloon.

"Wait!" Ramsay cried, running after him.

She thrust the shotgun at him. "Take this!"

Yakima grabbed the big double-popper. "You go on back to the house, lock up tight, and don't open the door for anyone again except me. Understand?"

She stared up at him, then slid her bright, anxious

gaze toward the saloon from which a girl's scream could be heard, ripped and battered by the unending wind. In an upper-story window, a light flashed. A shadow darted, dropped.

Yakima ran through the deep drifts that the snow had covered with a slick crust. His right side burned, and his head throbbed. He sucked air in and out of his aching lungs. Only when he reached the boardwalk fronting the saloon did he remember that he had only two shells for the double-bore.

They had to be the only two he'd need.

In one of the rooms above him, the shotgun blasted again, louder from this distance. He grabbed the knob of the closed winter door, jerked the door open, and stopped suddenly, his eyes widening in shock and horror at the carnage before him.

Slowly, he stepped inside the saloon and drew the door closed behind him. Just as slowly, he moved into the room, swinging his gaze from left to right and back again, his guts recoiling at all the blood and the strewn bodies, recognizing the staring eyes of Miss Venora, who lay beneath a table that had had the middle blown out of it.

The men—there were seven of them though it wasn't easy to count them amidst the sprawled, entangled limbs—had been forced to kneel in front of the bar, facing the room. There was the big leprechaun, Murphy, and the wolfer, Thunder Dodd, and the man whom Yakima had shot in the cheek—Jordan Tyree. The doctor lay belly-up across Tyree's legs, both Howe's soft, pudgy hands clutching the gaping hole in his chest. There were others Yakima recognized but didn't know the names of.

Some had been shotgunned. Others had been shot with a pistol or rifle.

The proprietor of the Canon House, Percy Crandall, lay near the bottom of the stairs. He must have tried to make a break for the staircase but had been cut down before he could gain the first step.

Looking around for a gun but not seeing any—the killer had apparently disarmed the men carrying guns, for the holster on Jordan Tyree's right thigh was empty, and there were no other firearms within sight—Yakima walked quietly toward the stairs.

An ominous, sepulchral silence had fallen over the place. He ran his eyes across the slats of the low ceiling—even some of those were blood-splattered—and beneath the wind he heard a creak. It had come from the second story, and Yakima saw a few bits of dust sift down from between the cracks in two ceiling slats beside a hanging kerosene chandelier.

He leaped old Crandall and climbed the stairs two steps at a time. At the first landing, the pain of the buckshot bit him hard, like sharp knives, and he had to pull himself up the second flight by the railing, wincing and grunting with every step. He gripped the shotgun's neck with his right hand, his thumb pulling back the first, rabbit-eared hammer.

He stopped at the mouth of the carpeted hall that was lit by four candle lamps guttering in the brackets on both papered walls. Two girls dressed only in underwear, one naked except for a pair of red silk panties, lay at the far end of the hall—entangled together like dead lovers. Their pale bodies glistened brightly from the blood of their many wounds.

Yakima swallowed. "Kelly?"

No response. The wind moaned.

Yakima walked ahead slowly, and checked the room from which he'd heard the floorboard creak. He found a dead Indian girl in there, along with a naked, potbellied gent with sandy muttonchops and a shocked expression on his face. He and the Indian girl had been shot with a pistol.

Yakima went out and slowly, cautiously checked out the rest of the second story. There were no more bodies here, but he found three more dead girls upstairs, the walls fairly painted with their blood. Two were alone in bed, a third had apparently been darning a stocking drawn over a chinaware egg before, hearing the commotion, she'd hid behind her bed. The killer had kicked her door open and riddled her, the stocking, and the far edge of the bed with buckshot.

Yakima walked slowly out of the room. Where was Tully? He neither saw nor heard anyone alive in the building. The wind continued to batter the building like the fists of drunken giants.

In the rooms and halls was the heavy, rotten-egg odor of cordite. Powder smoke wafted. The freshly spilled blood smelled like freshly forged iron. Yakima had seen a lot of carnage in his day, but none had equaled this. He'd never witnessed such savagery.

As he started down the stairs to check the second story once more, he heard a voice in the main saloon hall below. A female's voice, echoing softly, inquiringly. Yakima stopped, his index finger drawn taut against one of the shotgun's two eyelash triggers.

Ramsay's voice.

Yakima's heart hammered in his ears. A man's voice responded to Ramsay's, as conversationally as hers though the half-breed couldn't make out what either was saying. But then someone kicked a chair, and Ramsay exclaimed, "Oh, *God*, Jim—*why*?"

"*Ramsay!*" Yakima broke into a run down the stairs, dropping three steps at a time.

On the first landing, he stopped, raising the shotgun to his shoulder. Ramsay was near the front of the saloon hall, the door open behind her, snow blowing in. She was on the floor where she'd apparently fallen against a chair when she'd walked in and seen the carnage.

The barman, Tully, stood in front of the bar, wearing a long fur coat and a fur rabbit hat with dangling earflaps. Jim Tully held his double-bore in one hand, aiming the big blaster at Ramsay. In his other hand he held a whiskey bottle by the neck.

Yakima saw that both of the shotgun's hammers were drawn back to full cock.

Tully glanced at Yakima and grinned. The gold eyetooth flashed in the lamplight.

"Come on down here, breed. I got nothin' against Injuns . . . long as you lower that Greener." The barman turned his head toward Ramsay, who lay on the floor in front of him, her face white as the snow outside.

Again, Tully grinned. "I was just about to buy the mayor a drink. Looks like she could use one."

"Why don't we both put our blasters down?" Yakima said. "Then we can all take a seat and have a drink."

"Nah." Tully kept his shotgun aimed at Ramsay, who was still on the floor. "I like mine the way it is."

He tipped the bottle back, taking a long pull. Yakima

heard the whiskey splash against the neck of the bottle, then gurgle loudly as the big barman swung the bottle back down.

"Christ," the woman said in a pinched voice, staring at the dead men sprawled in front of the bar, on either side of Tully. "What's this all about, Jim? Why did you kill these men?"

"You're about to join 'em," Tully said with crazy menace.

Yakima started walking down the stairs, one slow step at a time. "Don't be a damn fool, Tully. She had nothing to do with what happened up at the preacher's lodge."

"Everyone in this goddamn town had somethin' to do with it," Tully said, showing his teeth like a rabid dog, his broad face reddening. "'Cause they all thought the preacher was the best goddamn thing since the invention of the spring wagon. Give all that money to the old bastard, so he could build that damn prison . . . that *torture chamber* . . . behind the church."

Tully looked at Ramsay again. As Yakima continued moving down the stairs, keeping his shotgun aimed, one-handed, at the barman, he gestured for Ramsay to rise and walk toward him.

"No one knew what was goin' on," Yakima said. "They couldn't have."

"Everybody in this goddamn town let him keep doin' what he was doin'," Tully spat, "because they didn't wanna *know* what he was doin'! Him and that bitch of his—Saul's ma. Wanted to give that old witch time to study on her son's death before I give her the same."

He laughed.

Ramsay slowly heaved herself to her feet, keeping her cautious eyes on the obviously insane barman. Yakima gained the bottom of the stairs and started weaving through the tables, toward the room's center. He wanted, ultimately, to position himself between Ramsay and Tully.

Haltingly, she said, "There were rumors . . . about him and the girls. Is that what you mean, Jim?"

"I had a little tour of the house," Yakima said, trying to buy the woman time. "Ekdahl had a trapdoor leading from his office into the girls' room above. He had another trapdoor leading from his bedroom"—he glanced at Tully, whose eyes had turned stony and bloodshot from the whiskey he'd likely been chugging for hours—"into the boys' room."

Tully scrunched his eyes closed and pursed his lips. Ramsay continued sidestepping toward Yakima.

When Tully opened his eyes again, he sidestepped toward the open front door through which the wind was blowing snow. The barman kept the double bores of that big cannon trained on Ramsay's middle. Yakima silently cursed as Tully moved on past the front door to the room's front center, sandwiching Ramsay about halfway between himself and Yakima.

Ramsay turned her body slowly, tracking Tully, holding her hands out from her sides in supplication.

"Jesus," she muttered in genuine shock. "I . . . I didn't know you were over there, Jim."

"Long time ago," the barman said, his Adam's apple bobbing in his stout neck. "I was born at Miss Venora's first place. She never did say who my ma was, just sent me over to Ekdahl. He and Ma raised me . . . till I ran away from the place. But that damn preacher followed me. No, not the man himself. But all he done to me . . . the other boys . . . and the girls. Him and that old witch mother of Saul Abernathy's."

He shook his head as though to rid his mind of a thousand barbed memories. "They wouldn't let me go. So I came back here, got a job here, in the Wild Coyote. Miss Venora didn't even reco'nize me." He chuckled, sneering, eyes glazed with long-bottled fury. "I decided to bide my time, wait for the right night, and kill every last one of the bastards and bitches holed up in this little perdition. Kill the memories."

"I don't understand," Ramsay said, her voice trembling slightly and her face blanching further as she cast a quick, disbelieving glance at the dead men sprawled before the bar. "Why . . . everyone?"

"Done told ya why. Everyone here's got blood on their hands, includin' you, pretty mayor. There was plenty o' whisperin' goin' on down here, about the lodge. Don't tell me there weren't, in a town this size."

"Fabienne?" Yakima was moving slowly to his right, to see around, possibly shoot around, Ramsay. "What'd she have to do with it?"

"She was so damn purty," Tully said, his eyes turning harder, his nostrils flaring. "Nice to me, too. But, ya see, I couldn't . . ."

He let his voice trail off, and his broad chest rose and fell quickly as a wet sheen slid down over his eyes. "And that goddamn Shade Darling thought she was his. He didn't deserve her!" A tear squeezed down from an eye corner to dribble down his cheek.

"Never could . . . with a woman, after what he done. Couldn't look at her no more and not—you know. So I killed her. Killed her after you was with her. To confuse folks, thinkin' you done it. Make 'em all easy pickin's after that. What a bunch o' stupid hoople-heads!" He sniggered through his teeth. "Killin' her's what started it all. That son of a bitch done cored me out like a goddamn apple, and you're all gonna pay!"

He slammed the butt plate of his shotgun against his hip and swung the barrels toward Ramsay.

The woman screamed and threw herself to the floor.

Yakima's double-barreled blaster exploded a half second before Tully tripped the triggers of his own gun.

The twin thunderclaps seemed to suck all the air out of the room.

The table in front of Ramsay exploded, slivers flying. Yakima's twin rounds of buckshot hammered through Tully, lifted him out of both his boots, and punched him straight back to the front of the room. He hit the window with an agonized scream, flew backward through the giant pane as though he'd been lassoed from behind, and disappeared in the snowy night.

The storm howled through the broken shards. The wind whipped the gun smoke and scattered it.

Yakima turned to Ramsay, who lay facedown on the floor, arms over her head. He went to her, dropped to a knee, set the shotgun down, and touched her arm.

She lifted her head.

"You all right?" he asked her.

She slowly climbed to her knees and stared toward

the broken window through which the wind moaned and gusted, as though through a cave mouth.

"How will I ever be?" she said after a time, her voice barely audible above the wind that blew her hair. She looked at Yakima as though only half seeing him, slowly wrapped her arms around him, and pressed her face to his chest.

"He left you alive so you'd kill him," she whispered. After a time, "Couldn't live with himself . . . any longer." She looked at Yakima in horror. "This is all the preacher's fault, isn't it?"

"I doubt he was a real preacher. Hell, I could parade around in a white collar if I was sick enough, and wanted a lodge full o' desperate children."

He snaked his arms around Ramsay's shoulders and held her tight against him, rocking her gently as she sobbed. "Oh, Jesus," she cried, mashing her head tighter against Yakima's chest, gritting her teeth. "Goddamn all of us to hell!"

Chapter 28

With the wind blowing through the shattered window, Ramsay sat at the very table that had saved her life and which wore a pumpkin-sized hole in its middle, and sipped a tall glass of whiskey.

Meanwhile, limping on his buckshot-peppered right leg, Yakima hauled in the coffins and the dead Jim Tully from outside. He fetched Ma Abernathy, whom Tully had apparently eviscerated when he'd first returned to town from the lodge. She'd made it halfway out her front door in a flannel nightgown and hair ribbons, before Tully had nearly cut the old woman in two with both barrels of his coach gun.

When all the dead were inside the saloon, Yakima went upstairs and emptied the coal oil from several lamps onto the carpeted floors. He tossed a candle lamp onto the mess and, with the fire *whush*ing and sighing and crackling behind him, limped his way back down the stairs to the main saloon hall.

He sat at the table beside Ramsay and sipped directly from her bottle. Neither said anything. Ramsay stared at the shattered window whose few remaining shards were stained with Tully's frozen blood. When the smoke began sliding down the stairs like gray, airborne snakes, Yakima corked the bottle, stuffed it into his coat pocket, then rose with a groan from his chair. He was about to wrap a hand around Ramsay's arm when he saw his prized Yellowboy repeater leaning against a curtained window on the room's far side.

Well, he'd be damned. He'd figured he'd seen the last of Ralph's trophy. The half-breed gave a rueful snort, wincing a little at the sting of the smoke now roiling down the stairs, and went over and picked up the piece. He wondered for a minute who'd saved it from the elements, and then he looked thoughtfully down at Thunder Dodd's blood-riddled corpse.

He walked back over to the bar, kicked Dodd onto his back. There, beneath the man's shaggy, thigh-length wolf coat, was Yakima's holster and shell belt. No sign of his horn-gripped .44, though. Frowning, he followed a notion outside, kicked around in the blood-slushy snow where Tully had fallen, and found the stag-gripped six-shooter on the gallery boards, near another revolver, the grips of which jutted from a pocket of Tully's coat.

The gun he'd probably killed Fabienne with, for the shotgun would have been too loud.

Finding his own weapons was the only bit of good luck the half-breed had seen tonight.

Looking around at the howling storm that peppered his eyes and slid icy hands down the back of his coat, he figured it was the last bit of good luck he'd see in a while. He wondered vaguely where Kelly was. The badge-wearing thief and killer hadn't been in the saloon. He hadn't been in the lodge, either.

Likely holed up somewhere on the shaggy outskirts of the storm-locked town with a bottle, a grin, and the twin bags of stolen loot.

Yakima slid the .44 into its holster thonged on his right thigh, rested the Yellowboy on his shoulder, and limped back into the saloon, noting his own blood tracks on the snow-dusted wood inside the door and on the heavy rugs beyond. He needed to get the holes plugged before he bled dry.

The smoke was making visibility as poor inside as out. But Ramsay remained sitting where she'd been sitting before, sipping her whiskey and staring.

"Let's get you home, girl," Yakima said, closing a hand around the woman's arm and tugging her gently to her feet.

She nodded dully, moved out around the table, and headed for the open front door. She glanced once more into the building's bloody, smoky bowels that would soon be a fitting funeral pyre for the town's dead, leaving only her, the mayor, alive, but having to remember all the bad things that had happened here, that had turned the town into a snake-infested perdition because of the unspeakable sins of one tall, fork-tailed demon in a white preacher's collar.

She nodded resignedly, turned dully toward the windy door, and wandered out into the stormy night. Both fires soon lit up the stormy, dark skies over Dead River.

* * *

The next day, at noon, the storm stopped suddenly. The clouds gradually thinned and lifted. A cold like that from deep space dropped over the town with its two black mounds of burned buildings, and the stars shone that night as though through a magnifying lens.

The day after that, the cold remained but the wind picked up, tossing the lying snow every which way and almost sweeping Pine Street clear. The cold, however, gradually lifted. A springlike warmth softened the wind that not so much melted the snow as scoured it from the earth, slowly revealing the rooftops, wood piles, trash piles, and rabbit brush it had covered. Icicles grew long from the eaves of Ramsay's cabin.

Yakima spent those days of recovery from his wounds with Ramsay and Alta Banos, in brooding isolation. Few words were shared. Alta remained in Ramsay's bedroom, healing from her own buckshot wounds, while Ramsay and Yakima slept on the parlor floor, making love not so much out of tenderness but from Ramsay's desperate need for comfort in the wake of the diabolical events for which she had not found the words to discuss.

Yakima would leave soon, and her fervent coupling with him was a way of clinging to him—the last man in Dead River—while knowing that once he was gone, she'd be alone here, unless Alta wanted to stay.

Alta had said nothing, only remained in her room in a silence even darker than Ramsay's. Ramsay dressed the girl's wounds and fed her, but they spoke little or not at all.

Before dawn of the fifth day after the fire, Yakima woke on the floor before the dead fire, hearing the front door click. He lifted his head, heard the crunch of snow outside. It dwindled gradually. Then there was only the caress of the mild breeze against the house, the sound of snowmelt dripping from the eaves, and Ramsay's quiet breaths touching his belly as she lay with her head on his chest.

Yakima frowned up at the ceiling.

"Where did she go?" Ramsay said as, a half hour later, they sat down to breakfast together.

"Reckon I'll find out."

But he knew. The day before, he'd spied a man's boot tracks in the mud outside Alta's window.

Ramsay glanced at the bedroll, saddlebags, and rifle he'd placed by the door. "You're going?"

He nodded. "You can come, too. No reason you should stay here alone."

"Alta might be back."

"Maybe."

She stared into her coffee. "This is all I have," she said with a half sigh, half groan. She raised her strong eyes to his. "I'll weather another winter. A few folks will be back in the spring."

She rose and pulled her bottle down from the shelf. "One last drink?"

When they finished breakfast and their whiskey-laced coffee, she went to him, pressed her head against his chest. He bent to kiss her, but she turned away, slipped quietly into her bedroom, and closed the door.

Yakima gathered his gear and went out to the stable behind Ramsay's shack, in which he'd stabled Wolf the morning after he'd burned the saloon, to keep the horse close for tending. Wolf was so excited at the prospect of getting back on the trail, he nearly tore the stable apart before Yakima could get him outside.

He put the horse onto Pine Street and rode south along the quiet town's vacant thoroughfare from which most of the snow had now melted, leaving large puddles in the depressions fronting the boardwalks. A warm breeze slid against him. He didn't wear his coat, but had it rolled up in his soogan. He was betting the passes were traversable now, in the wake of the melt.

He paused in front of the burned-out hulk of the Wild Coyote. Only a part of the facade stood, saved by the snow that had been falling that night, holding the fire to the confines of the saloon. The facade was fire-blackened. Behind, black and gray ash and a few charred sticks of furniture lay in several ragged heaps.

Holding Wolf to a trot, he kept his eyes on the ground, sweeping his gaze from left to right of the trail. He angled west along the main trail curving out of town along the stream of Dead River. The rushing snowmelt ruffled the glittering water as it made its way eastward down canyon.

He was just beyond the town when he discovered what he'd been looking for—the tracks of eight shod hooves swerving onto the trail from the collection of ragged shacks built along a northern fork of the stream, on the town's west edge. Two riders, one riding to the right and slightly behind the other. The tracks had turned to small mud puddles from the snowdrifts still melting along the north side of the trail.

The two riders were heading west, toward Grant's

Pass that loomed, cool, blue, and rocky over Wolf's owlishly twitching ears.

He was climbing the pass along its muddy trail between ponderosa pines when a gun cracked ahead and right of the trail. Yakima flinched, expecting to hear the bullet sizzling toward him, and jerked back hard on Wolf's reins. He fired a look up the slope through the heavy ranks of tall pines. Another shot cracked wickedly, echoing. Yakima reined Wolf off the left side of the trail, stopped the mount behind an outcropping of black lava, and leaped from the saddle. His boots thudded and made a squishing, crunching sound in the mud and pine needles on the downhill side of a dirty drift.

He dropped Wolf's reins, shucked his Yellowboy from his saddle boot, and peered over the rocks and into the trees on the far side of the trail and up the slope. Spying nothing, and hearing no more shots, only the angry cawing of distant crows, he stepped out from behind the outcropping, crossed the trail, and moved into the forest on the other side.

Yakima climbed the slope at an angle, moving around rocks and snowmelt-filled depressions. He climbed around the massive, muddy root ball of a blowdown tamarack, the air spiced with the smell of mud and pine needles, and stopped suddenly, dropping to one knee and raising his Yellowboy to his shoulder.

Footsteps crunched and thudded up the steep incline. A pine bough moved, and a figure stepped out from behind it, the bough springing behind her. Alta stumbled, floppy-footed, down the slope, her blanket coat open and her black hair tumbling over its collar, as tangled as ever. Her face was a copper oval inside her hair, her brown eyes wide and somehow vacant.

In her right hand, she held a .38 Remington straight down at her side. As she continued stumbling down the slope toward Yakima in her fur, calf-high boots, the gun in her fist popped. A pinecone leaped up around her knees. Her eyes found the half-breed, and she stopped too suddenly for her own momentum. She pitched forward, hit the ground, and rolled several yards downhill, arms and legs flopping like those of a child's rag doll.

She lay on her back, sprawled at an angle to the incline, staring up at the pine boughs angling high above her. Yakima ran up the slope, took a knee beside her. The .38 lay several yards away, near a pine sapling poking out of a small mound of pine needle–peppered snow.

Blood matted the front of her cream-and-brown calico shirt, over her belly. Her chest rose and fell slowly. She lifted her right hand from the mud and needles and extended it weakly toward Yakima.

"*Mierda.*" Shit.

Yakima took her hand in his gloved left one. "Why, girl?"

But he knew why. She'd had little else, and her baby had been dying. Kelly had offered money and escape.

Yakima squeezed her hand. It went limp in his grasp. Her chest and belly fell still, and the light left her eyes.

He reached up and ran his fingers down over her lids that were light as moth wings, closing them. Then he rose and continued up the slope, backtracking her. He felt sharp hawk talons tapping out a haunting rhythm along his spine. Ahead was a fairly level shelf in a clearing.

There were three horses—Yakima recognized one

from McMasters's livery barn. It was outfitted with a
wooden pack frame and bulging canvas panniers. The
saddlebags with the loot from Douglas were draped over
the big roan's rump. Kelly stood with his back to Yakima.
He was adjusting one of the pouches while the other two
horses foraged nearby, with their saddle cinches hanging. Kelly's rifle leaned against a rock to the man's left.

Yakima stole forward as quietly as he could. Fifteen
feet behind Kelly, he stopped and loudly racked a shell
into his Yellowboy's chamber, aiming the rifle from his
hip, index finger drawn taut against the trigger. Kelly
jerked with a start. Then he froze, facing his horse,
straight over the packsaddle and into the soggy, sun-
dappled forest on the other side.

"Goddamn it," Kelly said loudly, startling the pack-
horse.

One of the other horses whinnied.

Yakima caressed the Winchester's cocked hammer
with his thumb, keeping the rifle trained on the small
of the rogue sheriff's back. "Why'd you kill her?"

Slowly, hands raised to his shoulders, Kelly turned
around. His wool coat was open. Blood splotched his
lower right side. The wound had opened. Maybe it had
been open for days, and he'd had no one to tend it but
himself.

He'd probably been holed up pretty crudely in one
of those abandoned shacks at the edge of Dead River.
His face bristled with beard stubble, and there were
blue pockets under his bloodshot eyes. A bottle jutted
from a pocket of his coat. Yakima could smell the acrid,
sweet odor of the man's fever stench.

Kelly chuckled balefully. "She was gonna drill me,"

he said, a muscle in his cheek twitching nervously. "Can you believe that crazy little Mescin? I was gonna take her to Mexico, buy her all the dresses she ever could have worn." He made an exasperated sound. "And she was gonna shoot me and take it all!"

"When did she throw in with you?" Yakima said, his voice low and pitched with menace, his eyes colorless beneath his heavy black brows. "Back on the other side of the pass?"

Kelly nodded. "Me an' her husband, Christian, did some runnin' together, a few years ago. She made him quit to tend his family. Damn funny kinda joke, ain't it? Now she throws in with me—I figure she didn't have nothin' else—and then tells me she's gonna shoot me and go it alone from here."

Kelly shook his head. "There just ain't no figurin' women. Especially them crazy Mescins."

"No, I reckon there's no figurin' 'em."

Kelly stared at Yakima. "Back there . . . in Dead River. What the hell was goin' on down there, any-ways? Why the fires?"

"Killer on the loose," Yakima said with a grunt. "Old debts bein' called in."

"Alta . . . what was her part in it?"

"Alta just wanted to bury her baby on consecrated ground. This one, anyways."

Kelly looked befuddled. "Huh?"

"I reckon, in spite of everything, she believed the preacher's lies"

Lines cut deep across Kelly's pale, sweat-damp fore-head. "And then she was gonna kill me and take the loot?"

Yakima shook his head slowly, as genuinely puzzled as the sheriff was. "It's a crazy goddamn world, Kelly. Best not give it too much thought. Drop down on your knees. I'm tyin' you up, takin' you with me back to Douglas."

"Ah, Christ," Kelly said, glancing over his left shoulder at the bulging saddlebags, then stretching a seedy grin at Yakima. "Think what a good time we could have in Old Mexico, with all that gold! Hell, I'd cut ya in, fifty-fifty. Come on, breed—it'd be so damn easy!"

One of the horses stomped a hoof into the spongy earth. Yakima kept his thumb planted firmly atop the Winchester's hammer.

"I reckon it would at that," he said, staring at Kelly's slumped, infection-racked, feeble-looking frame. "But look what kind of man I'd be."

Kelly stared back at him. Gradually, the muscles in his face relaxed. His eyes acquired a gloomy, miserable cast, and he blinked slowly, wearily.

He lowered his hands to his sides, dropped with a groan to his knees in the mud, and stretched his arms back behind him. He hung his head like a man in deep prayer.

Later, after he'd buried Alta where she'd fallen, and mounded her grave with stones, Yakima led the string of horses to the top of the breezy pass. He felt bleak, as though cold, razor-edged Damascus steel had been pushed between his ribs. He wanted only to get Kelly and the money back to Douglas, and get Wolf down the trail to Arizona.

He had another grave to tend there, on the slopes of

Mount Bailey, and for some reason he felt drawn to that spot, as though it were his own sacred ground, the only home he had.

Amongst the rocks and dirty drifts piled waist-high around him, the pine boughs dripping, he halted Wolf and stared back in the direction from which he'd come. Dead River was little more than a splotch in the bowl-shaped, peak-hemmed valley below, under the clear blue, post-storm sky of a Wyoming fall. The river itself curved around the south edge of the town, between the town and the rugged southern ridge, the snowmelt flashing like sequins stitched into a brown velvet dress.

He couldn't pick out many details of the town, but he supposed the two black specks were the saloon and the preacher's lodge. Ramsay Kane's place would be near the saloon and east a ways. He could pick out the school, glowing white in the high-altitude sunshine.

Her cabin and stable would be there, between the school and that big cottonwood the storm had stripped of its leaves, about half the size of Yakima's thumbnail from this distance.

Maybe Ramsay was out there in her yard, gathering firewood for the coming night. Maybe she was gazing toward him, trying to pick him out of the rocks up here on this sun-washed saddle, wishing him a safe journey. He wanted to believe so, anyway.

"Yeah, you, too," he muttered as the breeze, cooler up here, slid against his broad copper cheeks.

"Who the hell you talkin' to, breed?" Kelly said with a snarl behind him, the man's wrists tied tight to his saddle horn.

"Nobody," Yakima said, reining Wolf around to the east. "Just another ghost, I reckon."

He jerked his hat brim down over his forehead. He tapped the stallion's flanks with his heels and started down the pass, the string of horses, including the big roan with the saddlebags, falling into step behind him.

ABOUT THE AUTHOR

Frank Leslie is the pseudonym of an acclaimed Western novelist who has written more than fifty novels and a comic book series. He divides his time between Colorado and Arizona, exploring the West in his pickup and travel trailer.

Also available from

Frank Leslie

REVENGE AT HATCHET CREEK

Yakima Henry has been ambushed and badly injured.
Thankfully, Aubrey Coffin drags Yakima to safety. But as he
heals, lawless desperados circle closer to finish the job—
putting his innocent savior in the cross fire.

BULLET FOR A HALF-BREED

Yakima Henry won't tolerate incivility toward a lady,
especially the comely former widow Beth Holgate. If her
new husband doesn't stop giving her hell, Yakima may
make her a widow all over again.

THE KILLERS OF CIMARRON

After outlaws murder his friend and take a young woman
hostage, Colter Farrow is back on the vengeance trail,
determined to bring the woman back alive—and send the
killers of Cimarron straight to hell.

THE GUNS OF SAPINERO

Colter Farrow was just a skinny cow-puncher when the men
came to Sapinero Valley and murdered his best friend, whose
past as a gunfighter had caught up with him. Now, Colter
must strap on his Remington revolver, deliver some justice,
and create a reputation of his own.

**Available wherever books are sold or at
penguin.com**